Black Sun

Carmilla Voiez

The right of Carmilla Voiez to be identified as the author of this work has been asserted by her in accordance with the Copyright, Designs, and Patents Act 1988

No part of this publication may be reproduced, stored in a retrieval system, or transmitted in any form or by any means without the prior written permission of the publisher, nor be otherwise circulated in any form of binding or cover other than that in which it was published and without a similar condition being imposed on the subsequent purchaser.

Vamptasy Publishing
www.vamptasy.com

I dedicate the final book in the Starblood Trilogy to endings and new beginnings.

Thank you, again, to Vanessa for her fine editing skills, and Sarah, Niccolo, Ricky and Michael for their help in kicking this story into shape. Thank you to those people who have supported me financially and emotionally over the past twelve months, and to my readers, without you none of this would be possible or worthwhile.

Chapter 1

The baby watches, spellbound. His mother lies before him on the soil, her body torn and her stomach open. The hilt of a dagger extends above the wound. His nostrils widen to drink in her scent, a heady aroma of blood and milk.

He crawls towards her and nudges her cheek with the crown of his head. Other than a gentle rocking in response to his pressure, she does not move. She has never opened her eyes, never held him in her arms or spoken his name. He isn't even sure he has a name, but he knows her name. Lilith told him. His mother's name is Star and she is beautiful.

He gives up trying to wake her and nestles between her inert arm and her breast. Clamping his teeth around her nipple, he sucks. Blood and milk mix and they nourish him. When his stomach is full he falls asleep beside her.

***

Star moves. She is some distance away from him and he only catches the movement of her arm from the corner of his eye, but he is sure he doesn't imagine it. His mother is awake.

He crawls closer and watches. Her body rests as always with both hands on either side of her torso at exactly the same angle as yesterday and the day before. He sniffs the air. She smells different. In addition to her usual scent of blood and milk he identifies an extra ingredient, the whiff of perspiration. He watches eagerly, frightened to move and miss anything.

She touches her stomach. Her fingers shake as they probe the dagger in her belly. The pressure of her touch makes the blade wobble. Bubbles of blood erupt from the wound and she screams. Letting go of the knife, she touches her lips. She stretches her tongue and licks the blood from her fingertips.

'Am I dead?' she asks.

He crawls closer.

'Who's there?' She waves her arms. The movement is weak and she only manages a few jerks before she gives up, panting.

He shuffles toward her. Star digs her hands and feet into the earth and tries to push herself away. Her efforts are slow and torturous. Unable to talk to her and calm her, he nudges gently against her cheek. He extends his tongue to lick her, to show her she has nothing to fear. She recoils at his touch and his chest feels heavy with the pain of her rejection.

'What are you?' Her hands flail wildly around her face. He backs away to avoid being hit. Her fingernails tear at her eyelids. Blood flows between her lashes. It congeals on her temples and in her hair.

He tries to lick her face clean. 'M-m-m.' Frustration bubbles inside his throat as he tries to form the word – mother.

'What do you want?' Her voice sounds terrified.

Tears burn his eyes. *This isn't what I want. Why do you fear me?* 'M-m-m.' He tries again, but he cannot make her understand.

Frustrated, he decides to let his actions speak for themselves. Perhaps then she might understand and accept him. He clamps his mouth around her breast and sucks. Warm milk squirts into his mouth. Piercing her skin with his teeth, he feeds on blood and milk. For a moment she is silent and he believes she understands at last. Then she screams.

He continues to feed until his belly is full then moves away. Today he does not wish to sleep nestled against the arm of his mother.

***

'What should we call the infant, Siloth?' Lilith asks. 'His mother refuses to name him. I suppose we should.'

'You want me to name him, Missstressss?' the wyrm asks.

'Of course not, Serpent,' Lilith shrieks. 'I want you to suggest names so that I might name him.'

Siloth bows his head. 'Well, may I sssuggessst a name that represssentsss both hisss mothersss?'

'Okay,' Lilith says. 'Like?'

'Moonsssstar or Edensssun?'

Lilith sucks air noisily and taps her clawed fingertips against her knee. Her brow furrows and she looks across at the baby. He returns her gaze.

'Edensun.' She nods. 'Edensun. I like it, Siloth. It suits him. Let's go and visit your mother, Edensun.'

3

Edensun crawls behind Lilith, down the bank of earth away from the villa and towards Star. Lilith's stride is too fast for him to keep up, but she remains in sight and he knows the route he must take. He has travelled the same way at least three times each day since he was born.

Lilith reaches Star and halts. Edensun overhears their conversation as he hurries to reach them.

'Good morning, Beautiful,' Lilith says.

Star's voice trembles as she replies. 'Why am I here?'

Lilith laughs. 'You branded yourself as mine. Of course you came back to me.'

Edensun reaches the women. His eyes follow the direction in which Lilith's finger points: a jumble of white scars on Star's thigh.

'What happens now?' Star's voice sounds stronger and steadier than before.

'Lie back and enjoy yourself. You'll find a wonder and beauty in the pain if you allow yourself to feel it,' Lilith replies.

'Never.'

'Then suffer.'

Lilith kicks Edensun, pushing his body towards Star's breast. He glances up in confusion and sees Lilith's frown. He understands that look and knows it means she wants him to do something. Shaking his head, he struggles to imagine what he is supposed to do. Milk dribbles from Star's breast. Ignoring the pain in his back, Edensun puts his questions on hold and clamps his mouth over his mother's breast. Star's arms shake and she tries to push him away. His teeth are

4

clamped around her and he pulls her nipple with him, stretching her breast. Star moans in pain and stops pushing. Edensun returns to her side and drinks.

'It has to feed.' Lilith's voice drips mock anger. 'What kind of mother are you?'

Edensun continues to suckle at his mother's breast.

'That's better,' Lilith croons.

Edensun crawls towards Star. She has changed beyond all comprehension. She no longer lies on the ground. Instead she stands within the jaws of Siloth, towering high above him.

He looks up at her and senses that she sees him too. The thought makes him smile and he grins at her. She shudders. Tears swell in his eyes. He disgusts her, his own mother. The sharp pain in his stomach reminds him that he hasn't fed in a long time. Lilith kept him locked in the villa. He had cried out, not understanding his banishment. Now he can see the reason, although he does not understand. Wondering how things can change so quickly, he weeps with the knowledge that he will no longer sleep on the ground next to her.

Hooking his claws into the serpent's flesh, he climbs. He senses the snake's pain. Siloth's body tenses as he ascends. He regrets hurting his friend, but he has no choice. He must eat or perish, his stomach tells him that much.

Edensun pauses at Star's waist, knowing her skin is more delicate than the wyrm's. He worries about the damage he might cause.

'Hello.' She smiles at him.

The warmth of her greeting and smile make Edensun giddy. He clings to the snake, confused. Tears of gratitude and love sting his eyes.

'It's okay, Baby. Everything is all right now.' Her voice chimes in his ears and resounds through his entire body.

He cannot believe what he hears. He has ached for her voice for so long. Perhaps he is dreaming? He reaches towards her.

'I'm sorry. I can't hold you. The snake has my arms.'

He studies the jaws around her waist. She is asking for his help. If he can help her now, she will love him.

'It doesn't hurt too much, but I can't move my arms. I'm sorry.'

He forces his tiny hands into Siloth's mouth and pulls. Slowly, the wyrm's mouth opens wide enough for Star to free her hands. Reaching forwards, she touches him. He shivers with delight. She lifts him to her breast. A beautiful harmony resonates through his body and soul. Desperate to communicate his adoration, he looks into her eyes. She thanks him.

Cradled in her loving arms, he suckles. He feeds gently, not wanting to hurt her or break the magic. He hums as he feeds. In his head a symphony praising his mother is composed. He wishes he could share it with her, but all he manages to communicate is a gentle 'M-m-m-m.'

Life continues this way. Edensun and his mother become closer, inseparable, or so he thinks. For the first time in his short existence, he is content. He loves and he is loved. The knowledge of this strengthens him more than her blood ever could.

***

Edensun awakes knowing this is the day that everything will change. Although she still cradles him, his mother's mind is far away. It journeys into the distance, too far for him to reach. The change frightens him.

It is the day he will meet his father and lose his mother, although he doesn't know this yet. He senses that things are changing too rapidly for him to comprehend.

He is feeding at his mother's breast when the man arrives. Star tips Edensun towards Satori. Hoping desperately that by ignoring the intruder he will push him away, Edensun continues to feed, clinging to his mother's breast with his claws.

Satori speaks to Star. His voice is low, full of pain and confusion. 'Star, I came.'

She answers him using the same soft voice she uses with Edensun. 'I never doubted you would.'

Edensun burns with jealousy. *She loves him too. Does she love him more than she loves me?*

'What is that thing?' Satori asks.

'My…our baby.'

'It survived?'

'Yes. I guess it did,' she answers.

It did? How could she? It? I'm not an animal. I'm your son!

7

Satori and Star are silent for a moment. Edensun wishes he could read their thoughts. *What are they thinking? Are they thinking about me?*

'How are you?' Satori asks.

Edensun's skin crawls in response. He fears his mother's answer.

'I don't know. Nothing seems real. One day I'm trying to discover what I want in life and the next I am a mother.'

My mother! Edensun wants to scream in rage. He swallows back the sound and keeps listening.

'Where's Lilith?' Satori asks.

'She'll be here soon. I have something of yours. Come closer.' Star bends forward 'Hurry up, Satori. What are you waiting for? Stay strong.'

One of her arms moves from Edensun's back. He claws at her breast afraid he might fall. Turning to look at Satori, he sneers at the frightened face of his father.

Star leans further. She holds a jewelled dagger in her hand.

'She's coming.' Star's voice breaks a little. 'From there.'

Edensun wonders whether she is afraid. His face turns towards the direction in which Star points. His eyes follow his mother's hand. He relaxes when he sees it is only Lilith and Siloth approaching.

Lilith smiles at Edensun and his mother. 'Hello, my darling.' When Lilith turns towards Satori, Edensun can no longer see her face. 'We're delighted you could join us at last, Magician.'

'Lilith,' Satori replies.

'As you can see, you had no reason to fear. Star has been well looked after.'

'Lilith, I've come for Star. Allow me to take her and we will leave without any fuss,' Satori says.

Edensun can hear the fear in his father's voice.

Lilith steps towards Satori. 'I have another plan. Star stays here and you give yourself willingly to me.'

'Why would I do that?' Satori asks.

'Because otherwise you will endure torture you cannot comprehend. Ask Star. Better still look at her. Do you think that you...you feeble, arrogant man, could endure so much? I am interested in you. You remind me of someone I once knew, and you have power. You are strong...for a man. If you give yourself to me and make me your goddess we can share this world and others. We will create wonders.'

'No. I am here to rescue Star, or to join her, whichever is my fate.'

'Stupid boy! Change your mind and beg my forgiveness. I am merciful.'

Satori screams. Star throws the dagger towards him before Edensun can stop her.

Satori catches the dagger and whispers a word he created from the black alphabet. A tornado widens around him.

Edensun feels the serpent shake. He clings tighter to Star. His mother tries to calm the wyrm. She must realise Siloth will not be calmed because she leaps to the ground with Edensun in her arms. 'Bury yourself, Siloth, until the storm has passed...Let go.' Star tries to pull Edensun from her breast.

9

He shakes his head and digs his claws further into her skin. *Don't leave me!*

Her fingers squeeze his arms. He wonders whether she will break his bones. With a vicious tug she tears him from her breast and releases her grip on his body.

He falls to the ground. Bruised he looks up at his mother in anger and confusion. His arms reach towards her. 'M-m-m-m.'

Lilith and Satori continue to argue. Edensun ignores them. He cannot understand what just happened. He shouldn't be on the floor.

Blinding light radiates from his mother. Edensun lowers his eyes. When he looks up again her body has vanished and in its place hovers a ball of golden light. The sphere, which was once his mother, rises above the ground getting brighter and brighter the higher she soars.

Satori's whirlwind splutters weakly then vanishes. He and Lilith fall to their knees. Lilith reaches towards the sky and Star.

Star's voice echoes around them. 'I do not envy you, Lilith, neither do I hate you. We are light. Merge with me and become complete again.'

Lilith becomes a white orb and rises towards Star. As the two bright balls merge, a wave of light blows out across Binah and sparks of fire hit the ground. Light embraces light. Edensun's eyes weep. It is too bright, but he cannot look away. The spheres separate and descend. Star and Lilith's forms become human again as they touch the ground.

Lilith speaks first. Her voice trembles. 'My love, after all I have done...after the terror and horror I have sewn within so many hearts...you forgive me?'

'I forgive you, Lilith.'

'You are both free to go or to stay. You have given me more than you could ever understand, more than I deserve.'

Noooooooooooo! Don't let her go. She's mine. She belongs here with me. Mother!

Star does not seem to hear the desperate plea inside Edensun's mind. She doesn't even look towards him. Her eyes are fixed on Lilith's face. 'Before I met you I was trapped inside the shell of a frightened child. What I have given to you is no more than I have received. Live well, Lilith. Look after our son for me.'

Edensun watches, powerless, as his mother walks away from him. Star takes Satori's hand and without kissing her baby good-bye, she deserts Edensun. Tears blur his vision as he watches her step beyond where he can reach.

Chapter 2

Star lies silently in the cell. Her black curls are wrapped around the front of her pale throat like a scarf. Satori's breath tickles the back of her neck.

'Star,' he murmurs. 'I found you.'

She smiles. 'Yes.'

His skin is warm against hers. She realises how much she missed that.

He wraps his pale, thin arms tighter across her stomach and she pushes against his angular body. He found her and she saved them both.

She sighs and snuggles closer. 'I love you.'

'We're home,' he tells her.

She laughs, but her laughter is gentle, not mocking. She is simply happy to be alive and with him, wherever they are.

The room is tiny. No more than two metres by three. An aluminium toilet squats in one corner. At the end of the bed, if it can be called that, stands a grey wall with a metal door.

'Well, almost home.' His laughter joins hers for a moment.

'Where are we?' she asks.

'My prison cell,' Satori answers.

'Your prison cell?'

'They arrested me for your murder.'

Star laughs louder this time. 'I wonder how that will work out, now I'm not dead…Oh shit, Raven.' Her laughter morphs into sobs.

'Shush, it's okay. You're dead. They can't try you for murder.' He strokes her hair.

She turns around on the bed to face him. Her wide eyes beg him to understand her fear.

'We won't tell them you're alive.' He kisses her forehead and strokes her tears away with his thumb.

Star scowls. 'Umm, I think they'll notice I'm here.'

'Not if we escape. Let's get out of here. We'll run far away.'

Satori's eyes shine in excitement. In the half-light one seems to glow red. Star shudders. She has seen this manic look before: the look that says anything is possible. Star swallows hard. She cannot argue the point. A few hours ago she was dead. Now she lies here in his arms. Her heart beats and her lungs draw oxygen from the air. *Anything is possible.* That is his law, not hers, and yet her reality confirms its validity in the same way the law of gravity is confirmed by her inability to float above this itchy and uncomfortable bed. For one second she hates him for being right.

Star sits up. Her back is rigidly straight. She stares at the metal door. 'Run? I feel that's all I have ever done. Maybe it's time I stopped?'

'We'll figure it out.' He places his body between her and the door, smiling gently.

She strokes his beautifully pointed face and gazes into his eyes. One sparkles with deep grey brilliance. The other is

13

damaged. She wonders when that happened. She kisses his lips and snuggles into his chest. His steady heartbeat calms her.

A fluorescent strip light flickers above them like a strobe on a dance floor. Energy crackles around the room, making their hair stand on end. Star clings to Satori as freezing air whips around the cell, like a hurricane. Satori sits up and touches her shoulder, instructing her to stay down. Star feels cold and unnaturally exposed in her nakedness. The light flickers again then fails and the cell falls into darkness. The air feels thick, almost solid. It punches Star's ears and throat and chills her skin.

'Satori!' she screams.

'It's okay.' Satori grips her shoulders and pulls her up towards him. They sit on the narrow bed together, shaking.

Air crushes her. She struggles to catch her breath. A vortex of wind drags Star from the bed to the centre of the room. Satori's hands fall from her shoulders. She cannot feel or see him. She stands up, alone. Air surrounds her, separating her from him. Her heart hammers and her legs shake. Wind swirls around her. She spins with it, not knowing which direction she faces when suddenly the spinning stops and she is pushed to the floor by a heavy blow. Crying out, she tries to push herself back up against the weight of air. The room stinks of blood and decay.

'What's happening?'

'I don't know,' Satori answers.

He sounds far away. Resting on her knees and one hand, she reaches into the space in front of her, searching for him. She cannot find him. Her fingers flail through the bitter wind.

'Where are you?' she yells.

'I'm here, Star. It's going to be okay.'

'How can you be sure?'

'Because we survived, I found you and we survived. We're not about to die here.'

She shakes her head.

'Talk to me,' he says. 'Keep talking and I'll move towards your voice.'

'Fuck! When will this punishment end? I don't deserve this. We don't deserve this. I never meant to hurt anyone. I don't know why things happened the way they did. It was like being in a dream.'

Satori's fingers brush against her knee. 'Here you are.' He moves to her side and puts his arms around her, squeezing her towards his body. 'It's going to be okay, I promise.'

As their eyes adjust to the dark, shapes take form in the air around them. Three terrifying faces, with hollow eyes and gaping mouths, drip blackness onto the floor. They move like reflections in agitated water. Arms appear, reach towards Star and Satori then vanish again. The faces remain: soulless, angry and tormented.

'I think I know what this is,' Satori says. 'They opened the vessel.'

'What?' Star can hardly hear him over the noise of the wind and his words don't make any sense.

The demons hiss at the huddled couple. 'Where issss he?'

15

'Who?' Star asks.

'The one who ensssslaved us. Where issss he?'

'They mean Paul,' Satori says.

'Didn't you tell me he was dead?' Star asks.

'He is. He's dead.' Satori's voice shakes.

'Where issss he?'

'Buried in the cellar of his house,' Satori answers. 'Or perhaps in the morgue? They, the police, they might have taken his bones there. I don't know. But he's dead. He can't hurt you anymore.'

'And perhaps we can't hurt him, but we can hurt you.' The voices are menacing. They echo around the room, moving closer and closer to the cowering couple until they are harsh whispers in their ears and sour breaths on their faces.

'Star!' Satori yells. 'Do something.'

Star pauses, confused. *Me?* Satori is the one who always has the solution. He lives for moments like this, the battles against magical forces. *Why me? Why now? Is he afraid? Are they too powerful?* 'Me?' she asks out loud. 'What can I do?' Her mind rushes through images. She thinks back to the toad she expelled from her mind and the goddess she tamed with her forgiveness. Star closes her eyes. She reaches for the light inside her. She searches through the dark tunnels of her mind, running through empty corridors, turning every corner. She cannot find the light inside her. She is lost in the labyrinth of her mind. 'I can't find the light.'

'Hold my hand. We'll do it together,' Satori tells her.

She squeezes his hand. His warmth guides her. She draws on his strength and magic, this tragic hero, the man who loved and destroyed her. She concentrates their combined energy inwards, searching. Her mind folds in on itself and the outside world ceases to exist. She floats through chambers and crimson interconnecting corridors. She finds a speck of light fluttering deep inside her mind; wills it to grow stronger and runs towards it, concentrating only on its brightness. The light gets bigger and she feels its warmth. She keeps running until her skin feels as though it will burn from her bones then she lets the light embrace her. She wraps it around her and stretches her mind, willing the sunlight to fill the dark cell.

Demons growl and Star feels the floor tremble. Air roars in rage as it rushes past her and out of the room. In the still silence, the oxygen feels thin. Star opens her eyes and clings to Satori's arm afraid she might pass out. Her light fades, back into her skin and the darkness feels deeper than ever. She tries to slow her breathing, but she is too afraid.

'There's not enough air. We have to get out of this room,' Satori says, wheezing.

Star crawls beside Satori, blindly across the rubber floor. Her outstretched hand touches metal.

'The door?' she asks.

'Open it,' he gasps.

'Me?'

'What the fuck? This again! Yes you. You're a fucking goddess, Baby! I think you can open a locked door.'

'How do I try?' she asks.

'Don't try. Just do it. Remember how you chased those demons away moments ago and those things you did in Binah. Remember the light.'

17

'I...don't know.' Her head spins and she collapses onto the floor.

'Look, Star. You can do it.' Satori's voice is weak and broken by gasps for air. 'We're running out of air. Please...'

Star rests her palm against the metal and closes her eyes. 'Open,' she says.

The door swings towards them. Cold air rushes into the cell. Star and Satori lie on the ground swallowing oxygen.

Satori laughs. The flickering light from the hallway highlights his face. He is beautiful.

They sit there, huddled together, unable to move. Their eyes glued to each other's face.

'What happened to your eye?' Star's words break the spell.

Satori sighs happily. 'A scratch. Don't worry.' He moves to stand up.

Star grabs his arm. 'Can I heal it?'

'I don't know. Lilith did it to me,' he answers.

Star rests her fingers across Satori's eye and cheek. She closes her eyes and breathes. Her fingers feel warm and tingly, then hot. She opens her eyes afraid she might be burning him, but he looks comfortable. He sighs again, deeper this time. She removes her hand and he opens his eyes.

He grins. 'Fuck! The world looks strange in three dimensions. I forgot what it was like.' He giggles. 'Thank you. Thank you.' He stands up, wobbling unsteadily on his feet and looks around. Frowning, he turns back to the cell.

His eyes focus on Star's face and his lips curl upwards in a warm and loving smile.

Star extends her hand towards him and he pulls her to her feet. Caressing her hand, Satori kisses her fingers and pulls her gently towards him through the cell door.

She holds his gaze for one eternal moment.

He looks away and shudders. 'It's too quiet. Where is everyone?' They stumble to the next cell. The door is shut. Satori opens the viewing flap and looks inside. 'Empty.' He checks the next and the next. 'They're all empty.' The pitch of his voice rises in panic.

Star shares his unease. 'We should leave, but my god, I feel so tired. I feel like I could sleep for a year. I wonder, maybe I'm not meant to use that power in this world.'

Satori rests against a cell door. He touches her cheek. 'Or maybe you just need to learn how to recharge?'

She shakes her head, grabbing his hand again, dragging him towards the barred gate at the end of the silent hallway. 'I don't trust it. Magic comes from Lilith.'

'I don't think it's Lilith. Maybe just take it easy, you know, until it feels natural. Although, fuck knows what those demons would have done to us back there if it weren't for you.'

Star coughs, embarrassed. 'You helped me.' She wants to tell him how he gave her strength to glow, but her chest aches and she cannot give him those words. Instead, she turns away and tugs at the gate. 'Fuck, this one's locked too. How are we going to get out of this place? Help!' Her voice echoes around the corridor. No noise answers her call, not even the rush of heavy booted steps.

'We should go to Donna. She needs to see you're okay,' Satori says.

'Donna?'

'Yes, she helped me reach you. She's in hospital. It's a long story, but it's important. She needs to know you're okay.'

Star looks around her. The corridor is empty. The demons, if they are still nearby, make no sound. She wonders where all the people are hiding. 'Okay.'

Satori nods. 'Let's get out of here.'

Star nods. Together they place their hands on the bars of the gate. Star closes her eyes. 'Open,' she says.

The lock clicks and Satori turns the handle, pushing the door open into another dimly lit but empty corridor. He leads the way through a maze of corridors and upstairs. As they reach the ground floor of the police station, the full effect of the rage of the demons becomes apparent.

Six bodies, dressed in police uniforms, block the hallway. Four of them are strewn face down across the floor. The other two, unfortunately, are not. The first face Star sees is male. His mouth hangs open wider than any natural scream would allow. His eye-sockets are hollow and pink liquid stains his cheeks. The flesh of his nose hangs in front of his mouth. The cartilage, which once supported the structure, clings to his Kevlar vest. His torso rests against a blood stained wall, facing the door to the stairwell.

Satori grasps Star's arm. 'Don't look.'

She shudders, turns away and steps over the fallen bodies towards the exit. The last of the six bodies is female. She lies on her broken, twisted back. One arm seems to reach for her colleague, seeking solace. Her fingers stretch across the floor of carnage just a few inches short of their target. Star cannot help but look at her face. Her skull is concave as though a giant fist pushed her features into the back of her head. Thankfully her eyes are closed. Her nose, cheeks and lips point inwards as if her face is a mould to create a mannequin.

Star's arm is tugged by Satori and she is pulled away from the horrors. No one alive, police, prisoner or civilian, crosses their path. Star wonders whether anyone else survived the demons. Each set of doors open for them and at last they reach the entrance.

'Come on,' Satori urges.

They run through the doorway, into the dark street. Turning back they see blackened windows of cracked glass. The building seems to shake in fear. 'It's going to collapse,' she whispers.

'Come on...' Satori urges.

Hand in hand they sprint past strangers who stare at them. Star imagines their shocked faces are in response to her nakedness and tries to cover herself with her arms.

Satori removes his shirt and passes it to her. 'I'm sorry. I don't know why...'

'Thank you.' She stops running to button it over her chest. She kisses his cheek.

They run onwards, hand in hand. She and Satori keep looking ahead, concentrating on their goal, Donna.

Chapter 3

'Satori!' Donna grins as she looks at the figure in the doorway. 'You're back. I thought...'

Star steps out from behind Satori and faces Donna.

'Oh My God! How?' Donna stares at Star in disbelief. 'Am I fucking dreaming?'

'We did it, Donna,' Satori says.

'We did it? Sarah, you're alive, but how? I can't believe this is real... How did you?'

Star steps forwards and smiles. 'He found me.'

'I knew he would.' Donna pulls herself upright. 'Come here, Sarah. Let me touch you. I can't believe my fucking eyes. I need to know this is real.'

Star crosses the hospital room and sits on the edge of Donna's mattress. She reaches out and grasps her friend's trembling hand. 'It's real. I'm alive.'

Tears pour down Donna's face as she squeezes the hand. 'I thought I'd never see you again.'

'We've come here to help you, Donna. Satori says you were in a fire.'

Donna snorts. 'Yeah, that was stupid.'

Star shakes her head. 'I understand.'

'Actually, I'm already healing. Whatever happened in those worlds with Satori, it healed me. The doctors say I'll have very little scarring and my breathing is getting easier every day. And now you! You've mended my broken heart.' Donna blushes and offers an embarrassed smile. She tugs at her fringe as if trying to hide.

'I'm sorry, Donna.' Star looks at Donna's shaking hand and squeezes the fingers tighter.

Donna's grip on Star's fingers tightens. 'Don't.'

Star shakes her head and forces a smile. 'We just came from the police station. There's been... fuck knows... some demons...' Star glances across at Satori, who smiles and nods. 'Donna? Look, I think I've brought something back from Binah. Some kind of power. I want to try and heal you.'

Donna shrugs. 'I'm okay, honestly. It's good to see you.'

'I want to do this. I need to. Please.'

Donna frowns and nods. 'Okay, sure.'

'Your scar from the bar brawl, shall I get rid of that too?'

'What? This?' Donna asks touching her eye. 'I haven't thought about it in a very long time.' Donna stares at Satori. 'What do you think?'

Satori nods. 'You've earned a fresh start.'

Donna nods. 'How will you do it?'

'Well, with Satori I touched his cheek,' Star answers. 'Look, his eye's all healed.'

Donna shrugs. 'Okay.'

'But for you.' Star leans across the bed and fixes her lips against Donna's. They stay there, motionless. Warmth spreads from Star's lips to Donna's. She opens her eyes and watches her friend's face glow with healing light.

As Star moves away, Donna's face reddens. Her lips are still pursed in a remembered kiss.

'Thank you,' Donna breathes.

Star feels light-headed. Her heart races. 'You're welcome.'

Satori steps towards Star and places a hand on her shoulder. 'Are you okay?'

She nods. Taking Donna's hand in her own again she says. 'It's over.'

'Really?' Donna asks. 'What about Satori? The police came to see me, but they wouldn't believe… Did they let him go, because…because you're alive? What about Raven, will they?'

Star shakes her head. 'The police station has been destroyed. I don't know what they'll do.'

'Destroyed?'

'Demons,' Satori replies.

Donna shivers. Her eyes widen. 'Did you bring them back with you?' She looks around the room. Her eyes wide open in terror.

'It wasn't us, I promise,' Satori tells her.

'No demons here, Donna. Just us three. So, what will you do now?' Star asks.

Donna looks away. 'I've decided, when I leave here, I'll go home with Mum. This city is finished as far as I'm concerned.'

'Donna…'

'Fuck it, Sarah, I love you. I know you'll never feel that way about… like Satori said… a fresh start…'

24

Star nods and kisses her friend's cheek. 'Promise me you'll write... from Exeter.'

'If you want.'

'Please. I have no fucking idea how, after all I've seen and done, I'm going to fit into this tiny world. I'd like to... you know... have someone I can talk to, about it all.'

'Yes. I'll write.' Donna nods. Tears soak her cheeks and nightie.

Star blows her one last kiss. 'We have to go.'

'Take care... both of you.'

'You too.'

'Thank you, Donna,' Satori says.

Donna nods. 'You're welcome.'

Satori and Star hold hands as they leave the hospital.

'What now?' Star asks.

'Got any more of that juice left?' Satori asks.

'A little, I think, maybe, why?'

'There's one more place I'd like to take you before we go home and start the rest of our lives.'

'Where?' Star asks.

Satori guides her away from the hospital in silence.

The traffic is busy. The occasional beeping of car horns reminds Star that she is only half dressed. In spite of this, she doesn't feel the cold.

Satori leads her to large iron gates set between high stone walls. The handle squeaks as he pushes it down. The gate judders as he pushes it open.

'What are we doing here?' she asks.

'One more friend to visit,' he answers. 'I made a promise.'

25

He steps through the gate. His skin glows in the soft twilight. Star watches him for a moment then follows. Loose stones on the driveway cut the soles of her feet as she walks behind him.

'Satori,' she whispers then speaks louder. 'Satori?'

He looks back at her for a moment and nods then he walks again, away from her. She hurries to catch up. Her stomach turns. She doesn't understand what he wants.

Graves mark either edge of the driveway: ostentatious statues of former leaders of the community. Satori turns left and starts walking along a mud pathway between two of the more modest marble sculptures. The earth is soft beneath her feet and her soles sink into the earth. She follows his footprints, striding wider than normal to match his path perfectly.

'What are we doing here?' she asks.

Satori doesn't answer. He keeps walking and she follows. Her vision touches the headstones at either side of the meagre pathway. Angels and dogs make way for simple crosses and the occasional teddy bear as they progress through time to the newer graves.

Satori stops in front of a black cross. A tree stretches its bare branches across the grave. Star reaches the marker and stands beside him. The name on the tombstone is Rhiannon. She looks at Satori. His head is bowed and his hands pressed together as if he is praying. She kneels at the edge of the turf, where grass has grown and died back for winter. The earth embraces her knees and she trembles.

'Raven.' Satori nods his head towards the grave. 'I promised her I'd bring you here when you returned.'

Star stares at the glossy blackness and remembers her friend. A teardrop gathers in her eye, rolls down her cheek and splatters onto the wet and yielding ground. 'I'm sorry.'

'Can you?' Satori asks.

'Can I what?'

'Can you bring her back?'

Star shakes her head. 'I don't know. Can you...give me a moment alone... please, Satori...Leave me alone!'

Star hears his feet pad softly back along the path towards the older graves. She breathes deeply and looks at the grave. A flower has shrivelled and sepia-toned petals are fused to the base of the cross, a lily perhaps. 'Oh, Raven. I'm so sorry.'

She leans forward as if in Islamic prayer and touches her forehead to the earth that covers her beautiful friend's feet.

She reaches out with her consciousness and tries to find Raven, or some remnant of her, within the ground. The earth teems with life. Industrious insects and worms push through crumbly soil. She reaches further, beyond a wooden barrier and into the satin embrace of Raven's coffin. The body looks peaceful. Her eyes are closed and there is the trace of a smile on her face as if she is in the middle of a happy dream. Pins hold her jaw in place and a chiffon veil softens her features, obscuring most of the damage to her once perfect bone structure. Star shivers. 'Raven, are you there?'

***

27

'I fucked Satori,' Raven says proudly. Her words are full of poison.

Star stares dumbly as the weight of Raven's words crash through her skull. She shakes her head to deny the image of Raven and Satori's bodies moving together. It fills her brain. Something wakens in Star's belly, *the baby?* She grabs Raven by the shoulders and pulls her into the narrow stall. Raven's ankles buckle as her boots slip on the wet surface. Star lifts the woman's head by her hair and smashes Raven's cheek against the porcelain toilet. She forces the face downwards again and again, pummelling Raven against the grubby white seat, now streaked with ribbons of red.

Raven's face cracks open like an eggshell in Star's hands. Rivers of blood pour from Star's fingertips and stain the veil, which covers the face in the coffin. Raven's dead eyes open. They are milky white and her right cheek and jaw are so badly smashed that her face hangs lower on one side, her mouth a triangle of pain.

'Why?' Raven gurgles blood as she moves her broken mouth to form the word.

Star shakes her head. 'I don't know. I'm sorry.'

'What do you want?' The words are wet hisses. Bubbles of blood explode like fungal spores and press against the veil.

'Satori, Satori wants me to bring you back.'

A sound between a laugh and a cough adds more redness to the darkening veil.

'Do you want me to try?' Star asks.

'You may have saved Lilith, but you can't save me. What you did, the way you smashed my skull into tiny pieces, it cannot be undone. Let me rest in peace. Tell Satori he is not to blame.'

'Who is?' Star's voice stammers and she instantly regrets asking the question.

'You are. Binah may have taught you what you needed to know, but to me you'll always be a murdering bitch.'

The venom of Raven's words makes Star jolt back. She hits the top of the coffin and smashes through it. Shards of wood tear and bruise her skin. The earth feels cold and damp around her. It presses into her nostrils. She coughs and swallows more as her throat convulses. As she pulls her body back into the chill evening air, she spits at the grave, rejecting not only the choking earth but also the vicious, unforgiving words. She hears Satori move towards her.

'I'm sorry. I can't.' Star turns away, bristling with fury, not wanting to see the pain in his eyes. Even the fact that he grieves for Raven makes her tremble with jealousy.

Chapter 4

'You can't or you won't?' Satori asks.

'I can't,' Star answers. 'I don't know how. I don't have that kind of power. Look, it's getting late. Where are we going to sleep tonight?'

Satori shrugs. 'Paul's?'

'Whatever,' Star answers. 'I'm tired. Let's go.'

Satori looks at her face. She will not meet his eyes. He embraces her and kisses her mouth, hard and deep. 'I love you.'

'I love you too.' Her words come automatically, but sound hollow. 'I'm sorry I couldn't help with Raven.'

He takes her hand and leads her from the graveyard. Wind whispers through the trees. He wonders whether Raven is trying to tell him something, but discards the thought. He has Star back now. Nothing else should matter.

Paul's house is dark. Star opens the gate. She stumbles across the lawn, complaining about stones and grass on the driveway. Police tape covers the front door. Star tears it open and pushes the front door inwards. The house exhales. The stench of death and suffering fills Satori's nostrils and he shudders. Star walks in front of him into the hallway.

'How did he die?' she asks.

'Lilith murdered him.'

'Why?'

'I don't know.'

'Where did it happen?' Star walks deeper into the shadows of the house. She turns towards the cellar door. 'In there?'

'No, the kitchen.'

'Can you hear them?' She turns away from the door and stares at him through frosted eyes.

He shivers. 'Who?'

'Children sobbing,' she says. 'We're not welcome here.'

'It's just for a couple of nights,' he tells her. 'Then we'll get that place you dreamed of: your little cottage.'

'How can we afford that?' she asks.

'We'll rent a place. I can get money.'

Star nods. Her face blurs as she moves closer and closer to him. Her lips are soft against his. His heart hammers in his chest. She removes his shirt. He reaches forwards and cups one breast. They kiss first then run up the grand staircase to Paul's room. Once again the room is filled with sweat and sex.

Between her thighs, Satori finds home. He knows that he will always love her and always need her. She validates him. She takes the poison in his veins and pumps life around his pale body.

He leaves Star in the cold light of morning. He hopes the house will not harm her. He considers taking her with him, but she says she is exhausted and needs rest. *Perhaps it is easier this way? I can get everything done and return armed with tributes of resolution. I can take care of her.*

He spots the headlines of the local daily newspaper on a board outside the newsagent. "Police Station Destroyed." He buys a copy and sits on the wall outside, scanning the story.

At the time it went to press the reporters had no idea as to what had caused the police deaths and the extensive damage to the building and equipment within. Bodies were bagged, tagged and extracted from the wreckage. Officials were unwilling to make a statement of any kind. An estimated ten police officers and five civilians lost their lives.

Satori folds the newspaper and carries it under his arm as he strolls towards his mother's house. The gentle sun warms his cheeks. The air smells sweet and fresh. He is free. He finds himself unable to mourn the lives lost to the wrath of Paul's demons. He warned them not to damage the vessel.

His house key remains at the police station probably covered with rubble. He knocks on his mother's door, hoping she hasn't left for work.

Marian opens the door and screeches in pleasure. 'Oh my god! Steve, you're home.'

'Hi, Mum.'

She pulls him into the house and embraces him. The hallway smells of fresh, rich coffee. Satori licks his lips and asks for a cup.

'Of course.' She grins and drags him into the kitchen. Filling two cups, she motions for him to speak.

When he takes the cup and devours the coffee in silence she taps his wrist and pouts.

'Well?'

'Have you seen the news?' he asks. 'Can I get some more coffee?'

With a look of exasperation Marian refills his cup. 'That nice lawyer, Ms...'

'Ms Wilson?'

'Yeah, she phoned this morning.'

'Oh?'

'She told me the police station exploded. Some sort of gas leak or something. It's chaos there at the moment. She wanted to let me know you weren't among the bodies they found.' Marian fusses about him, pulling at his clothes. 'You're not hurt?'

'No. I'm fine, Mum.'

'She wanted to know if I'd heard from you. She wanted to check you were safe.'

'Are the police after me?'

'She didn't know, but...'

'What?'

'Well, it looks as though the evidence room was destroyed. So she doesn't think they'll be calling you back in anytime soon. Apparently without evidence they can't hold you.'

'That's good news.'

'Yeah, right. Look, Steve, she sort of said something. Can you explain it to me?'

'I'll try.'

'She asked if you'd ever seen a psychiatrist.'

'Mum!'

'Yes, I know. It's not the first time we've...'

'Mum, it's not even the tenth time... I just don't get it.'

'Well...'

'I'm okay.' He leans against the back of his chair and stares into his lap. 'I am.'

'You wouldn't tell me if you weren't though... Look... I really don't want to push you away... you're my son, my life. But... I feel responsible, you know.'

'You're not responsible.'

'Perhaps if I...'

'Stop this.'

'Look, Steve, just let me speak, okay? I asked what she meant, but she wouldn't tell me. All I want to know, I guess, is... look, is this about magic or have you been passing out again?

'Neither really.' Satori exhales. 'Some of my explanations didn't make sense to her.'

Marian nods, her eyes hooded. 'I know how that feels. Well, you're an adult now. I wish you'd consider it though. You know I worry about you... Actually, Steve?'

'Yes.'

'If a psychiatrist is out...'

'It is.'

'I have some... friends. Maybe you could meet them.'

Satori shrugs. 'So did she say anything else?'

'Who?'

'Ms Wilson.'

Marian laughs self-consciously. 'I did ask her if we could sue if you were hurt or dead.'

Satori snorts.

'She said it wasn't her area of expertise, but probably. She did say, off the record, that if I were to see you I might advise you to just lay low.'

'It's good that she phoned.'

Marian nods then frowns. 'One other thing though, Babes. The police took stuff from your room when they searched the house. That's all gone too. I'm sorry.'

Satori embraces his mother. 'It's just stuff. With everything that's happened, I'm probably the luckiest bastard to walk the earth.'

'I was worried. I'm glad you're home.'

Satori rubs the back of his head. 'It's not just that, Mum.'

'Oh?'

'I saved Star.'

'Sarah?'

'Yes.'

Marian shakes. Satori takes her coffee cup and places it on a work surface. 'Come and sit down with me.' Supporting her arm, he guides her to the living room. 'It's a long story and maybe you need to get to work. I'm here because I need your help.'

Marian nods. 'You're on the run?'

'I guess so. It's complicated.'

'Of course. So Sarah is alive?'

'Yes.'

'But her body is in the morgue.'

Satori shrugs. 'I've no idea. Maybe it vanished when she came back.'

Marian places the palm of her hand on Satori's forehead as if checking for a fever.

'I'm not crazy. It's just, you know, kind of hard to explain. I don't know where to start.'

Marian's sigh sounds melancholy. 'My crazy, beautiful boy.'

Satori blushes and leans towards his mother. His voice is low and his words rushed. 'I went on a journey. I brought her back from the dead.'

'Oh Sith!'

'Huh?'

Marian's face flushes and she coughs. 'Excuse my French, it's just…'

'What did you just say, Mum?'

Marian looks away. 'Oh shit.' She turns back to face him.

Satori stares at her face. He sees no deception in her loving eyes. 'I wish I could explain it all to you... But, in the meantime, I need a favour. Will you help us?'

'Always, Love. What do you need?'

He asks his mother for money, promising to return it soon. She asks no further questions and simply retrieves what he needs. The embrace they share before he leaves is long and tight. Everything they want to say is communicated by that one hug.

'I'll be back soon, Mum. Thanks.'

Marian's eyes are full of tears and she bites her lip as if afraid to speak. As he opens the door she waves goodbye and blows him a kiss.

'I love you, Mum.' He turns from her and rushes away, pockets full of notes.

Wondering whether he is making a terrible mistake, he pays the deposit for a humble cottage beside the park. They can move in within the week. He is amazed at how easily he can exert his will on the world.

They are safe. No one hunts them. Star and Satori have their fresh start. He wonders what they will do with this second chance.

Chapter 5

When Star awakes Satori is gone. She searches the house for something to wear and settles on a pair of trousers that she has to roll up just to see her feet, and a soft silk shirt.

The phones in the house are all dead. She searches through Paul's drawers and finds some loose change. Heading out into the bright sunlight, she hunts for a public pay phone.

'Dad.'

'Who is this?'

'Dad, it's Sarah. Is Mum there?'

'What sort of sick joke is this?'

'It isn't a joke. Can I speak to Mum?'

'No you cannot. Who is this? My daughter is dead.'

'I'm not Dad. It was all a misunderstanding. I'll prove it. Remember the time our house was being renovated and we had to stay with Grandma by the lake? I fell in. Do you remember? I spent three weeks with a high temperature and you punished me by throwing away that doll I loved.'

'Don't call here again.'

'But Dad.'

'I mean it. I have no daughter. My daughter is dead. The shame of having a daughter who murdered a young woman, can you imagine what that did to us? Can you? All those journalists and TV cameras, my wife couldn't leave the house for months. Our friends shunned us. People blamed us. And now you phone here and tell me it was all a…what…a mistake? Whoever you are our daughter is dead. If you phone here again we will contact the police. Do you understand?'

Star puts her hand over her mouth and slams the phone receiver against the coin box. Shaking, she returns the receiver to her ear. The line is dead. Her father has hung up.

She wanders through the streets. Tears drench her shirt. People approach her and ask if she's okay. Their faces frighten her. She shakes her head and runs from them. They cannot understand. No one can, least of all Star.

She returned for this. Binah may have been torture, but she understood the rules. Lilith was angry and she took her anger out on Star. That's okay, because Lilith is a demon. She is supposed to be cruel. Her cruelty makes sense, and because of this, Star could help Lilith. She helped heal the demon and in return she was allowed to return home, to more anger, more hatred. Hatred that she has tried to understand for her entire life. *Why do they hate me? Why does my difference from them cause them to hate me, fear me? Why does it provoke such rage?*

Lilith told her once that she was hiding behind a mask. In Binah she removed that mask. For the first time in her life, bound in chains, torn and bleeding, she was free to be herself, to draw on her own unique strength. Lilith respected her for that strength. *Do I really have to hide myself again? Is that the price for love? With all I know, with all I've seen, how can I bear it?*

39

Holding her head in her hands, Star runs back to Paul's house. She heads for the kitchen. She searches through dozens of drawers looking for a knife. Nothing is left. The kitchen has been gutted. She runs to the bathroom and checks Paul's medicine cabinets. In the en suite bathroom she finds a pot of loose razor blades. They stick to each other. She rubs them between her thumb and forefinger to push the top one loose. Returning the rest to the pot, she studies the slender piece of metal. *My mask,* she thinks as she slices the top of her thigh with the blade. *Pain is my mask. Pain hides my pain. I can do this. I'm strong. Satori and I will make a home and we'll be happy. Fuck my parents. So I'm not Daddy's little girl. I never was. As long as Satori loves me, I can see my value through his eyes. Let that be enough.*

Chapter 6

Four years later.

Edensun runs across the soft earth, yelping with delight. He somersaults through the air oftentimes landing perfectly on his feet, occasionally bouncing on his bottom in fits of giggles. The twilight sky makes his skin look dark. He revels in his beauty and strength. Stretching his legs, he increases his speed. His imagination creates a hole in the sky ahead. The rift is darkness and chaos reigns beyond, air as active and directionless as his thoughts. He makes ready to leap through the hole, like a rabbit returning to its warren.

The earth trembles beneath his feet. Sealing the hole, he looks about, guiltily. A blunt nose pushes through the grey earth between him and the now closed gateway.

'Edensssun.' The voice in his head commands his full attention.

An eyeless face and a thick cylindrical body follow the nose. The giant wyrm curls itself in coils before Edensun's feet.

'Siloth.' Edensun's voice trembles. He sits beside the serpent and crosses his slender child-like legs.

'You know you are sssupposssed to ssspeak to Lilith before jumping.' Siloth's words fill Edensun's brain. The wyrm's huge jaws do not move as he speaks.

'I know, but...'

'Lilith knowsss you find comfort in chaosss. She undersssstandsss, but you mussst follow her rulesss.'

Edensun nods. 'I'm sorry.'

'You need not tell me you are sssorry. I am only her messssssenger.'

'Does she want to see me?'

'Not now. She is busssy. There is much work for her to do. Perhapsss you ssshould dissstract yoursssself with the charmsss of Magenta, Sssapphire and Violet. Keep yoursssself out of trouble.'

'Or in a different kind of trouble.'

'Indeed.'

Edensun stretches his legs and pushes himself from the ground. He changes into his demon form. His skin becomes grey and scaled, not unlike that of Siloth, and wings spread from his shoulders. Nodding at the blind wyrm, his powerful, leathery wings beat the once still air. Agitated sand rises in clouds as Edensun hovers above the desert. As if guided by a homing device, he shoots through the silver sky towards Lilith's villa, seeking the company of her three handmaidens.

The handmaidens rush to greet him as he lands in the garden. Exotic scents embrace him. The women's clothing outshines the glorious blooms which surround them. Edensun doesn't ask how they knew to expect him. Their soft hands caress his rough skin. Magenta's lips seek his mouth. She licks his fangs, cooing gently. Violet pulls his left arm towards her. He sways on the remaining two claws, clutching at the earth for stability. Violet pulls one claw into her accommodating mouth. Sapphire walks behind him and strokes the scales on his shoulders and lower back. As she massages him she sings. Her song fills him with lust and joy. It calls to his demon nature to dominate. If he had hands he would grab their breasts. If he had a penis he would thrust it into each and every hole in the sirens' bodies and perhaps create more holes with which he might sate his lust. Instead, he growls and bites Magenta's lip sucking at her sweet, warm blood. Soft flesh tears as he scratches the back of Violets throat with his claw. His body pulses with desire as the handmaidens croon and adore him, accepting each sensation of pain he offers them and begging him for more.

He gives them more, unafraid of Lilith's wrath when she sees her broken servants. He knows from past exploits that they will take a few days to repair the damage he does to their bodies, but he does not care. Let Lilith's whip tear the skin from his back, he too will repair and grow stronger until he becomes a man and can give these women what they really want from him.

His saucer-wide eyes gleam as he sees the wounds he inflicts. Torn mouths press against his skin. Blood coats his scales. Shredded breasts push harder into his mouth as the handmaidens moan with pleasure. He rolls onto his back and lifts each claw. He offers them as seats for the women to mount. Without hesitation they thrust themselves down on the vicious scimitar finials of his arms and leg. They bounce

43

on him, shaking their hair, panting and groaning ecstatically as they ride him. He watches their features in wonder. Their beautiful faces contort with the pain and pleasure he provides. He services Lilith's servants and all the while his razor-toothed mouth grins.

Chapter 7

The room is almost empty, but for the soft blue light which washes every surface and colours the air. Huge windows grace one wall. Azure light dances across the others as if reflected by crystals. The floor is tiled. The cool ivory stone shimmers like granite in sunlight. In the centre of the room stands a long table covered in lilac silk. Upon it a beautiful woman with auburn hair reclines on her stomach. A dark haired youth rubs her shoulders and back while soft music fills the perfumed air.

'Lilith,' Edensun says as he rubs scented oil into her back.

'Yes, my child.' Her voice is a purr.

'I think it's time I made the journey.'

'So soon?' She sits up on the silk covered table.

Edensun nods.

'I understand, Edensun. We all have our paths and they must not be denied. Pour me a drink and we'll discuss your plans. How will you find her? What if she doesn't want you?'

Edensun passes Lilith a tall glass of green liquid. Ice frosts the walls of the glass. She takes a sip and shivers deliciously. Her pupils dilate. 'Won't you join me?'

'Maybe later,' he answers. 'My thoughts are chaotic. I need to concentrate. There are too many possibilities to reconcile.'

'But you understand the basics. You know who the key players will be, your allies and your enemies?'

'I think so, Lilith, yes.'

Lilith takes another sip. 'So tell me. How do you imagine this will work?'

Edensun sits down beside her. 'I need to sever the ties Star has in Malkuth, then she will see only me and want to join us.'

Lilith smiles. 'To whom is she tied?'

'Her friends, my father mostly.' Edensun rotates his shoulders and straightens his back.

Lilith nods. 'I never expected those two to make it a month after leaving here. They've surprised me, but their bond is weaker now. I don't think he presents you with a problem.'

Edensun frowns. 'But they face adversity together. My mere presence could bring them closer.'

'There is one who has left the stage. If she should return, she will help you. She brings discord to their world - the one who is two.'

'You mean Freya?'

Lilith smiles at the mention of her protégé's name. 'Yes, if you find a way to reunite her with the key players she'll help you weaken the bonds between them all. There is another who might sever all links between Satori and Star.'

'Who?'

Lilith's smile widens. 'The woman who Star killed long ago. The lover of Satori.' Her index finger follows the rim of her glass, making circles.

46

'If she's dead how can I use her?'

'Satori has the power to cross the borders between worlds. Find him and guide him. He can bring her back.'

'Will he though?'

Lilith nods. 'If he is angry enough at Star, I believe he will. His arrogance has always been his weakness. Star drives him to the brink of madness and he will need to be mad to try it.'

Edensun mirrors Lilith's nod. He moistens his lips as the goddess takes another sip of her chartreuse brew. Saliva gathers in his mouth and he regrets his decision not to join her.

'So, you need to recruit Freya and Raven somehow. Do you know how you will do that?'

Edensun strokes Lilith's throat and shoulder. 'Give me time. I'll dream the answer.'

'Good boy.' She smiles proudly. 'How will you appear to Star?'

'What do you mean?'

'Well, you cannot approach her in your demon form. The last time she saw you, you were an infant. Four years have passed for her since. You could be a toddler in need of her protection?'

Edensun shakes his head. 'I don't think so. A toddler wouldn't have the strength or authority to move the other players into position. I should be a man.'

'No, not a man... a youth.' Lilith's eyes shine. 'A youth at the brink of adulthood. You will still attract her mothering instinct and awaken her sex drive. A youth is perfect. Your strength will not be anticipated.' She kisses his cheek.

Edensun grasps Lilith's hand. 'Yes. That's perfect.'

'I know,' she says. 'What else would you expect from me?'

He laughs. 'Nothing. I expect nothing. I am never disappointed, but frequently pleasantly surprised.'

She pouts and pushes him playfully. 'If I didn't know you better I would take that as an insult.'

'Don't, you know I believe you are perfect.'

Her frown becomes a smile. She mouths the word perfect. Her green eyes gleam like emeralds caught by moonlight. 'Yes.'

She stands up and claps her hands before her naked breasts. 'A party!' she shrieks, euphorically. 'We must have a party before you leave.'

Edensun's grin falls. 'I was planning to leave in a few hours.'

She strokes his cheek. 'Then delay a little. After all you still need to imagine the finer details of your plan before you leave. What better way than with chemical and magical assistance?'

Edensun knows better than to argue.

Lilith turns to face a raven-haired servant who walks into the room. 'Violet, get the others together. We're having a party.'

Edensun takes his time in the large pearl-coloured bath. Music and women's laughter rises through the villa. The party is for him, but he knows his lateness will be forgiven.

He sinks under the water. Strands of his hair float around his face attracting his peripheral vision. He remembers his mother. Her hair was dark too. He tries to recall her face, but it appears in soft focus, a distant memory. Her smile is warm, but her features blurred. He shivers, imagining her reaction when he calls her mother. His memory of her may have faded with time, but she will not recognise him at all.

Frowning he rises from the water and wraps a towel around his waist. Leaving a trail of wet footprints, he retreats to his room to dress.

The women turn to face him as he enters the ballroom. Soporific mist clings to his eyes and pushes vivid colours and wild ideas into his mind. He embraces three beauties at once, kissing them in turn: the blonde, the brunette and the redhead. The handmaidens stroke his skin and whisper words of love and seduction.

Lilith watches with amusement. Edensun hates her aloof moods. It is as though she is somewhere else entirely. A place he cannot reach. Great distance separates them, which he cannot cross and it frustrates him. The attentions of Sapphire, Magenta and Violet suddenly irritate him. He shrugs away like a petulant child and strides towards Lilith.

'What are you laughing at?'

She looks at him as if seeing him for the first time in years. Her eyes widen and her mocking smile softens. She passes him a drink.

'No thanks. I'm leaving.'

The servants protest. They ask him for one last passion-filled night before he leaves. His feet itch and his legs burn with an eagerness to stride far away. He feels no sexual desire, only the urge to experience new lands and new people.

'Thank you for the party, but it's a mistake. I love you all, but I need to go.'

Protests are renewed. Lilith holds a long nailed finger in front of her lips. The room becomes silent. Even the music ceases.

'Goodbye then,' Lilith says. 'Safe journey.'

Edensun wonders whether to hug her or run. This is his first true taste of freedom and he doesn't want to waste a second. He pulls Lilith's fingers to his lips and kisses her hand. Waving at the women, he takes one step to another world.

Chapter 8

Star opens the kitchen door and steps out into fresh air. Grass stretches out before her across the courtyard until it reaches the ivy-laden stone wall and blurs into shadow. At the centre of this wall is a wooden door. Sun and rain have faded the green paint, which has started to peel away in places. The door is bolted and locked. Beyond it, a Victorian park with trees and a duck pond waits. There are no swings or seesaws and children tend to visit other, larger parks. Instead, it is a space where people come to read or think or walk their dogs, if they come at all.

She crosses the lawn. Her bare feet sink into the damp grass. Between ropes of ivy she sees patches of light and darkness. Juggling her load, she steps towards the door and takes an iron key from her pocket. Reaching up, she draws back the rusty bolt at the top and unlocks the door with her key. She rolls the key across the palm of her hand, studying it before she returns it to her pocket. The key is anachronistic. It reminds her of churches and mausoleums. It has its own romance as though it would be more suited to unlocking other worlds, letting them bleed their magic into this one. She shudders. *More magic? I've had enough magic for a lifetime. Give me peace and tranquillity with space and time to paint and sculpt. Keep the demons at bay.* She turns the domed handle and lets the door sweep outwards. Taking care to scan the ground for sharp stones and broken glass, she skirts around thick trunks of oak and chestnut trees. Grass tickles her soles and moss caresses her toes. She finds the same spot as yesterday. The light is harsh today, brighter. She should have come earlier. She will have to adjust her palette to compensate. The bluebells looked rich, yesterday. Today, their hue seems dull.

She lays out her rug and sits upon it to open her easel and watercolours. The half-finished picture rests before her. The air thickens and shadows grow. She closes her eyes and breathes. Her mind opens to the magic of nature all around her. The plants and the trees all have voices and speak to her of legends. Her own story mixes with their words and she remembers, as she always does, her walk through the Scottish forest. What should have been her final walk, and yet here she is, living, breathing, almost unscarred, almost complete.

She picks up her brush and lets it dance across the paper. Greens, blues and purples stain the landscape. Bluebells spring up before her and between them glimpses of other lives and other worlds. Worlds which touch her own each time she sits and opens her mind, even if she would prefer to hide from them and forget.

The other world sent her home. Together, they survived its torments and Satori filled that desperate void inside her. His world became her world until the borders between the world she had spent so long taming and the wildness beyond blurred into shadow. Satori, the magician, her partner - theirs was a life too easily obtained and impossible to escape.

She still shivers in familiar yet exciting ways when he touches her. Her nostrils still flare to capture the scent of him. Yet what is their life? What have they gained from each other and what have they lost?

Each morning Satori leaves their cottage by the park. He returns late. He entertains believers and non-believers alike, reading tarot cards and performing illusions. Star wonders how much of the magic he uses is real. She is scared to know if he still plays with forces beyond his control. Satori's life is as speckled with light and darkness as the parkland behind their cottage. She knows he visits that grave. The thought of it humiliates her. She feels bitter and betrayed, but cannot grasp the source of these feelings. However often she asks, Satori will not tell her why he goes or what he gains from his time knelt at Raven's feet.

What of my own darkness? No, don't think about that. I left that behind. Binah cleansed and changed me. It gave me strength and it took away... what? A bastard child, an evil, twisted wraith with a greedy-toothed mouth. So why do I miss my son? Why is the feeling of loss getting stronger rather than weaker with the passing years? Why didn't we bring him with us?

Putting down her brush, she studies her painting. The violence of her memories is echoed in her brush strokes. From the shadows, half concealed faces with hungry eyes watch her. To the right, one bloom drips blood which congeals on its stem. Between her thighs, a sticky dampness spreads. She sighs. At least her black clothes will hide any

53

stain. Not that there is anyone here to witness. The park is empty except for her, the birds and the insects.

Star screws the lid back onto the jar of water. Pigments weave around each other, merging into russets and browns. She shakes the jar and stares at the dull brown liquid, folds her easel and rolls up her rug. Arms laden, she walks back to the cottage.

Leaving her things on the kitchen table, she heads for the bathroom and cleans herself. She studies her reflection in the bathroom mirror. Her blue eyes look dull to her. Too many troubled nights. Her curls need brushing and yet she cannot motivate herself to pick up the brush. How long has she felt like this, hours, days, months or years? She has to remind herself that she doesn't always feel this way. Some days are blessings. Sometimes lightness comes upon her, sending her dancing through the house and into the garden then she clings to the men she loves as surely as she will push them from her at other, darker, times.

Men, yes plural, my men. One is not enough, not anymore.

Leaving her soiled underwear in the linen basket, she wanders along the hallway and into her bedroom. The plum velvet bedspread wrinkles into valleys and peaks as she sits at the foot of the divan and tries to remember why she came into the room. *What is it that I am looking for, a touch, a kiss? Is it hours or years since fingers last sculpted my skin, remaking me, warming and softening my flesh?* She responds to the memory of a loving touch. Warm breath tickles her throat. Her breasts ache.

54

Closing her eyes, she searches her body for an answer, an answer to a question she has forgotten. She tries again with a new question – *is this where I belong?* The answer confuses her. Yes, no, not yet, soon... sticky warmth returns and she opens her eyes. Her fingers grip cool, brass handles and she tugs at her underwear drawer. Inside a mass of black lace, cotton and silk lies patiently. She holds her hand, palm down, above the selection of underwear and then grabs a pair of panties at random and pulls them up over her stocking covered legs. *What now? The dishes are clean, the floor swept and vacuumed, the bathroom polished.*

The house is quiet, like a breath held. *What is it waiting for? What am I waiting for? I have everything. I am free. I can paint all day if I wish.* She sighs again. The feelings she expresses in her art confuse her. They are echoes of him, like everything she does now. She yearns to be free.

Chapter 9

Satori sits at a circular table covered in black velvet. At its centre rests a crystal ball, between that and him, a pack of cards. The chairs opposite his are empty. People move around the room, women mostly. He lifts his gaze and smiles at a passing woman. She smiles back.

He has seen ten people already today, each with unique problems, all searching for solutions and guidance. He is their confessor. Their minds open to him and he strolls through their memories. Sometimes those memories linger in his mind long after the customers have paid him and moved on, unwelcome stories to add to his own. He shares their pain, some of it minor, others almost overwhelming: feelings of loss and degradation, confusion and humiliation. He understands. He too has lost. He thought he regained what he lost, but realises he is only fooling himself. Star is not the woman she was. She is more and yet she is less than he hoped. She doesn't need him. Perhaps she never did.

He thinks of her beauty: her fragile, ivory face, blue eyes full of sadness and regret and her soft lips. He wishes he could make those lips smile, and light her eyes with joy. *When she looks at me now, what does she see?* He has not lost his looks. Other women's reactions to his attention assure him of this. When he reaches for Star why does she pull away?

She holds him tightly at times, jealously keeping his cock inside her. Two days every two weeks, it is as though she is a cat on heat. Then when those times pass she walks away from his arms and closes a door on him. He wonders why it isn't enough and realises that there is no emotion. Her need for him is physical, his need for her spiritual.

His ears still strain to hear her speak of her love for him. He wants to be admired, he wants to be adored. Unlike Star's, his needs do not rest for two weeks and ignite for two days, to be used on her terms only, without love, simply for her gratification. To scratch an itch that obsesses her at times and leaves as quickly as it arrives. He wants her always. More than lust, it is a desire to be loved and needed.

His eyes follow a woman around the room. Her red hair bounces on her shoulders. Her white shift dress caresses her curves without clinging. She does not turn to face him. She handles crystals at a stall twelve feet away. *Perhaps I should join her? Find out what interests her. See her face.* As he moves to stand a teenage girl slouches into the chair before him.

'Hi,' he says.

'Hello.' She fidgets uncomfortably. Her fingers tug at her wavy, mousy hair. Her pale eyes dart about the air around him like butterflies, never settling on his face for more than a moment.

'Would you like me to read the cards for you?' he asks.

57

She shakes her head. 'Would you look at my palm? Tell me whether I'm going to die.'

'Die?'

'Soon,' she says. 'Will I die soon?'

Satori leans towards her. 'Let me see your hand.'

He studies the creases and lines that decorate her palm. Her story is told beneath them, within her skin. Her palm is a window, nothing more. Her hand trembles as he holds it.

'What are you afraid of?' he asks.

'Everything,' she answers.

He looks at her face. Her eyes are focused on the table. He peers through her lashes trying to see her eyes. He looks again at the palm of her hand. The life line is stunted, but that doesn't have to mean imminent death. More like a pause until her life is re-established.

'Who is he?' Satori asks.

She glances up at him then back at the table. Colour rises in her cheeks.

'She?' Satori asks.

The girl nods. 'She's my best friend, but she's popular now. I don't see her. She certainly doesn't see me, not even when I'm right in front of her.'

'And you want her to see?'

She nods again and a tear hits the table, exploding on impact. She pulls her hand from him and wipes her face with her sleeve.

'She will,' he tells her. 'She will see. Give her time.'

The girl shakes her head. 'She doesn't need me.'

Satori swallows. 'What we need and what we want are not always the same. Give her time. She'll see you and you'll have your answer.'

'I'm scared of the answer.'

'Don't be. Do you want me to tell you what I see, here in your hand?'

She nods.

'Potential. A life full of potential. You aren't going to die. Not soon anyway. You'll live, and she'll see and be proud of you.'

The girl nods and wipes her face again. 'Thank you.' She offers him a note.

He takes the money. It feels wrong. It cheapens him. It makes his gift hollow. But Star's art doesn't sell. Their house is full of her paintings. In spite of his encouragement she has never spoken to a gallery or even sold a picture online. She just sits and paints and thinks. *What does she think about? What makes her so sad? Why can't I touch her soul and make her smile.*

Chapter 10

Mark looks over his shoulder, but does not stop running. His feet propel him forward with wide strides. His heart pumps blood around his muscles. His lungs drag oxygen from the air. Movement is his medium. He cannot be still, not until he knows he has lost them.

Clothes cling to his body. Rain has plastered his black hair to his olive-skinned face. His green eyes dart around him, afraid of shadows in doorways and scowling faces.

His heartbeat quickens. He has no idea where he is. *Have I run this way before? The skip on the corner, did I see that half an hour ago? Am I running in circles? Will they be waiting for me around the next corner?*

He tells his legs to stop running and spins around. His eyes search every direction for potential threats. Three men gather near a doorway with a shivering dog. They are talking to each other. One gesticulates wildly about a subject he appears to feel passionate about. The others nod sagely and open their mouths to speak filling the gaps between the roars of their companion's excited voice. Mark cannot grasp the subject of their conversation, but reassures himself that they are oblivious to his presence. Ten metres or so further along the street, two children kick a football heavily against a stone wall. One boy turns to face Mark, frowns and looks quickly away.

Mark pushes wet hair from his eyes. To his left he sees an open door. It leads into darkness: an abandoned factory or warehouse. *Will I be safe in there? Will they find me? Are they waiting within the cold shadows of the room beyond?*

He creeps towards the building. One of the three men glances at him, smiles a toothless grin and holds Mark's gaze. Mark shivers. *Is he one of them?* The man keeps staring. Mark halts. He looks from the man to the doorway then in both directions along the dilapidated terrace. When he looks again towards the men, the two others face him. Their grey, weatherworn skins crease as they peer through the drizzle towards him. The dog barks. *They know. The dog can sense I am different. I don't belong here. I don't belong anywhere. That's the point, isn't it? If I find her, if she tells me why I'm alone, explains who I am and what I should do then I might be safe. Perhaps she could protect me?*

'Mother,' he whispers.

With a final glance towards the open door, he turns away and runs, faster this time. At the end of the street he turns left. *I didn't go left last time, did I?*

Chapter 11

Satori leaves the community hall. His crystal ball weighs heavily in his black sports bag. He slings it over his shoulder. He sees the redheaded woman again. She is placing boxes in the boot of her car. One of the stall-holders he presumes. As she shuts the boot, she turns towards him. He nods and she offers him a fleeting smile before disappearing into the car.

He marches towards home. His pockets bulge with notes. The air is warm and smells of freshly cut grass. He hopes that this means winter has ended. He hates the cold, has for years.

Without thinking, his feet travel pathways he usually avoids. He glimpses Ivan and Freya's house and hurries past. He turns a few more corners and stops walking. This isn't his way home at all. He's heading towards his Mum's house and here is the street where Star used to live with Raven and Donna. He treads carefully towards their old front door. It feels like a pilgrimage to his past. Memories resurface, parties hosted by Raven at the top of these stairs, including that fateful evening when he met Star. It seemed like a dream at the time. Her beauty, youth and fragility enchanted him. He sensed something about her she had tried to hide, still tries to hide, and it excited him.

He retraces his steps out of the cul-de-sac and decides to call on his mum before heading back to the cottage. It isn't far. How closely they had all lived. It was inevitable that their lives would tangle, although perhaps not as much as they had.

He passes the park gates and looks at the grass beyond. Even the park holds memories, some good, like drunken picnics on summer weekends and others bad, like the death of Freya's sister. It amazes him how interconnected so many parts of his life has become with those of his friends and enemies. He thinks of Ivan, Freya's brother, and wonders for a moment whether he is still counted as a friend. *Would a friend do what he is doing? Would a friend swoop in to steal the most important person in my life?*

He checks the time and wonders whether his mum will be home. He decides to risk surprising her. If she is there she's unlikely to have company. Satori has often wondered how such a beautiful woman hasn't had a string of lovers since his father. Perhaps it isn't important to her? She has never spoken about a man, or woman, with whom she has a close bond. After Satori's father left she seems to have lived a life of chastity. He wonders for a moment how she can stand it then wonders whether, in fact, it might be a better life than his own, simpler and purer: just her, her work and him. No one to make demands on her time or dictate her lifestyle, of course it also means no sex.

He ponders this as he walks to the house they once shared. The redbrick Victorian terrace house within whose walls he grew and became a man. As he turns into his street a thousand memories assault his mind. He remembers crouching and watching Star waiting on his doorstep the day he came home from Paul's. He recalls the day Donna visited and screamed at him until his neighbours rushed from their insular lives to help her. He even remembers watching from his bedroom window waiting for his father to return home. His mother cried when she told him Greg had left for good. Satori remembers hitting her, denying her words. She acted as though he had strength beyond his years and shielded herself from his tiny fists.

Satori touches his gate and pushes it open. He strides along the short path to his past and rings the doorbell. He has a key, but he is a visitor now. He hears movement within and voices. The blinds twitch beside him. He waves and smiles. Marian opens the door and embraces him.

'I'm sorry, Love,' she says. 'I didn't know you were coming.'

'Do you have company?'

'Yes, but they'll be gone in a moment. Come in. Would you wait in the kitchen?'

Satori nods and smiles. He kisses his mother's cheek and follows her through the hallway. As he passes the open door to the living room he turns and sees four faces stare at him. Two men, one old with white hair and stubble the other younger, around his mother's age, and two women, dominant, strong looking women with stern faces and cold stares sit on the settee and chairs with tea cups before them. The women draw his attention, one is older, perhaps she is the white-haired man's partner, and the other looks as though she may be younger than Satori himself. In spite of her scorn she has a pretty face; she holds a mobile phone against her ear, but does not speak. He smiles at the strangers and continues walking to the kitchen.

'Pour yourself a coffee, Sweetheart. I'll only be five minutes.' She closes the living room door behind her and Satori cannot make sense of the hushed voices beyond.

He pours a coffee and waits obediently at the kitchen table. Soon the people filter along the hallway, nodding, holding Marian's hands and saying goodbye.

'Who were they?' he asks, after Marian closes the front door behind them.

She shrugs and pours her own coffee. 'Friends,' she answers. 'So what brings you here? Not that I mind of course. You're always welcome, but I wasn't expecting to see you until Sunday.'

'I just wanted to see you,' he replies.

'Is everything okay?' Her mouth trembles and he waits a moment to see if she has more to say.

'Of course. It's just... things aren't how I expected?'

'Sarah?' She frowns.

He knows Marian has never approved of Star, but in spite of their troubles he still feels protective of his girlfriend. 'In part, I guess. It's not her fault.'

Marian nods. 'It isn't yours either.'

'Mum, did you ever fall in love again after Dad left?'

'I have plenty of love in my life. You, my work and my friends, I'm not lonely. Look, Baby, you can come home whenever you want. It doesn't have to be this way. You said you needed to prove you could be a man. Well, you've done that time and time again. If it isn't working between the two of you, you don't owe her anything. You repaid that debt in full, remember?'

Satori nods. 'It's not that simple. I still love her.'

'Does she love you?'

Satori stares into his mother's eyes. Her eyes are grey like his own, but with golden haloes around her pupils. He shakes his head.

'You deserve love,' she tells him. 'You deserve someone who will make you happy.'

'Maybe I'm like you, Mum. Maybe I'm destined to be alone.'

'I'm not alone, Steve, and neither are you. Look, Baby, come home. Stay here a while. Let me spoil you.'

'I don't know, Mum. You have your own life and she needs me.'

'Are you sure?'

Satori shudders. Marian's words remind him of those spoken in another land years ago. "Are you sure she needs you to save her?" 'Yes, I'm sure,' he answers.

'Steve?' Marian asks.

'Yes, Mum.'

Marian's eyes dart towards the hallway and back to her son. 'It's nothing. I'm just... you know, I worry about you.'

Satori looks at the empty hallway. Shadows of Marian's friends pass through the door again. The images tug at a distant memory. 'Do I know those people?'

'You met most of them years ago. I doubt you'd remember. We just support each other. Steve, you were always so strong headed. You have never taken my advice.

You keep secrets from me. Look, years ago you chose your own path. I didn't approve, but what could I do?' Her cheeks flush.

Satori exhales, sharply. 'You worry too much, Mum. I'm still standing. I want to know about those people. Who are they? What do they mean to you?'

Marian frowns. 'So you are allowed to keep secrets, but I must tell you everything? More coffee?'

Satori glances at his empty mug and nods. 'I just... I feel I'm missing something.'

Marian fetches the pot and pours dark liquid into both cups. Replacing the pot on the hot plate she speaks without turning to face her son. 'We're just helping a friend who's in trouble. Do you remember Freya?' Marian turns to face him and returns to her seat.

Satori's chest tightens. He shakes his head. 'I haven't seen her for years.'

'She moved away. I... Mike... well anyway, we were just looking out for our own.' She takes a large sip of coffee and purses her lips.

Satori reaches across the table towards Marian. She leans back, out of his reach.

'Is Freya okay?' he asks.

'Sure. She has a baby now. They're coming home... I... oh, Steve, Steve, where did I go wrong?' Her eyes grow moist with the word baby and she gazes wistfully across the table.

Satori smiles, stretches his arm further and reaches for his mother's hand. 'You never did anything wrong, Mum. You're perfect.'

She looks down at their conjoined hands, pulls away and wraps both palms around her mug of steaming coffee. 'I just wish… I could protect you.'

Satori shakes his head. He feels confused. She is hiding something, he can feel it. 'What are you talking about? All I've gone through and you think I need your protection?'

She faces the front door. He turns to follow her gaze, but all he can see is an empty hallway. When he refocuses on his mother she is shivering. He stands up and moves around the table to her. He squeezes her tightly.

'This is to do with those friends. Who are they? You don't need to protect me, Mum. I thought you knew that. What are you afraid of? Let me help you.' His voice sounds higher than he planned. The sense of calm he wanted to share is tainted by his eagerness to understand.

'It isn't like that,' she says.

'But this sadness and worry… it has something to do with those people who were here, right?'

'No,' she answers.

'Who are they?'

'I told you. They're my friends. We've been helping Mike.'

He shakes his head. His mouth tastes bitter. 'No, it's more than that. I can feel it. I can taste your lies.'

Marian's eyes narrow and colour rushes to her cheeks. 'How dare you?'

Satori breathes deeply, trying to control his anger. He doesn't want to fight with her. *Why can't she understand that?* 'Mum, remember all those times I would say things and you'd despair because I didn't make any sense?'

She nods.

'Well, now I know how you felt.'

'I'm sorry.'

'Don't be. Just tell me. Who are those people and why are you afraid for me?'

Marian stands up. She places her cup on a work surface. She looks out of the kitchen window then turns back towards him. Her shoulders rise and fall as she breathes deeply. Even so her voice sounds unsteady when she speaks. 'It's too late. If we'd made different choices...' Marian covers her eyes. Her body shakes to the sound of her sobbing. 'I have a splitting headache. Can you get me some pills please, Love?'

Satori heads for the medicine cupboard, brings her some paracetamol and fills a glass with water. She downs the pills and he returns the glass to the sink. He holds her shoulders, hoping to reassure her.

'I think I should go and lie down, Love, until the headache goes away. Are you okay to let yourself out?'

Satori frowns. 'Don't avoid me Mum. If you really think I need protecting at least tell me from what.'

'Shhh, Love. My head... ouch... it really hurts.' She closes her eyes and rubs her forehead. 'Look, I just don't know, okay? All I know is something's coming. It's angry and powerful. We think we might be able to stop it, but I'll feel safer if you're here, with me.'

69

'Who thinks you can stop it? Those friends?'

'I can't do this right now, Steve, please. I'm your mother. You can trust me.'

Satori shakes his head. He feels dizzy chasing her around in endless spirals of logic. At times his eloquent and intelligent mother gets stuck like this and acts as though she is as muddled as him. Perhaps he can fit the pieces of this particular puzzle together more easily if he does leave? 'Are you going to be okay?'

'I'll be fine. I just need to sleep. Thank you. Give my regards to Sarah when you get home.'

Satori watches as Marian leaves the room. Her shoulders hunch over as she walks. Suddenly, she looks ancient and weak to him. He feels bereft without her strength. 'Sleep well, Mum. I love you.'

Chapter 12

Mark pulls his coat around him. A fire crackles in a metal bin at the other side of the tunnel. Its promise of warmth calls to him like a siren, but the crowd around the flames warn him to stay back. *Who knows whether they are friend or foe? Hiding is safer.*

He wonders whether he will see his mother tomorrow. *If I do, will I be too frightened to confront her? Why should I be afraid of anything?* Fear consumes him. Greedy faces look at him in expectation, fear in some eyes and desire in others. Everyone seems to want something from him, while all he wants is to be left alone. *If only I could wear a cloak to shield me from their prying eyes.* The filthy stink of his body should be camouflage enough, but it isn't. They see him, the real him, through the grime and they want him. He doesn't know exactly what they want, but he is certain it is something he isn't willing to give.

A can rattles at the end of the tunnel. Mark looks up and sees a group of young men stride through the darkness towards the fire. The men move confidently and appear strong. They do not shuffle or wheeze. This is not their home. *So why are they here? Is it for me?* He hears cruel laughter and his body stiffens.

The people around the fire notice the strangers approach. Mud-stained heads turn and grimy bodies jerk inelegantly around the flaming bin. The light in the tunnel shifts and dances. Through strobe-like illumination, the men approach. They look more menacing than ever as their shaven heads are thrown alternately into shadow then light.

The leader twists his arm and a heavy chain uncoils by his side. Mark pushes himself further into shadow as the strangers move closer to the hobos around the fire.

'Fuck off!' A drunken man lurches from behind the fire bin towards the group of skinheads.

'What did you say, Grandpa?' The leader strides towards the swaying man.

The drunk shakes his head, thinking better of his plan and moves to walk away.

The man with the chain lifts his hand and cracks his metal whip against the skull of the staggering drunk. The vagrant's knees buckle and he falls to the floor. Stagnant water rises around his body. The skinheads gather around the fallen body like hyenas. Mark notices a thread of blood flow from the man's head, making the water around him pink.

With a growl, one man pulls back his leg and kicks the hobo in the lower back. Bones crunch, but the man does not cry out. Mark supposes he is unconscious or already dead.

Stifled gasps of shock and confusion rise from the vagrants as they watch their fallen comrade. Mark wonders whether any of them will help. The homeless people in the tunnel outnumber by far the three angry men. Yet the audience leave the arena, fleeing from the brutality like rats scuttling from cats.

Mark stays where he is to watch. The unconscious body becomes a rag doll, lifted by kicks and crushed by chains and the stamping of boots. Red liquid trickles across the ground towards Mark as he tries to comprehend what joy these men might gain from damaging the lifeless body of a stranger.

The kicks become slower and less intense. The men put arms around each other's shoulders like teammates after a win. They turn in the direction from which they first arrived. As they turn one of the men catches sight of Mark through hazy eyes.

'Over there,' he says.

Mark looks left then right, ready to run.

'Enjoy the show?' the leader asks him. 'Waiting for an encore?'

Bending his back, the man holds his forearms towards Mark and gestures with his fingers. Eight fingers waggle a beckoning and behind them the man grins. His knees are bent slightly and his head cocked to one side. His head is shaven and his heavy, black boots and the turned up cuffs of his jeans are smeared with blood.

Mark stares at the man. The other two move to flank him, cutting off Mark's escape routes.

'We're good here,' Mark tells the jeering skinhead. 'Just move along.'

The three men laugh. Sounds crash off the curved brick walls and vibrate against Mark's eardrums.

'Yeah, we're good,' one of the tribe echoes.   The others nod.

Mark closes his hand around something from the floor and stands up slowly.

'Uh, uh, uh.' The leader shakes his head. 'I hope you weren't considering leaving so soon.'

'Of course not,' Mark answers. 'Not when the fun is just getting started.'

The men look at each other. Their faces betray confusion.

Mark shakes inertia from his limbs. 'Are you going to let me pass?'

'I don't think so,' the leader says. 'Did you know this guy?'

Mark shakes his head.

'Then why didn't you leave when you had the chance?'

Mark shrugs. 'I don't know.'

The leader drops his chain to the floor. Its clatter echoes around the tunnel. Mark's teeth shudder to the frequency of the sound. When the echoes stop, he balls his hands into fists. The leader steps closer and the other two follow. They are an arm's reach away.

Mark breathes deeply. *Now or never?* He ducks and lunges forwards, punching upwards and knocking the leader off his feet.

'Fuck!' The leader sits in a dark puddle and rubs his jaw. 'Wait,' he tells the others as they move to grab Mark. 'How old are you?'

'Thirteen,' Mark answers.

'Thirteen.' The man rises to his feet. He nods at the other two and motions for them to join him. 'I reckon we could make some money here.' He nods towards Mark. 'That boy has a killer right hook.' The others mumble their agreement. 'Hey, kid. Want to have a drink with us? I reckon you could make a pretty penny or two.'

'Doing what?'

The leader laughs. 'Nothing kinky. I ain't no ponce. Fighting, lad. You're a lot stronger than you look. Of course, if you prefer not to let me manage your fighting career and get you out of this dump, we can always go back to plan A.'

He bends down to retrieve the discarded chain.

'I'll think about it,' Mark says.

'Sure, but think about it over a drink. We'll get some beers in and go to Kevin's.'

Mark glances towards the motionless body of the hobo. 'What are you going to do about him?'

'Nothing to do. He'll be okay. He'll wake up with a sore head and drink it away. Stinking wreckage, just like my ol' man. Yours too I bet.'

Mark shrugs. 'Maybe.'

'So what do you say? Fancy getting pissed?'

Mark pockets the rock clenched between the fingers of his right hand. 'Sure,' he says. 'Why the fuck not?'

Chapter 13

A baby cries. The wail pricks at the edge of Freya's mind nudging her into consciousness.

'Oh, for fuck's sake, shut up,' she shouts.

Her eyes open in slits. Dawn light nudges between the curtains decorating the white wall with a peach bloom.

'It's your turn.' She reaches behind her to poke Rob in the ribs. *Lazy bastard!* Her finger sinks into his side, but he doesn't respond. His t-shirt feels sticky. *The night wasn't hot. It's still early spring. Why would he be wet?*

She struggles to turn around. Sleep doesn't want to free her from its grip yet. Midnight feeds and restlessness take their toll. She has never felt so tired. *Why won't he wake up? It's his fucking turn.* Turning slowly, degree by tortuous degree, she braves the light from the window and opens her eyes. Rob's face looks pale. His eyes are open.

'For Christ's sake, Rob, Jasmine is crying. Go and sort her out. I need to sleep. I can't keep doing this by myself.'

He doesn't respond. His face doesn't move. His lips are slightly open but do not tremble with breath. She pulls back the black duvet to shock him awake with the coldness of the room, and screams.

Her scream drowns the baby's cries. Long after she has drawn breath the echoes of it shake the room. 'Rob! Oh my god! Rob!'

His torso is red. Covered in blood, his t-shirt is torn. She touches his cheek. It is cold. She jumps out of bed and stares in horror. *How? Why?* She runs out of the room and checks on the baby. Jasmine has wriggled out of her blanket. Her arms reach towards her mother. The screams grow more demanding as Freya steps towards the cot. Jasmine is okay.

Freya reaches into the cot and picks up the beetroot faced infant. Bloody handprints smudge her yellow babygro. Freya shakes, not knowing whether to return her daughter to the cot or take her to her dead father. The room spins. Freya blinks. Her stomach does somersaults. She puts the baby back into the pine cot mere seconds before her back folds and she vomits on the nursery floor.

Jasmine's screams grow louder. Freya covers her ears and feels the slicks of blood from her hands tangle her hair and stain her cheeks. She looks at her hands and screams again. Jasmine's legs and arms punch air. Freya turns and runs back to the bedroom.

The duvet is pulled back. Rob's inert body lies there. Crimson wings curve across the mattress on either side of his chest. His t-shirt is sodden. Shaking, Freya approaches and with trembling fingers she pulls the t-shirt up towards his throat. Six deep splits, like eyes or cunts, gape across his blue-grey chest. *Knife wounds. Who?*

Freya backs away and turns around, searching the room for clues. Shadows skulk in corners. *Is anyone still hiding here, waiting for the right moment to push me to the bed and stab me too? Rob was adored. Who would do this to him?*

Freya opens cupboard doors and looks behind the curtains. She moves from room to room in the apartment checking behind every door, checking the shower and below the sink, opening each cupboard in the kitchen. No one, not even an unlucky black cat, pounces out at her. The only sound she hears is the insistent scream of her six month old daughter.

She heads to the front door. It is bolted on the inside. She rushes around opening every curtain. Every window, large enough to admit anyone, is closed and locked. Almost blinded by tears she searches the apartment again, still no one. Jasmine's cries become more frantic. Panic makes Freya feel faint. She tastes iron on her tongue. Her limbs feel heavy and her legs shake. *The attic?*

She grabs the hooked pole and snags the handle of a trap door in the ceiling. As she pulls steps unfold across the hallway. The attic is dark. Anyone could be hiding there. She keeps the pole as a weapon and slowly climbs the stairs. As her eyes peer over the rim she sees boxes of old books and Christmas decorations plus a chest of summer linen, stored until needed. Any of the boxes might hide an intruder. Her eyes flick around the room as she climbs. She wishes the baby would be quiet. Over the noise of screaming she wouldn't hear footsteps until it was too late, but she cannot stop now. She has to know what happened.

She steps onto the plywood floor and tiptoes across the space. The attic is self-contained. There is no access to attics of other apartments. Only 20 feet by 30 feet in which someone could hide, but in that space dozens of boxes create bolt holes, sheltering anything or anyone from her gaze.

She looks behind them all. Ready to strike with her hooked stick should she see anything lurking in the shadows, but there is no one. She is alone. Jasmine's voice screeches through the floorboards. If she doesn't quieten the child soon, a neighbour will call the authorities. *Bloody neighbours.* They're always complaining, never sympathetic to the mother of a demanding child. A child who slowly wears Freya's soul into dust while she watches her skin age with disinfectant and her clothes grow tatty from scrubbing at baby vomit.

She descends the steps and pushes the trap door closed. After stashing her pole in a cupboard for safety, she grimaces at the irony of maintaining such a routine and rushes to pick up Jasmine.

Jasmine feels hot to the touch. Freya suspects it is because she has cried for so long, but she undresses her anyway and leaves the blood stained babygro on the nursery floor.

'What are we going to do, Jaz?'

The only answer is a weak hiccup of a cry in protest to having been left so long. Freya opens her pyjama top and lets Jasmine latch on for her feed. She paces around the nursery, frightened to return to her bedroom. *What if I imagined it? What if I didn't? What if he's really dead? What do I do?*

'Should I phone the police, Jaz?'

The baby suckles contentedly.

'What if they take Mummy away? What then sweetheart? They might think I killed him...Fuck! What do I do?'

Jasmine finishes feeding and falls asleep in Freya's arms. Freya places her back in the cot and tucks the blanket over her. She does not look for a clean babygro or redress her daughter in the blood stained garment on the floor. She hopes Jasmine will be warm enough in her vest for a couple of hours.

She watches the baby's body relax. It is one of the moments she enjoys best about being a parent. Watching tension fall from Jasmine's sleeping body, through the cot and the floor below, is like watching meditation. The effect is soothing. Freya sits beside the cot, crosses her legs and places her palms face up on her knees. She breathes in and out, concentrating on her breathing. She tries to let the tension drip from her own body, but, as she visualises losing negativity and stress, the image changes and becomes her stabbed and bleeding boyfriend. Blood rather than tension seeps into the floor. She squeezes her eyes tighter, trying to push the image away, but it refuses to be ignored. Her mind will not let her pretend the carnage does not exist, not even for one blissful second.

She tiptoes silently into the room. In the back of her mind she wonders if this is a trick Rob is playing on her. *Rob and his sick sense of humour. Of course it is make-up. If he doesn't hear me creep into the room I'll catch him grinning, amused at how easily I fell for his joke.*

Except, when she returns, he isn't smiling and he hasn't moved. If anything the crimson wings have grown wider and darker as if blood still pours from his wounds. She walks across to him. Approaching him by a circuitous route so that the window is behind her and her shadow is cast across him. The position also allows her to keep her eye on the open door and check for movement in the hallway in case the killer returns, or never left.

She grips Rob's wrist, no pulse. She wasn't expecting one, but the knowledge that he is truly dead makes her feel weak and she lowers herself to the floor, kneeling beside him as if in prayer.

'Who did this to you?'

Rob's corpse does not reply.

His mobile phone is on his bedside table. She picks it up and dials her brother's number. It's early. When he answers the phone, Ivan's voice is a yawn.

'Rob?' Ivan asks.

Freya weeps into the receiver.

'Sis?' Ivan's voice trembles.

'I'm in trouble,' she says.

'What sort of trouble?'

'Rob's dead.'

'Did you kill him?' Ivan asks.

'No, of course not. How could you ask that?'

'Then call the police.'

'I'm scared.'

'Of course you are, but the police will help you. Is Jasmine okay?'

'Yes, she's sleeping. I can't call the police,' Freya says.

'Why?'

'They'll think I did it. They'll lock me up and I'll lose Jasmine.'

81

'No they won't. Look, I'm hours away. It'll take me at least five hours to reach you. You'll have to call the police.'

'I can't.'

'You and Jasmine can't stay in the flat with…'

'A corpse?'

'Uh huh.'

'Tell me what to do, Bro.'

'Call the police.'

'No.'

'Then get out of the flat. Take Jasmine. I'll call you when I reach York. Then we'll go back to the flat together. Shall I call you on this number?'

Tears run through her fingers onto the screen of Rob's phone. She shakes her head. 'No. I'll take my mobile.'

'Are you going to be okay?' His voice is soft and full of concern.

Her chest squeezes her heavy heart like a vice. 'I don't think so, Bro.'

'I'll be there as soon as I can.'

'Thanks.'

'I'll bring Dad,' Ivan says.

'I don't know…'

'He'll be more use than me, Sis.'

Freya sobs into the receiver. 'He'll hate me.'

'But you didn't kill Rob.'

'It looks like I did.' Freya's weeping grows louder. Her body shakes. She feels the threat of hysteria grip her shoulders.

'But you didn't.'

She breathes deeply, choking on tears. 'No, I didn't,' she whispers.

'We'll sort this out, you, me and Dad. It'll be okay. Look, I'm going to put the phone down and ring Dad. We'll call you when we're on our way, okay?'

Freya wails.

'Okay?' Ivan asks again.

'Okay,' Freya answers. 'But hurry.'

Chapter 14

The flat is dingy. Empty cans and bottles cover the floor around sofa and chairs like pebbled shores around volcanic islands. Mark steps across reefs of glass and aluminium and curls his legs up on an empty armchair. The arms of the chair are pitted with black circles as if someone has used them as an ashtray. He rubs his fingers over the scars. The melted fibres scratch his skin.

He looks across the room at the three guys shoulder to shoulder on one sofa. They use beer cans as ashtrays. When they offer him a cigarette, he shakes his head.

'Wise. I wish I'd never started. A slave to nicotine now.' Simon lifts a bottle of Grolsh to his lips and pours the lager into his throat. 'This stuff will kill you, but who wants to live forever, huh?'

Mark nods and leans back in the chair. His eyelids feel heavy and the oppressive warmth of the room pulls him towards sleep.

'Sure kid, get some sleep. You're safe here,' Kevin assures him.

He isn't sure whether he thanks them or not before sleep claims him. In his dreams three faces drift just beyond his reach, two women and a man. One face is well known to him, the others feel like distant memories. He's here to refresh those memories.

When Mark wakes, the settee before him is empty. He picks his way across the carpet, between mounds of debris to the kitchenette. An old looking fridge hums and the meagre surface space is covered in dirty plates, dishes, take-away cartons and mugs full of cold, half-drunk tea. The bin overflows and the oven, covered with unwashed crockery, looks grimy and black.

Mark returns to the living room and walks towards the front door. He knows beyond the door a staircase leads to the world outside. The door has three keyholes and two sets of heavy bolts. Neither bolt is drawn. Mark pushes the handle down and the door opens. The staircase is empty. He could leave.

He closes the door and looks at an alcove to his left. Two other doors hang between magnolia walls. Both stand ajar. He peers into a dark room. A bed rests in the centre. A pale body in boxer shorts is sprawled across the sheet. The upper sheet and blanket have been kicked away and lie tangled like a caterpillar beside the shaven-headed sleeper.

The second door leads to a tiny bathroom. This room, although grubby, does not have rubbish strewn across the floor. A small blue bathtub, sink and toilet huddle together around a grey towel, which has been spread across a vinyl floor. The towel has imprints of feet. Mark touches the fibres. They are hardly damp, but the imprints are deep and dark in colour.

85

Mark wonders whether to leave or stay. *Sleeping in a chair is preferable to the dank tunnel, but what will the men demand in return?* He suspects they want violence from him. While he is not afraid he has other plans, a different purpose for being here. *Will these thugs get in my way or can they help me?* He decides to wait and see.

He heads for the kitchen and searches for bin liners. The empty cans, bottles and cartons Mark stuffs into four large sacks, carries down the stairs and out of the building, placing them in a nearby bin. He looks for washing up liquid but finds only hand soap. He uses this to drag grime from plates and dishes and tidies them away into empty cupboards.

By the time the sleeper rises from the bedroom, the kitchen and living room have both been cleared of rubbish. The carpet looks as dirty without cans and bottles scattered upon it as with, but it is less hazardous to move around the room and easier to find a vessel from which to drink water.

'Did you do this?' Kevin asks.

'Yes,' Mark answers.

'Why?'

Mark shrugs. 'I had time to kill.'

The man returns Mark's shrug and sits down on the sofa. 'Thanks. Get us a cuppa will you, Kid?'

'Sure.' Mark heads to the kitchen to fill the kettle.

A cloud of cigarette smoke and the chatter of a television waft into the kitchenette. *Still it's better than urine*, he tells himself.

Chapter 15

Edensun wanders through labyrinthine city streets. The contrast between this place, so full of buildings and people, and his home, Binah, makes his head spin. He touches a rich ochre and black wall of stone. It feels colder than the colour suggests. He pulls his hand away and studies his palm. A fine layer of grey dirt clings to his skin.

He weaves through crowds of people along narrow cobbled streets. To his left a huge Cathedral dominates the skyline. He walks towards it. Dozens of camera lenses focus on the structure, capturing its memory for people to carry with them when they leave.

A horse and trap wait outside. The cart is black and has a sign on its side offering York City Tours. A man and woman sit on a bench at the rear, a well-wrapped driver at the front. The man and woman grip each other's hands and look around them, at the looming York Minster, the snug taverns and shops, the bright green lawn of the parkland behind them and the multitude of people walking past or pausing to pet the horse.

He stays for a moment, until the punching weight of human sounds makes him feel giddy. Turning away, he follows the quietest street he can find and weaves between shoppers and tourists. When Edensun reaches the city wall, he climbs the steps to the narrow walkway at its summit. As he marches across wooden boards laid on stone, he watches the world rush by below. Every so often he needs to squeeze against the wall and make himself narrow for others to pass. His eyes scan the rooftops of the ancient buildings to his left and the modern ones to his right. It is hard to see the two as parts of the same whole.

He wanders aimlessly. The sun sets, and streetlights are lit. People dress in brighter costumes to compensate and the old city seems more alive than ever. Hours pass as Edensun explores. This is Malkuth. He had struggled to understand Lilith's descriptions of this world. He could not imagine that such a crush of souls could exist. Seeing it now he realises they wander around oblivious to each other, making walls out of air to protect themselves. He thinks of his mother and wonders whether he will get past her wall. *Is she as lonely and resigned to her fate as the rest of these plumed humans? I will find out soon enough.*

The crowds of people thin and dissipate, returning to their homes drunk and loud. Cobblestones make them stagger. Edensun watches with amusement as high-heeled, short-skirted women topple and fall.

Like a shadow, he glides through the quiet streets towards his destination. He could have gone there first, but this was more fun. Watching the lives of people, feeding off their energy, before he severs the mortal coil of the one he hunts.

He climbs a red brick wall to a first storey window. He balances cat-like on the windowsill. The curtains beyond the pane are drawn. He sees only the faintest glow of light through the narrow gap between them. The only part of the window he can open is a narrow strip at the top about thirty centimetres deep. He tugs at its edge, pulls it open and leans towards the gap. His body alters to fit. It squashes down like rolled pastry and he feeds himself into the room beyond.

Standing behind the curtains, he studies the room. At its centre stands a cot. Through the gaps of its white wooden struts he sees a sleeping infant covered in a pale green blanket. He shuts the window behind him to make sure the baby's room doesn't get cold.

The room is silent. He moves to the door and hears a soft purring, vibrating noise. Stepping into the hall, he follows the noise to a door that stands ajar. He pushes it open slowly and quietly. Before him is a double bed. Two sleepers lie together beneath a crumpled duvet. The one on the right is a blonde haired woman. The one of the left is a man with fair, but not quite blonde, hair. The sound comes from the sleepers. It is the noise they make when they breathe.

Edensun creeps across the room. The woman, Freya, stirs and he freezes, but she doesn't wake. Her contribution to the purring, vibrating duet resumes.

As he stands above Rob, the sleeper awakens and his eyes flick open. Edensun places his finger before his lips and Rob stares up at him unable to comprehend. The man moves to reach out to the woman beside him. When Edensun shakes his head Rob's fingers tremble then slowly withdraw, away from her shoulder.

'What do you want?' Rob whispers.

'I need to send Freya somewhere,' Edensun answers.

Rob shakes his head. His eyes widen as he sees the glint of metal in the youth's fist. Edensun strikes before Rob can articulate a scream. Air wheezes from the wound on impact. Rob's eyes grow dull and his body sinks into the mattress. The youth pulls his knife from Rob's chest and slams it into his victim again and again, enjoying the cracking, wheezing sounds the body makes. When he is satisfied, Edensun watches blood spread through the fabric of Rob's t-shirt.

He wipes the blade clean on the sheets and pockets it before leaving, as he arrived, through the narrow window in the baby's room.

Chapter 16

Star lies on her bed. She lifts her legs and turns her ankles, watching the play of shadow and light on her skin.

A face fills her head: a male face, similar to Satori's but with darker skin and vivid green eyes. She reaches out to stroke the soft warm cheek of the familiar stranger and smiles as his lips move to kiss her fingertips. The feeling is as soft as butterfly wings against her flesh.

She moves her hand between her thighs and strokes the velvet flesh beneath her panties. Other faces join the stranger's. They watch her mouth open and close with the sounds of pleasure. Satori is there and Ivan and another, a face in shadow. She screams as the shadow lifts and she recognises her father's disapproving stare. Her hand jolts back is if electrified. 'I'm sorry.' She turns from them in shame and weeps.

Clutching her burning stomach, she curls her body and sobs into the pillow. 'I'm sorry. I'm sorry. I'm sorry,' she repeats until she falls asleep.

When she wakes the room is dark. She checks the clock and wonders whether Satori has already returned. She tidies her skirt before leaving the room to check.

'Satori?' She wanders around her silent home. 'Are you here?'

There is no answer. She grabs a plate from the kitchen and fills it with salad leaves. Sinking into an armchair, she switches on the television and watches the news. There is a story about a dog that saved a little girl and her father, and a few words about a murder in a drainage tunnel. The weather prediction is for a cold snap before spring sets in properly.

Star sighs and eats without relish. Boredom grips her in its bony fingers. Ideas flick through her mind of things she might do to distract herself, paint, read or dance. Inertia keeps her seated before the chattering television set. She leans her head against the back of the chair and thinks.

I am the mother and the sun. In Binah I was everything, lover of a goddess, mother, mistress of a giant snake. Here I am a failed artist whose sex drive peaks beyond all measure. Did I make the right choice? Did I choose at all or did I just follow him home?

She imagines her son, the tiny sharp-toothed infant she had so easily discarded. He would be four now, walking and talking. *Does he speak about me? What does Lilith tell him? Does he think I hate him because he is different? Just like my father and mother hate me.* 'I shouldn't have left you.'

She leans forwards and changes the channel. Black and white images of Morticia and Gomez fill the screen. *Now there's a real goddess*, she thinks as she snuggles into the chair to watch.

Three episodes later she starts to wonder whether something might have happened to Satori. She tries to phone him, but his mobile is switched off. She growls in frustration. For as long as she has known him he has always been

92

unreliable with his phone and timekeeping. It's another thing on the long list of things about him, which annoy her now.

Chapter 17

Freya pushes the pram around the town. It bounces over cobblestones at the Shambles. Voices fight each other for her attention, offering her the best deals on fruit, vegetables and electrical goods. She glances at her phone. The signal is strong, but no message yet.

Jasmine wakes and starts to cry. Freya pushes her faster around the marketplace. She ignores other people and stares at her daughter through a veil of tears. She is grateful for the size and weight of the old fashioned pram. No one tries to push past her; they avoid her as if she is driving a tank rather than pushing a baby.

Jasmine's wails squeeze Freya's skull. The pressure in her head makes her brain pound and her thoughts chaotic. Nothing makes sense. She thinks of the room: Rob in bed covered with blood, her unharmed. She didn't hear a sound as he was slaughtered. *How could the murderer have been so quiet? How did they get in and out of the flat? Who would murder him? Was it someone Rob knew? Rob was always so sweet to me and Jasmine. How could he upset anyone to the point that they would want him dead?*

She checks her phone again, still no call from her father or brother. It has only been two hours. They won't arrive for ages. In the meantime she must try to keep calm, not draw attention to herself, and stop Jasmine crying.

Freya pushes the pram into a coffee shop at the edge of the market. She sits at a table with plastic flowers in a metal vase. She lifts her baby from the pram and opens her blouse. Instantly Jasmine settles. She is hungry. She is always hungry.

A woman comes across the room, holding a notepad and pencil. She smiles at the baby and then at Freya.

'It's lovely to see a woman feeding her baby,' she says. 'What can I get you?'

'Tea, please,' Freya answers.

'Do you also want some water? You know, to top your fluids back up.'

'Sure, thanks.'

'How about something to eat?'

'Ummm, what?'

'We're still serving breakfasts. Can I bring you one?'

Freya shakes her head. 'Just tea for now, okay?'

'No problem. Let me know if you change your mind. Nursing mummies have to stay strong, right?'

Freya shrugs. 'Yeah, I guess. Look, I don't want to be rude, but...'

'I'm sorry.' The woman blushes. 'I'll leave you in peace. Your tea and water will be with you in a minute.'

Freya nods. 'Thanks.'

Freya looks at her phone again. She considers dialling Ivan's number, but what good would that do? She can hardly talk about the murder scene on the telephone in a café. She's better waiting until they get here and they can see for themselves. *Maybe they can help me understand what happened?*

Jasmine falls asleep in Freya's arms. The waitress returns with a pot of tea and a cup. She nods at Freya's open blouse and exposed breast. Freya frowns, looks down and blushes. She lays Jasmine back in the pram and buttons her blouse. Within seconds the baby wakes and starts screaming again. The waitress pulls a sympathetic face and walks away. Freya sighs and picks Jasmine up again. The baby reaches for her mother's breast. *Always hungry.*

Chapter 18

'Are you busy?' Star asks.

The telephone line goes quiet for a moment.

'Ivan?' she asks again.

'Hi, Star.' Ivan answers. 'Look, I'm sorry it's a bad time. I'm on my way with Dad and Bill, out of town for a couple of days.'

'Shit!' she says.

'Call Satori.'

She bites her nails. 'I can't.'

'Of course you can. He'll want to help.'

'Anyway he's busy.'

'I'm sorry. I really am, but I'm busy too.'

'Fuck!'

'Take a few deep breaths. Meditate. Stay at home. What time's Satori due back?'

'I dunno. Eight-ish.'

'I'm really sorry, Star. You know I'd help if I could. You can do this. You can get through it. It's only a few hours.'

'Sure. Sorry I bothered you,' she answers.

'Don't…'

She hangs up without listening to Ivan's reply.

Should I phone Satori? He would come home. Ivan's right. But I don't want him, do I?

She goes to her drawer and takes out a ten inch vibrator. She looks at it and strokes its length. It will have to do. It's all she has for now. She pulls off her panties and holds the dildo by its vibrating base. She straddles the latex cock and pushes herself onto it. She is wet enough, thinking about Ivan and playing with herself for an hour before even calling him. She moves herself up and down, imaging him inside her, imagining any man inside her. She feels empty. She needs to be filled. Her body aches. Her vagina cries out in pain and longing. *Why do I feel like this?*

Lilith? All that time as Lilith's plaything, is this the result? Did the demon taint me? Are we the same - insatiable? No, not all the time, only when...only when the moon is full or when it's new, empty, black. Then I am afraid to go outside. Afraid of what I might do and yet afraid to be alone. It hurts. I can fuck myself for hours and yet when I stop, when my arm is so tired I can hardly move, I still need more.

She rides the dildo more frantically, bruising her cervix. Her body vibrates, but she doesn't orgasm. She isn't there yet. She can never get there, not like this.

She throws the vibrator across the room. Batteries spill from its guts. The pink rubber is smeared with white from her body. She stares at it, her eyes full of hatred and accusation.

'Fuck you!' Her hatred is for Ivan, Satori, Lilith, herself, the vibrator and all of mankind. Everything hurts. Everything aches. The butterfly inside her breaks its wings against its cage. She has to get out. *No, I can't go out. What if?*

She falls onto the bed and screams. Tears stream from her eyes, soaking the duvet. She reaches for her mobile and dials

Satori's number. The call goes straight to message. 'Fucker!' she screams. 'Fuck! Fuck! Fuck!'

She sweats. Her body is on fire. She tears off her clothes and pushes her fingers deep inside her cunt. She can't reach far enough. She replaces the batteries in the dildo and, tilting her pelvis towards the ceiling, she tries again. However vigorously she pushes it inside her she gets no relief. She cannot come and the moment it moves out of her she feels empty and bereft.

She dresses carelessly, pulling a thin summer dress over bare skin. She slips her feet into her boots, grabs her keys and purse and leaves the house. The corner shop isn't far. The man behind the counter looks at her strangely. She asks for a bottle of tequila and he asks her for ID. She checks her purse and pulls out her student ID. It takes everything she has to smile and pass him the ID rather than throw it at him. He looks at her photo and the information. She taps her foot. He returns it to her, smiling.

'Eighteen pounds, please,' he says.

She passes him a twenty pound note. He gives her the change before reaching for the bottle. She strides out of the shop and unscrews the lid. The liquid burns her throat. She coughs. Somebody says something as they pass her. She looks up and watches an old man walk away. Hot between her legs, she imagines falling to her knees before him and taking his cock in her mouth before riding him until his semen fills her.

He keeps walking and she lets him go. The fantasy replays in her head, horrifying her. She takes another mouthful of tequila, screws the lid back on and walks towards the cottage.

Shadows lengthen. They reach across the path, trying to touch Star. Her eyes sweep the ground as she steps over the dark bruises cast by branches, adapting the Christopher Robin game she played as a child, when her mum would recite the rhyme while the young Sarah avoided treading on cracks in pavements so the lurking, unseen bears couldn't trap her. All the while she would check frantically behind walls and through gates, knowing, even then, that her mother would not protect her.

Star wraps her arms around her body. The thin material of her summer dress offers no resistance against the cold evening air. Her carrier bag swings in her hand. The glass bottle bounces off her thigh. The pain feels like a bad omen: a bottle thrown against the hull of a ship on her maiden voyage that does not smash. It is unlucky and warns of troubled waters ahead.

Chapter 19

Freya's phone buzzes. She picks it up, *Ivan.*

'Where are you?' she whispers, frantically.

'We've just got here. We're outside your apartment. Where are you?'

'At a café off the Shambles, shall I come to you?'

'Dad's heading inside. Do you want me to come and meet you?'

'Meet me at the city wall. I'll be there in fifteen minutes.'

'Okay, Sis. I love you.'

'I love you too, Bro.'

Freya pays the bill and tucks Jasmine back into her pram. Her cup of tea sits untouched on the table. It looks grey, like dead flesh: cold and lifeless. She never even got to taste it.

The waitress looks at her sympathetically. Freya has sat there for hours, cuddling her daughter through sleep and wakefulness. Staring out of the window at the Medieval city beyond. Lives passed her by while she sat motionless, cradling her child.

Other people have come and gone. Conversations overheard: tourists, students, lovers, families, each with their own lives. *I have no life. I have only clung to the pretence of a life since my sister died when I was thirteen. I thought Rob would breathe life into my days, and for a moment it felt as though that might be true. Then Jasmine arrived. Jasmine's life usurped mine. I exist to feed and change, cuddle and soothe my tiny baby. I am an appendage. No more and no less. I have no life.*

'You're a good Mum,' the waitress says.

Freya shrugs. 'Thanks.'

She weaves the pram between tables and through the café doorway. The metal frame rattles as its wheels bounce over cobblestones. Jasmine sniffs the air.

'Shhhh,' Freya urges.

Jasmine pushes her blanket up with her tiny feet and looks into her mother's eyes. She makes the hiccupping sound which precedes tears.

'Please don't.' Freya blinks tears from her eyes. 'Don't cry.'

Jasmine smacks her lips noisily and reaches for the blue and green giraffe beside her pillow. Freya picks it up and passes it to the baby, steering the pram one handed, glancing up every now and again to avoid other pedestrians. 'It's okay, Grampy and Uncle Ivan are waiting to see you.'

Jasmine suckles the misshapen nose of the giraffe and settles back to sleep. Freya pushes the pram faster towards her destination - the wall and Ivan, Uncle Ivan.

She spots Ivan in the distance under the ancient arch of the city wall. He waves at her and starts walking. She smiles, forgetting for a moment her fear and grief until it all comes flooding back and she starts to cry. Ivan puts his arm around her shoulder and pulls her towards him. He bends his neck to glance into the pram. 'She's beautiful.'

102

Freya nods. 'I know.'

'Let's get you guys to Dad. May I?' Ivan touches the handlebar of Jasmine's pram.

'Sure.' Freya hooks her arm through his. Elbow to elbow, they walk slowly under the arch. Out of the old city and into the new.

'Thanks for coming.'

'What happened?'

'I woke up this morning and Rob was dead. He's been stabbed. I don't know how or by whom. His blood, so much blood, soaked through the bedding. I don't know how I slept through it.'

'Who would want to hurt him?'

'I don't know.' She studies her brother's square jaw and troubled frown.

'We'll see what Dad and Bill say when we get there.'

'Bill?'

'Dad brought a friend. I'm fucked if I know he is. Bill something.'

Freya shudders and looks away. 'It's not much further.'

'I know.'

'I'm sorry.' Freya's voice breaks into sobs.

'I know.'

'What will we do?'

'I don't know. I haven't even seen the flat yet,' Ivan answers.

They turn the corner onto Freya's street.

'Where's Dad's car?' she asks.

'It was here.' Ivan pulls out his mobile phone and calls his father. There is no answer.

Freya unlocks the front door and pulls the pram inside. 'Dad?'

The house is silent. Leaving Jasmine and the pram in the hallway, Freya and Ivan push past, climb the stairs and head for the bedroom. The bed has been stripped. A dark stain on the mattress is the only trace of Rob which remains.

'Help me,' Freya says, lifting the side of the mattress.

Together they flip it over, but the stain is much larger on the other side so they turn it back.

'I guess Dad couldn't fit this in the car,' she says. 'Do you think we can wash it?'

Ivan sits on the floor in silence shaking his head.

'He's protecting me,' Freya says. 'It looks like I did it so he's protecting me. He always protects me.'

Ivan looks away.

'I don't know what we'll do about this mattress though.' Freya knows she is rambling, but cannot stop. She feels despair stalking her. She cannot give it room to grow. 'Maybe I should burn it? Help me drag it into the garden, Bro.'

Ivan shakes his head. Worry lines cast the shadows of his doubts across his forehead. 'We should have called the police.'

'Well, we can't now. Dad's made sure of that,' Freya answers.

'Rob has work. He has family. It's only a matter of time before people come looking for him.'

'Jasmine and I won't be here.'

'Where will you be?'

'With you.'

'Then they'll find you.'

Freya shakes her head.

'How do you know?'

'Trust me. Now help me get rid of this mattress.' She drags at the heavy corner, cursing its weight and bulk.

'You can't burn the mattress in the garden. Think of the smoke. Someone will call the fire brigade.'

'What do you suggest?' Freya snaps angrily. *What use are you? What did I expect?*

'We wait for Dad and Bill to get back.'

'Wait here?' Freya shudders. Her eyes fix on the bloodstain.

Ivan reaches towards her. 'Yes.'

Freya sniffs and takes a deep breath. 'Okay. Do you want a cup of tea?'

Ivan stares at her. His thoughts seem to dart behind his eyes as if he is trying to piece together this stranger he calls sister. 'No thanks.'

Freya walks from the bedroom and into the kitchen to switch the kettle on. She cannot sit still and wait. *Why should Dad make all the decisions anyway? Because I called him to help me. No I called Ivan, but what help is he? Dad's doing what needs to be done. He's saving Jasmine and me. I can wait for him to get back. Maybe he does know what to do. How does he know? What part of being a taxi driver and a father prepares a person for this? And who is Bill? Do I know him?* The kettle bubbles as the water warms. She holds her hand in the column of steam. It scolds her skin, but she does not pull away. *This is insane,* she tells herself, and moves reluctantly away, grabbing a cup and a teabag.

She takes her tea into the hallway, stands at the top of the stairs and watches her daughter sleep: a calm spot in the centre of a hurricane. She imagines Rob kissing her goodbye and walking past her and out of the door for work. 'Have a good day,' she whispers.

As if her words summoned him, the front door opens and her father steps inside.

'Hi, Daddy.'

Mike bends to look in the pram then turns his face towards her. His face looks as white as smoke around his dark eyes, but he is smiling. 'Hey, Freya. Good to see you.'

'Where's Bill?'

'He's not coming back with us. Look, Freya, I need to make a quick phone call before we finish here. Is that tea? I'm parched. Could you make me a cuppa?'

Chapter 20

Satori cannot bear to go straight home. Instead he heads to an old local drinking hole, *The Full Moon*. The woman behind the bar smiles warmly and he orders a single malt. He sits on a stool at the bar and turns around to study the other patrons.

It is still early and the men and women gathered around the wooden tables of the public house are all much older than Satori. He sees in their faces a well-worn resignation to the pointlessness of existence. He pities them, takes a large sip of his whisky and starts to pity himself as well.

I could have had it all. My life was so full of potential. There was nothing I could not do. How much can one man change in four short years?

The bar keeper approaches him and asks in her syrupy voice whether he would like another. He nods and thanks her. She is attractive in the heavily painted sort of way that women in the service industry seem to prefer. Her hair is long and ash blonde with waves which she tucks behind her ears, revealing large gold hoops. She has a perfect smile with the whitest teeth Satori has ever seen, the sort of smile that lights up a room. He asks her name.

'Gloria,' she answers.

'Great name.' He looks steadily into her soft blue eyes.

She blushes slightly and smiles again. 'I haven't seen you before.'

'It used to be my local, but I moved away.'

'A local boy,' she chimes. 'So where do you live now?'

'On the north side of town.' He extends his hand across the bar. 'I'm Satori.'

She takes his hand and shakes it. 'Pleased to meet you.'

She moves away to serve another customer then returns. 'What do you do for a living, Satori?'

He grins and licks his lips. 'A bit of this and a bit of that. I read tarot. I tell fortunes and I can bless or curse pretty much anything you can name.'

'Are you a gypsy?'

He shakes his head, laughing softly.

'Would you do it for me?'

'Tell your fortune?'

'Yes. I've never had my cards read.'

'I could, but not here. When are you free?'

'I get off at twelve,' she says.

He considers her reply. 'I'm sorry. I'll be long gone by twelve tonight. I could come back another day to see you, if you like.'

Her smile is wider and brighter than ever. 'I'd like that very much, Satori. I can even ply you with free booze while you wait for me to finish.'

'Tempting though that is, I should keep a clear head when I'm working. Maybe we should share a bottle after we're done?'

'Perfect.' Her long lashes cast shade over her eyes and she moistens her lips.

Satori swallows hard. His cock stirs inside his boxers. 'Then I'll see you soon. I had better be on my way. It was a pleasure meeting you, Gloria.'

'And you, Satori. Hurry back.'

'I will.' His grin doesn't falter as he leaves the pub. He doubts he will return to accept her offer, but her attention and flirtation make him feel good.

Chapter 21

Mark passes a mug of strong, sweet tea to the man, who grunts. 'Thanks, Kid.'

'I need to go out,' Mark tells him.

'Sure. Wait ten minutes and I'll come with.' Kevin lights a cigarette and takes in drags of smoke between sips of tea.

Mark shakes his head. 'I need to go out alone. There's someone I'm looking for.'

'Your mam?' Kevin adjusts his position, straightening his back and tensing his torso. His body language is alert and interested, ready for action.

Mark blushes. The man's gaze feels heavy with expectation. 'How did you know?'

'The state of you. What happened? Did she walk out on you?'

'Yes.'

'Women. Can't fucking trust the cunts.'

Mark bristles. Adrenaline heats his muscles. 'Watch your mouth. It's not like that.'

The man laughs. 'Sure, kid, relax. Whatever, but I need you here at two o'clock. Got someone who wants to meet you.'

'Who?'

'My mate, Garlow. So we can go out and come back, but I'm not about to let you go wandering off. What if you get lost and end up back in those sewers? I'd never forgive myself.'

'I know where you live.' Mark feels indignant. He is not a child.

'Kid. This is a big city, a dangerous city. I'll look after you. We can get some lunch. You like burgers, right?'

Mark shrugs. 'Dunno.'

'The bitch never even fed you burgers?'

'My mum isn't a bitch. Stop calling her that.'

'Sorry, Kid. Force of habit. My mum weren't no good at all. Just wanted to sleep around and stay drunk enough not to remember my name.'

Mark sighs. He grabs Kevin's empty mug and takes it to the sink.

Kevin pushes himself out of the chair and yawns. 'Give me two minutes. I'll get my kit on and we'll head out.'

Mark nods.

'Where you gonna look first?' Kevin's voice echoes through the apartment.

Mark wanders back into the living room and waits. He hears grunts and the rustling of denim and cotton coming from the bedroom. 'I don't know. I don't know anything other than her name.'

'Really? How long since you've seen her?'

'Most of my life.'

Kevin strides into the room, fully dressed. 'Oh shit, kid. But she's here, is she?'

'I think so… I can feel her.'

'How old is she?'

Mark shakes his head. 'About your age, maybe.'

'No fucking way, Kid. I'm only twenty-six. I couldn't have a kid your age.'

'Yes you could.'

Kevin looks at Mark askance. 'One for the ladies already, huh?'

Mark shrugs.

'You really are dark horse, scrawny kid like you, a fighter and a lover. Colour me impressed, but it doesn't help us figure out where your mam will be. Maybe we should hang tight and ask Garlow. He's a man with connections, right. If anyone can tell you where to start looking, he can.'

'Okay. I'll ask him. But I want to go and walk about anyway. Just to see, you know?'

'I have no idea, Kid, but sure. What harm can it do?'

Mark wanders among the shoppers. Flattened cobblestones underfoot give the illusion of an ancient city, a city with history. The glass ceiling above reflects thousands of lights, which look like stars against the indigo of the sky beyond. Everyone is rushing. He walks calmly among them, recognising no one.

'Anything?' Kevin asks.

'Not yet,' Mark answers.

'Wait here a minute,' Kevin says. 'I just wanna pop in this shop.'

Mark nods and wanders with the older man towards the glass front of a high-end supermarket.

'Want anything?' Kevin asks.

Mark shakes his head. He looks at his reflections in the window, in triplicate. In each his face is twisted and his eyes look hollow. He turns towards the centre of the arcade. He watches men in suits and women in high heels hurry past. A movement in the corner of his eye attracts him. Something large and white moves slowly between the shoppers, it heads towards him.

Mark looks at the shop doorway then back at the figure. Its white coat billows like a spectre. Its steps are slow but purposeful. Mark looks in the opposite direction and sees another figure in white. Motionless, it watches him.

Mark's heart hammers as he looks left and right between the two men in their long, white coats. He looks back at the supermarket and sees Kevin in a queue. He taps on the glass with his knuckles, but Kevin does not look up. One figure is only a few metres away now. The other stands some distance from them and watches. Mark balls his fist. He considers running into the store, but what can Kevin do? What would Kevin do? Mark is no one to Kevin. Why would he interfere?

'Hello.' The man in white smiles at Mark.

'Hello,' Mark answers.

'Come with me.' The man's smile seems fixed. His mouth barely moves as he speaks.

'What do you want?' Mark's voice is loud. A woman turns to look at them. An auburn curl falls across her eyes. She frowns, tucks her hair behind her ear, shrugs and moves on without another glance.

'Just to talk,' the man says. 'Somewhere quiet.'

113

'I can't. I'm waiting for someone,' Mark answers.

'We know who you're looking for,' the man says. 'We can take you there.'

Mark's eyes widen. 'You do?'

The man nods. The top of his head has a bald patch the size of Mark's fist. The skin glows pink within the halo of black and grey.

'What's her name?' Mark asks.

'Not here,' the man answers.

Mark sees a movement to his left and realises the other man is walking towards them. He reaches behind and knocks on the shop window again.

The bald man in white looks past Mark through the window. 'He won't help you.'

Mark's arm shakes. He wants to grind his fist into the smile before him.

'What's going on?' Kevin strides towards the trio.

'Kevin!' Mark says.

As Kevin steps closer, Mark feels stronger and protected. 'Are these men bothering you, Kid?'

'Do you know this boy?' the bald man asks.

'Sure,' Kevin answers.

'Do you know what he's capable of?'

Kevin sighs. 'We're not interested, Grandpa. Get lost.'

The man nods towards his companion who is less than two metres away. His hand slips inside his coat.

'Run!' Kevin shouts.

Kevin's punch catches the bald man off balance and he stumbles. Kevin grabs Mark's arm and they sprint away from the two men in white.

'Who are they?' Kevin asks as they keep running, out of the mall, across the road and up some steps onto a grass bank overlooking the river.

They run until they reach the walls of the ruined castle. There they crouch with their backs against a cold stone wall. Their chests inflate and deflate as they catch their breaths. 'Who were they?' Kevin's chin drops towards his shoulder as he studies Mark.

Mark blinks. 'I don't know.'

'What did they want?'

'They wanted me to go with them.'

'Fucking perverts.' Kevin spits. 'There's too much of that shit around here, Kid. This city ain't what it used to be.'

'Do you think they'll come back?'

'Nah, they're long gone. I'd like to know what that bastard was going to pull from his pocket though, wouldn't you? Couldn't get into a fight there, anyways. Too much fucking security. What do you reckon he was gonna do?'

Mark shakes his head. 'I don't know. They said they know who I'm looking for. Maybe I should go back.'

'Huh?'

'Maybe they know my mum.'

'Didn't seem that way to me, Kid, but if you want to go back I'm right beside you. Those nonces will be long gone, though. Trust me...and anyway, look it's late. We can't be late for Garlow. It just doesn't happen. We can come back tomorrow if you want.'

Marks nods. 'Sure. Oh and Kevin.'

'What, Kid?'

'Thanks.'

'No problem. Gotta keep my prize winner in good nick, huh?' Kevin punches Mark's shoulder playfully.

'Huh?'

'Don't worry. Garlow will fill you in. Just know I'm looking out for you.'

Chapter 22

'I'm sorry, Daddy,' Freya says.

'What the fuck happened?' Mike asks. 'I haven't seen a mess like this for…'

'I don't know. I just woke up and…' A tear rolls down Freya's cheek. 'I found him. He was already dead.'

Mike looks at Ivan then back at Freya. 'Okay. We can talk about it later if we need to. First, we'll clear the apartment of everything. It'll look like you've skipped town, but no more than that. Help me with the mattress, Ivan.'

Ivan and Mike grab each end of the mattress and pull it out of the room. Freya sighs and shakes her head. She hears the door shut behind them then soft whispers that she cannot understand.

Do they think I did this?

Well did we?

No, of course not.

Are we sure?

Yes. Maybe we don't know who did it, but we know it wasn't us.

Freya checks on Jasmine in her pram. She is fast asleep.

How could we do this, Freya?

We didn't, Deya. You'd remember if we did. Now think. Dad wants us to get rid of everything.

Passports, credit cards, clothes.

Yes that's right. Grab a suitcase and we'll start packing.

Freya opens every drawer. She leaves cutlery and kitchenware behind, but packs everything else. Toiletries, books, clothing, money and identification all get pushed into the four suitcases she can find. Her tears dampen fabrics as she presses layers of cotton onto velvet and satin. She does not fold anything. It is thrown in without a care for creasing or other damage. Her skin itches. She wants out. She wants to leave this place and never return.

It was a mistake coming here.

We're leaving now.

But, Rob.

You can't help him.

I never helped him. Now he's dead and my baby has no father.

But she has a mother.

Two mothers.

That should serve her well. As long as no one suspects us.

Daddy does.

Daddy loves us.

He always has. He forgives us everything because he doesn't want to lose us too.

I know.

Freya, do you think it's odd that he knew what to do?

Who, Daddy?

Yes. It's like he's done it all before.

Do you think he has?

Surely, not.

No one found those boys, did they?

Do you think?

Do I think he killed the kids who murdered our sister? Yes. I think it's possible.

Should we ask him?

Absolutely not.

By the time Ivan and Mike return, the belongings are packed. Ivan stares silently at the floor.

'Is this all of it?' Mike asks.

Freya nods.

'Are you sure?'

'Yes, Daddy.'

'Good girl. Now give your old man a hug.' A nerve beneath his eye pulses.

Freya kisses his cheek. 'What did you do with it all?' she asks.

'Bill's taking care of it.'

'Daddy, you need to know. I...'

'Sweetheart, all I need to know is that you and that beautiful granddaughter of mine are safe. You're coming home with us.'

'Won't they look for me there?'

'Who?'

'The police.'

'Why would the police look for you, Baby?'

Freya looks around her. Her jaw drops. She shrugs.

'Trust me,' Mike answers.

'I do, Daddy.'

Chapter 23

Satori stops at the front door. He hears sobbing. Slowly, he pushes his key into the lock. His skin prickles and he shivers. *What now?*

'Are you okay, Star?' he asks as he steps through the door.

She doesn't reply, but the sounds of crying become louder.

He closes and locks the door behind him then strides across the living room. The hallway is dark. The door to their bedroom stands ajar. He pushes it open a crack further and looks inside. She is there.

Her dark hair is wild and tangled. An empty bottle of tequila lies on its side on the bedside table. Her head is bowed and her nose is red from tears. She rocks herself back and forth. In her hand she holds a vibrator. There are traces of blood on its shaft.

He rushes towards her and envelopes her with his arms.

'Shhhh,' he whispers. 'It's okay.'

He takes the vibrator from her clenched fist and places it beside the empty bottle. He strokes her hair, pushing tangled and damp strands away from her face. Ginger roots show against her black-dyed locks. He pulls her face towards his chest and holds her tightly. 'Did it happen again?'

He feels her forehead brush against his chest as she nods.

'Why didn't you call me?'

She sniffs. The sound is loud and wet. She shakes her head.

'You can always call me, Darling. Whenever something like this happens, if ever you need me, just call. I'll come home.'

She shakes her head again.

'Can you tell me what happened?'

Her sobs get louder. He strokes her hair again and hushes her. Their bodies rock together. 'It's okay now, Star. I'm here. You're safe. I love you. We'll get past this, okay?'

She neither shakes nor nods her head but presses her cheek harder against his chest.

'I love you,' he whispers.

She does not reply.

Her silence stabs him in the chest. Her body is stiff and unyielding. She feels as though she is simply tolerating his touch.

'Star, what's happened to us?' he asks.

'I don't know.' Her voice sounds thick with resentment.

He doesn't ask her anything else. He holds her in silence letting anger gnaw at his stomach. He wonders if he is beyond caring and realises he is not. Whatever happens, she will always be his responsibility. He will care for her and hope that one day she will come back to him, just like she did four years ago. The memory of his temporary success chills him. If he knew then what he knows now, would he have bothered to travel worlds to save her? He has no answer to that question and is thankful he has never borne the burden of foresight.

121

When he saw her in Binah, her body was torn apart. It had been torture just to look at her. He had never suspected how deep those wounds went. Lilith's taint on Star remains. Now it is internalised. The damage the demon inflicted has never healed. Star's obsessive behaviour is becoming more pronounced and more dangerous month by month. She has no doctor they can turn to. Officially she is still dead. It had seemed simpler that way at first and now it is too late. He is powerless to help her and day by day she pushes him further and further away.

Chapter 24

'I should go back,' Star whispers.

Satori stirs beside her. He yawns and opens his eyes. 'Did you say something, Star?'

'I should go back.'

'Is this because of your compulsion, your dreams or us?'

'I – we have a son.'

'And we left him four years ago. Look, I know it's getting harder for you, but give it time. Give us time, please.'

'How much time?'

'Star, Darling, you survived. You survived a nightmare. I couldn't have done what you did. That place was torture and yet you got stronger not weaker. Why now?'

'I miss my son.'

Satori sighs. He puts his arms around her and pulls her wet face to his chest. 'Our son isn't human. Who knows what he is or what he will become?'

Star puts her arms around his shoulders and squeezes. Her ear and cheek press against his warm skin. She wants to squeeze until she crushes them both. He doesn't struggle. Instead he strokes her hair. Gradually the tension flows out of her and her grip loosens.

'Why do I feel like this?' she asks.

'I'm not sure,' he answers.

'Am I insane?'

'Of course not. Neither of us is insane. We just know things other people don't.'

'But what about this compulsion, as you call it? Why is it happening to me? It took all my strength to resist today. I'm scared, Satori.'

'I know you are. Maybe it's a taint from Binah or Lilith? Let's meditate together. We can wash your spirit clean. You can start again. Be who you are meant to be. Fulfil your potential.'

'My potential.' Star snorts.

'Remember when we came back? You healed me. You got us out of prison. You helped Donna accept and grow from all that had happened to her. What makes you think you can't do that for yourself? Why did you stop?'

'It made me tired.'

'Baby, you just need to recharge. I told you that. Use my energy, or the earth's or the sun's. Meditation will help. It's stupid to turn your back on who you are, again.'

'Stupid?'

Satori shrugs. 'You know what I mean.'

'You mean I'm stupid because I don't want to mess around with this stuff like you do. Because I think it's dangerous. You say I am strong because I survived where you couldn't and yet you still question every fucking little thing I do, and then you wonder why sometimes I can't stand being around you. So who's stupid?'

He pulls away from her. His eyes narrow and he stares at her hateful face. His body shakes with anger. 'I'm not as stupid as you think.'

'What's that supposed to mean?' Star trembles as she waits for his answer.

'Just that I know, but it's your body, your life. I have no right to decide what's best for you or who you should be with.'

'No you don't.' Defensive anger makes her answer harsher than she planned.

'I wish you'd told me though.' Satori looks down at the duvet as if it is covered in a puzzle he must solve.

'He didn't want me to.' Her voice is softer this time.

'Why?'

'Maybe he's scared.'

'I doubt it. What does he want from you, Star?'

'To help me heal and give me time out. Pretty much what you want, except he understands that the answer isn't always magic. Magic, magic and more magic, that's all you understand, Satori. You don't know me or what I need. When you look at me you see yourself with tits. I'm not you. I don't want to be.'

'But Ivan knows you?'

Star shrugs. 'I think so. As well as I know myself, anyway.'

'Do you want to be with him?'

'I don't want to always feel bullied and challenged. I don't want to always hear that you know best when you clearly don't.'

'You think I bully you?'

'I think you live your life assuming that you are the most important person in the world and deserve to have everything you want. I think you want me to be someone I am not. In fact I think as soon as I finish this sentence you'll try to convince me that you only want me to "fulfil my potential", my potential as you perceive it, of course.'

Satori frowns. 'Maybe I should go?'

'Maybe you should.'

He stares at her in silence and she wipes her nose with the back of her hand. She returns his stare. 'I'm sorry,' she whispers.

'What for?'

'For not being what you want me to be.'

Satori shakes his head. 'I only want you to be happy.'

'Exactly.'

Chapter 25

Mike drives towards the motorway. In the reflection of the rear view mirror Freya catches glimpses of his face. His eyes watch the road with cold concentration. Ivan keeps turning around in his seat to frown at her or smile at the baby. She knows what they are both thinking.

'I'm sorry,' she says.

'It's what Dads are supposed to do, Sweetheart, get their daughters out of trouble.' His eyes darken then clear again.

'I wish I knew what happened.'

'Did he hurt you?' Mike asks.

A rush of hot anger floods the car. She realises her father sees her as the victim not the killer. Through all these years he has never blamed her, always himself. Now he must make up for letting her sister die by ensuring nothing can ever hurt his little girl. Even if he saw her as a cold-blooded murderess he would still want to save her, whatever it took.

'He didn't hurt me...and I know it sounds crazy, I don't understand it myself, but I swear I didn't hurt him either.'

Ivan turns to face her again. His stare penetrates her skin. His jaw is clenched and his mouth trembles.

'I didn't, Ivan. I loved him.'

'We know, Love. No one is saying you killed Rob, are they, Ivan?' Mike's voice is hard.

Ivan turns to face the windscreen and the road ahead. He doesn't answer.

'Who's Bill?' Freya asks.

'Yes, Dad. Who is he?' Ivan echoes.

'Just a friend. Someone I know I can rely on.'

'How do you know?' Ivan asks.

'I just know. Look, this isn't something I'm prepared to talk about.'

The three of them and the baby travel silently for half an hour.

Freya rubs the handle of Jasmine's car seat. Her stomach feels hollow. The void grows, stretching throughout her body, pressing against her lungs making it hard to breathe. 'Do you think I'm mad?'

'Insane?' Mike says. 'No, you're not ill. You're strange but who wouldn't be after all you've been through. You're a survivor, Freya.'

She stares at her brother's ash blonde hair. He watches the road steadfastly. She is sure he can feel her watch him, but he does not respond.

'I searched the flat when I found him like that. There was no one else there.' She is unsure of whether she is speaking to herself, her father or brother. Words spill out of her. 'I looked everywhere. The house was locked. What could have done that to him if not me?'

'I don't know, Freya, but if you say you didn't kill him, I believe you. We just need to get you away from there. Things will work out. You'll see. You have your family to take care of you and your daughter to love you. Things will get better, I promise.'

'Dad.' Ivan's voice trembles as if from the weight of his thoughts or fear of his father's reaction. 'What about the police?'

'We didn't leave anything there. There was no murder. Rob, Freya and Jasmine left town. No one knows where they went.'

'What did you do with the body, Dad?' Ivan asks.

'There is no body. Leave it, Son.'

'I can't, Dad. How can you be so calm about this? You... you... I don't get it. What are you not telling us?'

'Drop the subject.' Mike growls.

'Dad?'

'Ivan!' Mike roars. 'Shut the fuck up!'

Jasmine wakes and starts to cry. Freya places her hand across the baby's stomach and sings softly to her. Her mother's voice and the movement of the car soothe Jasmine back to sleep.

'I'm sorry, Freya, I didn't mean to wake her.'

'It's okay, Dad, she's asleep again.'

'Your mum's looking forward to seeing you both. We've all missed you and that beautiful little girl.'

'Thanks, Dad. We've missed you too. All of you.' Freya studies the back of her brother's head. He stays perfectly still, eyes forward, as if meditating. She wonders what he is thinking. *Is he working through all the questions their father refuses to answer or has he escaped to his sacred space?*

She remembers her own sacred space, modelled on her brother's tree of ribbons. She remembers the snakeskin, the shell, skeleton and athame. She remembers leaving then returning to a body she created with magic. She remembers everything so clearly. So why doesn't she remember killing Rob?

Chapter 26

Satori lifts his bag onto his shoulder. 'See you Monday,' he calls through the bedroom door.

Star stirs in bed. 'Oh, yeah, okay. Have a good weekend.'

He considers kissing her. Her lips are soft and supple just above the edge of the duvet. The black cotton covers her body, making it look as though she has been beheaded. Her head left on his pillow as a warning, but a warning about what? Their life has been one battle after another. He had hoped when they came back from Binah things would be different, she would be different, but she hadn't changed. She never will. Still he loves her, but now he wonders whether this alone is enough.

Star is selfish. She goes through life unaware of everyone other than herself. She manipulates me. Her softness and beauty make me love her. I want to protect her from the world, but I cannot protect her from herself. Perhaps it is time to start again. At least one of us might be insulated from her wilful self-destruction. Four years – I've spent four years of penance making up for the fact that I made a terrible mistake. I couldn't see it then. I couldn't see that she and I do not belong together. I could be happy. I could have a life worth living, but not here and not with Star.

He sighs and blows her a kiss across the room. Her cheeks twitch in what might be an attempt at a smile. *Where did it all go wrong? I've done everything for her, but I couldn't make her happy. Perhaps part of Binah returned with her, a shadow inside her that grew and corrupted her over the years. Or perhaps this is simply who she is and I was too busy saving her to notice.*

We both need this break and it will be good to see Mother again.

He turns away and leaves the cottage, locking the door behind him.

'Steve!' Marian kisses both his cheeks and ushers him into the house. 'I made up your bed for you. Your room will always be yours. Dinner will be ready in half an hour. Do you want a drink, a shower or to settle in before I serve?'

'Hi, Mum.' He embraces her. 'Good to see you. Can I help with anything?'

'No, no. Just relax. Wine, whisky or coffee?'

Satori nods. 'Thanks. Whatever you're having will be great. I'll just pop my bag upstairs, shall I?'

'Yes, please do. There's a pot of coffee already made. Shall I bring a cup up or do you want it when you get back down?' She studies his face, perhaps searching for cracks in his armour.

He protects her from his tears, holding them back with a smile. 'I'll grab it in a minute. Thanks, Mum. It's great to be here.'

'Yes. I've made loads of plans for us for the weekend, but I can cancel them all if you want. We'll talk about what you want to do this weekend after dinner, shall we?'

Satori kisses his mother's cheek. 'Sure. See you in a minute.'

'There's no hurry, Love.'

Satori smiles and carries his bag to his old room. His possessions drag on his arm as he puts one foot before the other and climbs the stairs. His door groans softly as he opens it, protesting his long absence. Little has changed. Still the same bare floorboards and the same duvet on his single bed. The bookshelves are now filled with his mother's overspill of novels and there is a dark red armchair beside the window, but the rest remains the same. He opens his old wardrobe. Empty hangers wait to be filled. He closes the door again and drops his bag onto the bed.

He sits beside the bag, bouncing gently on the bed, remembering times spent in this room, studying, practising magic, making love. Memories flow through his mind, not swamping him with their weight, simply visiting, saying hello and making way for the next one. He sits with his hands on his lap and closes his eyes, letting each memory come and go in their polite and orderly fashion. This was where he lived. He may have been flawed, he may have been selfish, but he truly lived.

He sighs and opens his eyes. *Star.* He should leave her, probably. Start again. Put it all behind him and be free. *Why is it so hard to leave? What is this stranglehold she has on me? Do I still feel responsible for her? She's a grownup, a survivor. She doesn't need me. She never has. I needed her once, but now? I should leave. This weekend I'll find out whether I miss her. Maybe I won't?*

He stands up and unzips his bag. His clothes are folded neatly inside. He places them on the bed, smoothes out tiny creases and hangs them in his wardrobe. Removing the clothes, he uncovers a toiletry bag, two books, three pens, a journal and his personal MP3 player. He pushes the toiletry bag under his bed and places the books, pens and journal beside the headboard on the floor. He unravels the wires of his MP3 player and places it on top of the bookcase.

He checks his bag to ensure he hasn't forgotten anything, zips it up and pushes it under his bed. He sits with a pen in his hand and his journal on his lap. He writes one word – Star, followed by a question mark. He turns to the next blank page and scribbles a strange figure, like and elaborate figure 8 drawn diagonally. He taps his pen on his bottom lip then closes the journal and replaces them beside the headboard. He sits silently for a moment then returns downstairs to his waiting mother.

Chapter 27

Jasmine's frantic crying jolts Freya from her dreams. She opens her eyes and looks around. For a moment she cannot understand where she is. Then she remembers. She is home.

Freya pushes back the blankets and swings her legs out of bed. She rubs her head and presses her eyelids with her fingertips. 'It's okay. Mummy's coming.' She straightens her arms and pushes herself off the bed. Eyes half closed, she pads across the bedroom floor to the cot. 'Okay, okay.'

Jasmine's face is beetroot red. Freya picks her up and rocks her, but the baby refuses to calm down. 'Shhhh.' Freya hums a melody as Jasmine tugs her pyjama top. 'Okay, I get it.' Freya carries the anxious and hungry baby back to her bed.

Snuggled with her daughter, t-shirt pulled up to her neck, Freya dozes to the rhythmic suckling until both mother and daughter are asleep once more and the house is silent.

'Good morning, Freya.' Her mother's wide smile welcomes her into the kitchen. 'Did you sleep well? How's that beautiful little granddaughter of mine? Yes, you are beautiful. Yes you are. May I?' Lorraine holds her arms open wide in the international symbol of let me have a cuddle and a sniff of those gorgeous head pheromones, please.

Freya returns the smile. Teardrops form in the corner of her eyes as she struggles to remember the last time she was the subject of maternal affection. 'Of course.' She passes Jasmine across the narrow space between her and her mother which had once seemed an unbreachable gulf.

Freya sits at the breakfast table and watches her mother rock Jasmine. Coos of pleasure are vocalised by both grandmother and granddaughter. A new start, reconciliation and all it took was a baby.

'How's Rob?' Lorraine asks, looking across at Freya.

Freya swallows hard. 'We split up, Mum.'

Lorraine gasps. 'Oh, Darling. I'm so sorry.'

Freya bows her head. She leans across the table, resting her forehead in a nest between her arms and weeps.

'Baby.' Lorraine sits opposite Freya at the table, still rocking Jasmine. 'You can stay here for as long as you need. Do you want to talk about what happened?'

Freya lifts her face from the table and shakes her head.

'Well, whenever you do…'

Lorraine stands up, leans forward and kisses Freya on the forehead.

Jasmine grabs a fist full of Freya's hair and pulls it as Lorraine straightens her back and rises. Silently, Freya touches the baby's hand and unhooks her hair. Jasmine reaches out her arms towards her mother and makes a noise somewhere between a cry and a hiccup.

'Do you want her back?' Lorraine asks.

'It's fine, Mum, enjoy.'

Her mother grins with joy and gratitude. 'Babies are wonderful, don't you think? They're full of potential. It is too easy to damage them, even when you try hard not to, even when all you want to do is love them.'

Freya sees tears gather in her mother's eyes. 'Mum, don't.'

'I'm so sorry, Freya. All I've done is let you down. This precious little angel is so lucky to have you for a mother. I know you'll do a better job than I.'

'You were a great mum. No one should lose their daughter. We were fine until Tanya died. I understand what you did, how you felt, I really do. What happened isn't your fault. It isn't Dad's fault either, although he seems to think so. The world is full of evil. You did your best to protect me and I love you.'

Lorraine nods. 'Here, you take her. I'll be back in a minute.'

Sobbing, her mother leaves the kitchen. Freya rocks Jasmine in her arms, smiling at the look of peaceful oblivion on the infant's face. 'You are lucky,' she whispers.

.

Carmilla Voiez

Chapter 28

Kevin nudges Mark's shoulder.

'Hello, Mr Garlow, sir,' Mark says.

Mr Garlow sits in the corner of the public bar. His back is so straight and his face so proud that he could be seated on a golden throne rather than a grimy leather couch. The man nods, a subtle movement of his glistening bald head. His beard is black and grey and his suit a deep blue. He doesn't smile but his pale blue eyes shine.

'Hello, Mark,' Garlow replies. 'Kevin has told me a lot about you. Please, take a seat.'

Mark strides across to the man and sits on a wooden chair beside him. The difference in the chair heights mean that Mark towers over the man. He wonders for a moment whether this is appropriate then uncomfortably slouches in his chair to reduce the height differential as much as he can.

'Tell me about yourself, Kid. Why were you in the tunnels?'

Mark shrugs. 'I don't have a home, or didn't until Kevin took me in.'

'Is he taking good care of you?'

Mark nods.

'He tells me you're searching for your mother.'

Mark nods again.

'How did you lose her?'

'She left me. One day a man came and she left with him. I haven't seen her since.'

'How old were you?'

'I dunno, a baby, I guess.'

'How much do you remember?'

'She had black hair, a soft smile, and she would rock me in her arms.'

'Kevin tells me she was very young.'

'Yeah, I guess so.'

'Do you know why I wanted to see you?'

'Kevin says you want me to fight.'

'I have this little business. I hear you're a fighter. Perhaps?'

Mark nods. 'Sure.'

Garlow stares at the boy. 'How old are you?'

Mark shakes his head.

'Thirteen?' Garlow asks.

'Yeah, thirteen.'

Garlow leans forward and taps Mark's knee. 'I wonder…'

Mark looks at the man waiting for more. His eyes widen as Garlow stands up and pulls his coat over his shoulders. He nods at Kevin who follows him out of the room.

Mark straightens up in his chair. Dotted around the room are five other bald-headed men. Some wear suits, others jeans and short sleeved shirts. They drink and chat together. Occasionally one or two of them glance across at Mark then resume their conversations. Mark sighs. He feels twitchy. He wants to follow Kevin and Mr Garlow and find out what they're discussing. He feels angry that they are talking about him without his presence. His cheeks prickle and he shifts in his chair.

All eyes turn to him as he fidgets then the faces turn away one by one and the murmur of conversations begins again.

Mark presses the palms of his hands together. Folding his fingers over his knuckles, he bounces his chin against their peaks. He scratches the top of his head, then his neck. He shuffles his shoulders and moves about in his chair again. He leans forwards, rests his elbows on his knees and breathes into his palms. He starts again from the beginning, pressing his palms together, repeating the ritual until he can stay sitting no longer and stands up. He starts walking towards the door.

A large man moves in front of him. 'Where are you going, Kid?'

Mark glances at the door then faces the man. 'Toilet.'

The man nods and steps aside. Mark can feel eyes upon him as he walks towards the door marked "Gents".

As he washes his hands the door opens and Mark sees Kevin's reflection in the mirror.

'He's gone,' Kevin says.

'What did he say about me?' Mark asks.

'He's got a job for you.'

'Oh?'

'Not a fight, nothing happening there for the moment. A delivery.'

'Oh?' Mark reaches for the towel and recoils when he notices its black and cream patina of mould. He rubs his wet hands on his jeans instead.

Kevin takes a package from his pocket and passes it to Mark. It feels light. He goes to open it.

'No.' Kevin shakes his head emphatically. He passes Mark a piece of paper. 'The address is on that.'

'Are you coming with me?' Mark asks.

'Not this time, Kid. Meet me back at the flat. Do you like curry? It's curry night.'

Chapter 29

Satori stretches across his bed. He rubs his back against the familiar cotton cover, creasing the duvet around his body like a nest. *Home.* In spite of the fragrant fabric softener in the weft and weave below him and the slender webs of plaster cracks above, his room feels as alien to him as the cottage he shares with Star. He tries to remember the last time he felt that he was in a place where he could truly be himself. Somewhere no one would judge him for his imagination, his creativity, his love of adventure. The Planes – they were the only places he was free, the only worlds which understood and accepted his true value. He went there to find Star and ended up finding much more. He found faith in his abilities and acceptance of his frailties. There he could be anyone and do anything.

He closes his eyes and tells his mind to return to Yesod with its violet shifting sky and bone white earth. He yearns to see Gabriel again, share stories and experiences with the angel, touch him.

When he opens his eyes the brightness of the sky is blinding. He holds a hand across his forehead to shelter his eyes. The air moves around him, touching him, stroking his body, embracing him.

The ivory soil beneath his feet is hard and cool. He leaves no imprints as he steps forwards. He scans the horizon for some hint of life, a shadow or column of smoke as before, something he can head towards. The agitated sky makes him feel dizzy. He closes his fingers around the metal object in his fist. Lifting it up, he sees his athame, his magical dagger, and smiles. He lifts it to the sky and calls 'Gabriel, come to me.'

Light bounces off the curved blade and whirls in a vortex. The air moves more quickly, a tunnel or typhoon ahead of him. Gabriel does not appear within its frantic walls. Satori waits a moment. The air keeps spinning, but nothing appears. He takes a step then another until he is surrounded by the whirlwind. He holds his knife in the air again and whispers. 'Take me to him.'

His body is pulled to the right. His neck jolts violently and he grabs it with one hand trying to relieve the pressure. He orders his bones to be supple - *don't snap*. Satori is thrown to the ground, landing awkwardly on his knees. As he looks up he sees the beautiful naked man towering above him. With a gentle smile on his perfect lips the angel reaches an enormous hand towards Satori who grasps it and allows himself to be pulled to his feet. Even standing Satori barely reaches Gabriel's chest.

'Have you grown taller?' Satori asks.

Gabriel shrugs. 'Welcome back, my friend. It's been a long time. How are you, traveller? Did you save the woman?'

'How long has it been?' Satori asks.

'Many years by human standards, I think, since the sun and moon embraced.'

Satori nods. 'The sun was the woman I was trying to save, Star.'

Gabriel's eyes widen. 'You said she had power. I did not realise she was so magnificent.'

'Not anymore,' Satori answers.

'You sound bitter, friend. Tell me what troubles you.'

'She doesn't love me.'

'And?'

'I don't think I love her anymore.'

Gabriel shakes his head. 'Is that a terrible thing?'

'I don't know how to do anything else.'

'Nonsense.'

Satori shrugs.

'You are merely feeling sorry for yourself. Remember how much more you are. The loss of love can wound, but it cannot make you empty. You are love. Not just for one woman but for everyone and everything you see. All is one.'

'And all is nothing.'

'Yes. We are both everything and we are nothing. Does that frighten you?'

'Sometimes.'

'It shouldn't. It's a beautiful truth, if you can accept it. Satori, I'm about to make crupta, will you join me in my meal?'

'I can't. The rules will not let me eat here.'

'Then what can I offer you, my friend?'

'Your love.'

'You already have it.'

Satori smiles. 'May I?' he asks widening his arms.

Gabriel smiles back. 'You wish to hold me?'

Satori nods. 'Very much.'

Gabriel cocks his head and stares at Satori. 'Why?'

'It's hard to explain. I guess love for me needs a physical expression if it is to feel real.'

'Physical expression?' Gabriel shrugs. 'You need the physical to express the metaphysical?'

'Ummm, yes. I guess so.'

'Very well then, friend. You may touch me.'

Satori wraps his arms around Gabriel's waist. The angel's muscles feel hard and lumpy against his skin. Gabriel's energy prickles him and Satori's hair stands on end. He shakes as he tries to keep hold. His teeth chatter and his eyes roll back in their sockets. He bites his tongue and feels hot blood drip onto his chin. He lets go and looks up at Gabriel.

'Did it hurt?' Gabriel asks.

'Less than I expected,' Satori answers.

Gabriel smiles. 'Will you forgive me if I prepare my meal? You are welcome to sit with me. I enjoy listening to your wisdom and folly.'

Satori sits on the hard earth beside the newly made fire. As before, a pot stands above the flames. The gentle aroma grows stronger as the broth warms.

In the distance Satori hears the splintering of glass then a cry of rage. 'Did you hear that?'

'Hear what?' Gabriel asks.

146

Satori strains his ears. He hears shouting and the thud of something heavy hitting the floor. The violet sky stops moving. Colours fade until he is surrounded by the whitewashed walls of his bedroom. He sits up on his bed, in his room and hears his mother scream.

Chapter 30

Mark looks again at the address on the piece of paper. The streets all look the same and he has no idea in which direction he should travel.

'Excuse me,' he calls to a woman striding past. If she hears him she fails to show any indication.

Mark sighs and sits on a bench turning the paper over and over in his hand. 'What now?'

He looks up at passing business people, mothers, children, elderly couples and lonely looking people wandering solo. He wonders what he's doing. *These people: Kevin and Garlow, they're a distraction from my purpose. I know why I'm here and it isn't to deliver packages.* He lets his eyes wander between the people who surround him, ever moving, and wonders whether they have a purpose and what has distracted them from completing it. *Is this what life here means, doing things without a goal? Living in the moment, getting by second by second, how can they stand it?*

Clutching the paper in his hand, he walks towards a white haired man who sits quietly on a bench a dozen metres or so away.

'Excuse me.' Mark sits beside the old man.

'Hello, Son,' the man replies.

'Can you help me?'

'What's the trouble, Kid? Hey, shouldn't you be in school?'

'Day off.' Mark passes the man the piece of paper. 'Do you know where this is?'

The man pulls a pair of glasses from his coat and studies the note. 'Yeah, sure. I grew up around there. You need to catch the...now which bus is it? ...hmmm, oh yes the number 9 bus. You'll head out of town and under the motorway. When you get to a rank of shops...hmmm, what's there now? Yeah, I reckon it's a ladies hairdressers, ummm, a hardware store, and a flower shop, yeah.' The old man nods thoughtfully. 'I'm pretty sure they're all still there. Oh and there's some supermarket and an estate agents, yeah that's right. Or is it a travel agents? Hmmm... no estate agents, I'm sure it is. Well, get off the bus at the shops and you'll be on a hill. Walk up the hill towards a telecommunications tower. You'll see it. Pierces the sky, it does. It would take me about 20 minutes, I reckon, so it should only take you five. You'll see a road called...Church Lane, no Church Terrace, well something like that. Walk along that road, past the church and you'll come to a bend in the road.' The man's body sways as if he is turning a corner in his mind. 'Go round that bend, there used to be an old play park on the right hand side. Don't know if it's still there though... probably houses now. Go past the play park, if it's still there, and you'll see a narrow road which is kind of steep. That's the road you're looking for.'

Mark scratches his neck. 'Thank you, sir. So the number nine bus?'

'Yup, I reckon so lad. They're pretty regular. I think there's a stop close to the cinema, just over the way. I can't remember the name of the cinema. It's one of the old ones. Pretty. I remember having dates there when I was young. Always took my lady friends to the cinema. Do you like films, Son?'

'Ummm, yes sure. Look, thank you. I guess, I guess I'd better go or I'll be late.'

'No problem, Son. Have a great day.'

'Thank you, sir. I will. Thanks again.'

'No bother at all. It's a pleasure chatting with such a polite young man. You take care and don't forget school's important. Best days of your life.'

Mark smiles. 'I'll remember, Thanks again. Goodbye.'

'Goodbye, Kid.'

Mark stares at the road sign and checks the paper in his hand, a match. He starts climbing the steep hill. Blocks of flats on either side make the space feel claustrophobic, narrower than it should be, like a tunnel. He looks up half expecting to see a roof of rock or concrete, but the sky hangs above him, dull and grey. Dark clouds threaten rain.

He reads numbers on the sides of the buildings. 'Forty to Fifty two… Fifty four to sixty six… Sixty eight to Eighty.' He checks the note again, one hundred and six. 'Eight two to Ninety four… ninety six to one hundred and eight.' He walks up to the narrow door and studies an arrangement of buttons on the right. He locates 106 and presses. No answer. He waits a few moments and presses again.

'Hello.' A female voice crackles.

'Hi, it's Mark.'

'Mark who?'

'Garlow sent me.'

'Wait there a moment. I'll be right down.'

Mark turns around and looks along the street. So many dwellings, so many lives and yet the street is deserted.

The door clicks behind him and he turns around to face a woman with short, blonde hair. A dressing gown or housecoat is pulled tightly around her. She exudes a smell like nothing he has encountered before: repugnantly sweet and bitter. His nostrils are filled with the evil scent. It disturbs him and he considers thrusting the envelope into her clawed hand and leaving. He dips his hand into his pocket. She shakes her head and touches him arm so gently it feels like a butterfly flew between the hairs of his forearms.

'Come inside,' she says.

He looks around at the empty street again, longing to be gone from this place.

'Inside,' she whispers in his ear.

Her breath makes his stomach churn. He stands at the doorway shaking.

'What's wrong, Kid?' she asks.

'I have to go,' he says.

'This won't take long,' she answers. 'Come on. Hurry up.'

He takes his hand from his pocket leaving the package inside. She nods and moves back from the doorway into the shadows. Her insistence that he follow her makes him bristle, but he does so anyway. He breathes the external air as though he expects it to be his last breath and follows her.

She mounts the stairs. He watches her from the bottom.

'Well, come on then,' she urges.

They climb three flights. The sharp bones of her slender hips stab at the air as she moves. He has never felt more uncomfortable in the presence of a woman.

She draws a key from the deep pocket of her velour robe and opens the door to her flat. The windows are shuttered and the room is dark, but she does not switch the light on. She moves effortlessly around the room, seeming not to notice the darkness. He watches her movements with fascination as she bends to remove papers from a drawer.

She opens the drawer and pulls two envelopes out. One has the letter G scribbled on the front.

'This is for Garlow,' she says, passing the envelope to Mark. 'Do you know where you have to take this one?'

Mark shakes his head as she passes him a second envelope with the letter J written in what looks like a red felt tip pen.

'Okay. I'll write the address down for you, just make sure you destroy the paper after you've used it and remember the address. Safer in your head, right?' She taps the right side of her forehead with her forefinger. Her nail is long, curved like a talon and stained brown along its edge.

He nods in reply.

She scribbles an address on some paper and passes it to him. He checks he is able to read her writing. 'Thank you.'

He stores her instructions in a segment of his head and uses the rest to study her. She is young and yet old. Perhaps the magic she accesses has aged her. She does not care for herself or her environment. Her appearance, like that of her home, is chaotic and he feels the same chaos radiate from her mind. Yet with all the power she holds she seems oblivious to the presence she has welcomed into her home. He would have expected some sign of recognition. A positive or negative reaction to his existence, but she displays neither. So wrapped up is she in the chaos in her head, she appears detached from the world outside.

She snorts and holds out her hand. 'What have you got for me?'

He pulls the package from his pocket and passes it to her.

'Ta,' she says. 'Is my address written down anywhere?'

He nods and passes the scrap of paper to her. 'You know where I am now, Kid. I'll dispose of this.'

'Can I go?' he asks.

'You don't want to stay for a cuppa or something stronger?'

'No thanks. I'd better get on.'

'No worries. Pass my regards to G.' She leans past him and pulls the door open. 'You can find your own way out, right Kid?'

Mark nods and hurries down the stairs.

As he rushes out of the building he pinches his nose, trying to squeeze remnants of the smell from his nostrils. He coughs and gulps air into his lungs. *What the fuck?* he thinks. *What the fucking fuck was that?*

He looks at the new address in his hand and remembers her instructions. He considers heading back to Kevin's first to sort out Garlow's envelope, but discards that thought. The directions the woman gave him were precise and he uses

153

these as a mental GPS to guide him without the need for thought.

While he walks he considers what he has achieved so far and realises it is very little. Like a game of chess he has positioned his pieces with care. He will win this game and achieve his final goal, but distractions tire him and he wonders why he has decided to align himself with Garlow and his thugs. He isn't present in this world at this time to become a delivery boy for a megalomaniacal gangster. Something cautions him not to be too eager to burn this bridge. The thugs may be useful.

Chapter 31

Satori hears the scream again and sits bolt upright. *What is it?* He pushes himself to his feet shaking the remnants of Yesod from his mind. *Mum!*

He races down the stairs, leaping over the final four, and runs into the living room. His mother is there, the neck of a broken wine bottle in her hand. At her feet, curled into a foetal position, is a boy.

Satori rushes to his mum and grabs her shoulder. She looks at him through glazed eyes as he removes the broken bottle from her hand.

'What happened?' he asks

She nods towards the boy on the floor. His black hair is matted with blood. His skin looks frighteningly pale.

'Help me tie him up, before he wakes up again.'

'What?' He steps towards the teenager.

His mother yells. Her voice borders on hysteria. 'Rope, get some rope, Steve. I need to tie him to a chair.'

'Who is he? What did he do?'

'I'll tell you, I promise, but first we need to make sure he can't hurt us.'

'Hurt us? He needs an ambulance, Mum. Is he still alive?' Satori bends down and touches the boy's wrist. The pulse flutters, weakly.

He looks around to speak to his mum but she isn't there. He stands up and walks towards the door. He hears his mother's voice from the kitchen. '…That's right. Yes, hurry.'

She puts the phone down as Satori joins her. 'How long will they be?'

'Not long,' she answers, picking up a chair.

'What are you doing, Mum?'

'Just in case, Steve. It will make me feel safer.'

'Mum, you can't!' Satori shouts and tries to wrestle the chair from her.

Her grip is firm and, however hard he tugs, she does not let go.

'He came in here to rob us, Steve. Maybe he was going to kill us.'

'I couldn't see a weapon. What makes you so sure?'

He pulls the chair again, but she refuses to release her hold. He gives up and sidesteps to stop her moving towards the living room and the unconscious boy. As he takes a step, she swings the chair. The blow knocks him to the floor. His head bounces off the edge of the freezer and he blacks out.

Chapter 32

Mark delivers the second envelope without incident. As he turns away from the street he feels a furious tug in his stomach. He closes his eyes and investigates the feeling. His chessboard appears in his head. He stands at the edge of the game and watches. The queen is moving freely, unhindered by whatever shadow made her cautious before. The black bishop fades out of the game. His image becomes translucent. Heat and power surround the piece like an aura. Satori is practising magic. Somewhere in the city the magician is leaving Malkuth and travelling back to the Planes of Existence.

Mark considers reasons for these changes. He senses that the relationship between his queen and the bishop has altered. He feels the presence of another player rise, a knight coming into play and realises if he is to win the game this piece must be sacrificed. The knight cannot be allowed to protect the queen or stand in the way of the king.

For a moment he considers reaching out to Star. He might go to her, speak to her, offer his help, but the risk of failure is too high. While she is tied to the people around her, she is likely to resist his offer and pull away. Her strength is such that he cannot force her to love and accept him. She must do it of her own free will. Her free movements across the board are part of his plan for her. If she is impeded by another it will make things more difficult and more challenging, at worst it could mean stalemate or even his defeat.

Mark must visit Satori. It is time. He tucks Garlow's envelope back into his jacket pocket and hurries towards his destination.

The moment Marian opens the door Mark becomes acutely aware of his oversight. She is one of them, a daughter of Sith. She is one of the robed worshippers who have shadowed his every move on this plane. Her eyes darken and he knows she has recognised him. She invites him inside. His mind works quickly to change this unexpected problem to his advantage. When she raises a brown bottle from an occasional table he sees his chance. He blusters around the room as noisily as possible, begging her at the top of his voice to have mercy on him. When she swings the makeshift weapon he does not dodge its blow, but falls to the floor, eyes tight shut.

He hears Satori plead with Marian to see sense. Others join them and discuss how they will secure their prisoner permanently. Mark's body bounces around as others struggle to move him. A violent jolt loosens their grip and he is lifted onto a shoulder. Satori runs from the house as Mark hangs limp over the man's body. A soft smile makes Mark's cheeks twitch. The magician is resourceful and brave. For a moment his body warms with pride.

'Help me.' Mark's voice sounds weak.

'I am,' Satori answers.

Chapter 33

Satori hears whispers. His head throbs. A door closes: the front door. He tries to sit up, but his head spins and he vomits. The whispers grow louder. He lies on the floor. His eyes open the merest crack. A woman in a white robe moves into the open doorway and looks at him.

'He'll be out for a while,' he hears his mother say.

The woman's voice is deep and soft. She speaks as though she expects to be obeyed without question. 'What will you tell him when he wakes?'

'I'll think of something.'

The woman turns away and leaves the room. Satori wiggles across the floor, his ears alert for sounds of their return.

'How did you find him?' the woman in white asks.

'He rang our doorbell. He said he was drawn here.'

'By what?'

'Sith only knows. I just invited him in and…'

'Did he attack you?'

'No, but he insisted on seeing my son. When I said he couldn't he was about to leave so I stopped him.'

'Well done, Sister Marian. Brother Bill, help us get the demon into the van. We need to get him out of here before Marian's son wakes up.'

Satori hears a groan. 'He's heavier than he looks,' a male voice says. 'Can you help?'

The woman snorts. 'Put you're back into it, man. What's wrong with you? He's only a child.'

'He isn't only a child though, is he?' Marian says. 'I'm right, aren't I? He is the one she predicted.'

The doorbell rings again.

'Ahhh, this will be Mike. Between you two you should be able to lift a teenager, right?'

'Of course. As you will it,' the male voice replies.

Satori hears footsteps move along the hallway to the door. He isn't sure how many. He slithers to the kitchen door and looks. Two female forms in white robes stand beside the door. One opens it and Ivan's father steps into the house. As he crosses the threshold he pulls the hood of his robe over his bald head and bows. Satori pulls himself to his feet and hides.

He hears footsteps move to the living room again. Feeling stronger, he takes a key from under the breadbin, walks to the backdoor and unlocks it. He opens it slightly. Breeze freshens Satori's face and he feels his strength return.

He returns to the hallway and listens to grunts of exertion as the two men struggle with the boy. He sees the white edge of a robe nudge backwards into the hallway and runs towards it. With the full impact of his elbow, he knocks Brother Bill to the floor and grabs the boy.

Mike looks at Satori in anger and amazement, holding empty arms towards him.

'Satori!' his mum shouts as he sprints towards the back door with the boy over his shoulder. 'Satori, come back!'

160

Satori runs. The boy's body slams against his stomach and lower back.

'Help me!' A weak male voice pleads.

'I am,' Satori answers.

'They're after me.' Mark says.

Satori struggles to speak as he sprints along a shadowy lane. 'I'll get you to the hospital.'

'Don't. They'll find me there.'

'Your head. You need to go to a hospital.'

'I heal fast. Look, you can put me down. I can walk from here.'

Satori stops running and places the boy on his feet. 'Are you sure?'

'Yes, but I'll need somewhere safe to go. Somewhere they won't find me.'

The boy and man walk side by side as they talk. Their steps are urgent. They keep to shadows and lanes away from traffic, afraid of being found.

'I'll take you home,' Satori says.

'I don't have one,' the boy answers.

'Okay. I know a place. I'll take you there. But, tell me, who are you? What were you doing at my house?'

'My name's Mark. I was looking for you.'

'Why?'

'I was drawn there by your magic.'

Satori halts and looks into the teenager's vivid green eyes. He frowns and narrows his vision to a graphite stare. 'My magic...so why did Mum hurt you?'

'I don't know. They've been watching me for weeks, trying to get close to me, trying to kidnap me. I don't know why.'

'Who?'

'The people in white.'

'Who are the people in white? Mum, Mike and the others… It doesn't make sense.'

'It doesn't make sense to me either.'

Satori paces back and forth blocking Mark's passage along the lane. 'I have so many questions. I need to understand. My mum is one of them, those people in white. Yet, I didn't know about any of them until today. Why do they want you?'

'All I can gather is they think I'm special.'

'Earlier. I heard one of them call you a demon. You don't look like a demon. You don't feel like one either, although you do feel familiar. Do I know you?'

'Perhaps. A long time ago.'

'Who are you?'

'Don't you think we should get somewhere safe first? What if they find us?'

'You're right.' Satori stops pacing and marches forward without checking whether Mark is following in his wake. 'We'll find a taxi. There's this place. I think it's empty still.'

Mark's reply sounds breathless. 'Thank you. Thank you for all your help. I don't know what would have happened to me, if…'

Satori slows his pace a little. He doesn't want the boy to pass out. 'We're not out of the woods yet. And you still need to tell me who you are.'

'I know. I will.'

Headlights sweep around the street corner. An orange rectangle glows above.

'Taxi!' Satori shouts.

The taxi pulls up to the kerb and Satori and Mark climb onto the back seat.

'Where to?' the driver asks.

'Snuff Mills,' Satori answers.

Chapter 34

'Hi,' His voice is soft, almost a whisper. It caresses Star's ear.

'Ivan,' she answers.

'Hey, Star. Sorry about the other day. You okay?'

'Satori left me.'

'When? Why? Does he know?'

'About us? Yes.'

Ivan sighs.

'He's not stupid, Ivan.'

'I know. Did you tell him?'

'He knew. I didn't deny it. What's the point?'

'What now?' Ivan asks.

'I don't know.'

'Should I come over? We can talk.'

Star bites her lip and makes a soft clicking sound with her mouth. 'Yes.'

'I'll be about twenty minutes.'

'Thank you.'

'No problem.'

Star fixes them both a drink. She pours a generous measure of Satori's favourite whisky into a tumbler and adds some ice cubes. She opens a bottle of beer for herself. She takes a gulp of amber liquid from the brown bottle and takes both drinks to the table beside the sofa. She crosses and uncrosses her legs. Pressing firmly with her thumbs she massages each palm in turn. She sighs and sinks back into the second hand settee. She closes her eyes, opens them again and sits up straight to reach for her ale. She takes another gulp and cradles the bottle in one hand scratching off the label with her thumb nail. She sinks back again, still holding her beer and thinks. *Is this what I want?* She has no answer. Ivan will come and comfort her. He will talk to her as his friend then they will embrace like lovers. *It's easy.* She doesn't have to pretend for him. He expects nothing from her. *What if that changes? What if he wants a relationship with me now Satori is gone? What if he doesn't?* She realises she has no idea how Ivan feels about her. *I could ask him, but then he might have to change. My words might change him. I could stay silent and hope that nothing changes or I could hope that it does change. I could hope that this will be the love that elevates me and makes me whole. Lilith told me* "There is no shame in love, only completion." *A life without shame, what would that feel like after all these years?*

A gentle knock at the door breaks into her thoughts. *He's here.*

She puts her half-finished bottle of beer next to Ivan's drink and rises from the settee. Tip-toeing towards the door, she can almost hear him breathing on the other side of the wooden barrier.

She fumbles with her key and pulls at the handle. He looks flushed, fresh and warm. The smell wafting from him to her is intoxicating. He smiles as she opens the door fully and moves to embrace him. He wraps his arms around her and chuckles softly.

'I've missed you,' he says.

'I've missed you too,' she replies.

She pulls herself away from his warmth to let him move inside the cottage then locks the door behind him.

'I made you a drink.' Star nods towards the whisky glass on the table.

'Thank you,' he says. 'Although I'm driving. I probably shouldn't.'

'You can stay here tonight,' she says quickly.

He turns and looks at her. She blushes. He nods and smiles, lifts the drink and sips the rich golden liquid. She shudders. *Is this a mistake?*

He lifts her bottle and passes it to her then sits on the settee watching her intently.

She squirms under his gaze and blushes again.

'It's not like we…'

He shakes his head and grins.

'Ivan…' she says.

'Yes.'

'How do you feel about me?'

He coughs and splutters. His face reddens. She cannot tell if it's from nervousness, embarrassment or the whisky burning his throat. She wishes she could take back the question. Her feet itch and she has the sudden urge to run from the room. She doesn't need to know how he feels. *What was I thinking?*

'I feel you're the most interesting, complex and sad woman I have ever met.'

She stops shaking and sits beside him. 'Sad?'

'In a beautiful, soulful, melancholy way, but yes – sad.'

'Does that bother you?'

'Should it?'

'I don't know. It bothered him.'

'Satori?'

'Yes. He couldn't understand it. It was as though my sadness was a threat to him. It's the one constant in my life. I don't know how to stop.'

'You experience joy sometimes.'

'Yes. Those moments are exquisite, but fleeting. Do you know what I mean?'

'Of course.'

'You're sad too, aren't you?'

Ivan nods.

'Why?'

'Why am I sad?' Ivan cocks his head to one side and inhales. 'Wow! You're all about the big questions tonight, aren't you?'

'I'm sorry. You don't have to answer.'

'To be honest, I'm not sure I can answer. Not accurately anyway. I can tell you why I think I am sad, events which have changed and tainted me, but maybe it's deeper than that. Maybe it's part of the human condition. Perhaps we are all sad, but some people hide it better than others. Some people reject sadness in almost pathological ways. They cannot stand to be around it or feel it inside them. We are not those people.

We can experience the spectrum of emotions and find value in them all.'

'Yes,' she whispers. 'Yes, exactly. Hold me.' She tilts her face and brushes her lips across his. The whisky tastes peaty on his mouth.

He takes both drinks and puts them on the table beside him then leans across and envelopes her body in his arms. His whiskers scratch her chin. The feeling isn't painful. It awakens her senses. She feels her body crush against his until there is no space between them. She swings her legs up and across his lap, clinging to his torso with all her strength. Their lips bruise each other as they kiss. She explores his mouth with her tongue and tastes freedom: freedom to be herself, to never have to justify any thought or emotion.

Chapter 35

Boy and man approach the high iron gates. Satori pushes against the gates grunting, but they do not move an inch.

'We'll have to climb the wall?' Satori says.

Mark nods. He looks between the bars of the gate at the long driveway and Gothic mansion beyond. 'Who owns this place?'

'An old friend. He's dead, but I don't think it's been sold yet. We should be okay to stay here for a while.'

'Should?'

'There are no guarantees in this life, Kid.'

'Please, don't call me Kid. Everyone calls me Kid. Call me Mark.'

'Sorry, Mark, of course, no problem. I think there are some trees around the side, in that garden, back there. That could be the easiest place to climb over and the drop shouldn't be too challenging on the other side.'

'Go through the neighbour's garden?'

'Well, their wall is a lot lower at the front.'

'Do you know them?'

'No.' Satori snorts and shrugs.

Mark smiles and makes a sweeping movement with his right arm. 'Lead the way.'

Satori nods and grins at Mark. 'You feeling strong enough for this?'

'Never better.'

'How's your head?'

'Ahh, it was just a scratch. Your mum hits like a girl.'

Satori laughs. 'When we get inside you're going to tell me what all that was about.'

'I would if I could. I'll tell you what I do know though, okay?'

'Deal.'

Satori and Mark scramble up the side of the neighbour's wall. As they drop to the other side they hear barking. Three large Rottweilers race towards them. Their jaws hang open and saliva soaks their chins and drips onto the claws of their huge front paws. About a metre away the dogs stop, eyeing the intruders suspiciously and growling.

Satori backs away.

'It's okay.' Mark's voice is low and calm. He bends his knees slightly and crouches down, putting his arms out at either side of his body. 'You're not going to hurt us.' He looks at each dog in turn. The dog at the centre growls louder. The others quieten down.

Mark turns and makes eye contact with the middle dog. 'You have nothing to fear from us. We're just passing through. Do you understand?'

The Rottweiler takes a step towards Mark.

'Watch out,' Satori urges.

Mark stays where he is. He continues to stare into the dog's eyes.

The dog shakes its head and saliva sprays in every direction. Mark wipes some from his cheek and laughs. 'Thanks.'

The dog takes another step forwards. Dog and boy are muzzle to muzzle. The Rottweiler's nostrils expand and contract as it sniffs the intruder, trying to make sense of the situation.

Mark moves his right hand towards the dog and it growls again.

'Mark!' Satori warns.

'It's okay. Isn't it, girl? You don't want to hurt me.'

The growling softens and Mark continues to move his hand towards the dog. The bitch breaks eye contact to look at his hand. Then she looks back at the boy's face. She stands like a statue in silence then cocks her head as if trying to make a decision. Mark keeps moving his hand until he is able to stroke the crown of her head. She growls the moment he touches her.

'That's good isn't it?' Mark says.

She looks at his feet and stops growling.

'Good girl,' Mark tells her. 'We're going to climb the wall over there. Neither of us is going to hurt you and we won't stay in your territory longer than we have to.'

Mark stands and turns to face Satori who is staring open mouthed. 'How?'

'I have a way with dogs,' Mark answers.

Satori nods.

'Shall we?'

Satori stares at the dogs. 'Are you sure it's safe?'

Mark grins. 'Nothing can be guaranteed, right?'

'Right.' Satori grins back. 'Okay. Let's do this.'

They cross the well-kept lawn. The three Rottweilers follow on their heels. They keep a measured pace and stick to the edges of the garden and the shadows of the wall. A conifer stands about forty metres ahead.

'There?' Mark asks.

'Looks likely.' Satori moves to overtake Mark, but growls of warning make him change his mind and he continues to match the boy's pace.

When they reach the wall, Satori tests the branches of the tree. They are supple and bend when he pulls them, but should hold Mark's weight if not his own. He looks at the wall, testing for hand and foot holds. He remembers scaling the sheer wall of the obsidian mountain in Yesod and feels this should be much easier. Only a twelve foot drop onto grass if he fails.

'Stand clear. I'm going to work my way up using these cracks in the surface. I'll check what the drop on the other side looks like, okay?' Satori says.

Mark shrugs. 'Sure, but you know I can scale that tree in five seconds flat, don't you, old man.'

Satori scoffs. 'Go on then…Kid.'

'Touché. See you on the other side.'

'Wait. Check the drop before doing anything stupid.'

'No problem.'

Mark pulls himself through itchy branches. They scratch his face and hands as he pushes past them to the top of the wall. He twists his body to sit on the apex, the king of the proverbial castle, and swings his legs like a little boy. He smiles down at Satori.

'What's it like on the other side?'

'Drop and roll.' Mark launches himself with a grunt. He bounces on the earth, stands up and brushes his sleeves. Mark turns around as Satori hits the ground behind him with a thump.

'You okay?' Satori asks, standing up.

'Sure.'

'We'll try and get in through the back. If not there's always his summer house.' Satori points to the white building to their right.

Satori walks ahead and Mark strides behind him through the plants. Many have browned, perhaps temporarily with winter. The lawn they cross is crushed in places by cruel weather. Around the summer house and trees the grass stands as high as Mark's waist.

'How long has it been empty?' Mark asks.

'Four years,' Satori answers.

'What happened to the owner?'

'Official version or truth?'

'Huh?'

'He was murdered by a demon,' Satori replies.

Mark stops walking and looks towards the large house. The windows are dark. He wonders what waits beyond their glass panes. 'Which demon?'

Satori pauses and turns to look at Mark. 'So you know they exist?'

Mark shrugs. 'I dunno. Your mum, she called me a demon. I reckon her definition might be different to yours.'

Satori nods and walks towards the house.

Mark hurries to catch up. 'Which demon do you think murdered this guy?'

'Lilith.'

'Nobody important then?' Mark laughs, nervously.

'I'm impressed. You're what thirteen…fourteen and you know your demons.'

'I bet you did too.'

'I guess you're right. So do you practise?'

'Huh?'

'Magic.'

'Not really. I've just picked up a thing or two along the way.'

'No doubt.' Satori shudders. His body feels cold and his hands numb as if his heart isn't beating strongly enough to provide adequate circulation. He forces himself to look forwards rather than turn to face the strange boy. Too much has changed in the last hour of his life. He cannot make sense of it. His mum, the woman who grounds him, has kept secrets from him for how long? All his life, perhaps. *The people in white, Sith, why didn't she tell me?*

He thinks back to when he turned thirteen, the year his father suddenly stopped sending him gifts. A memory lurks in the corner of his mind, something his mother said. He tugs at the memory, but it just makes him dizzy. There is too much to think about. Later he'll examine the memory, in his dreams.

They reach the edge of the house and follow the wall around the rear. Satori gasps and Mark sprints the last few steps and peers around Satori's shoulder. 'Oh.'

'It looks as though there could be squatters here,' Satori says.

A panel of the French doors has been smashed and the left side door forced open. Glass covers the entrance to the kitchen. Across white tiled walls, words and drawings have been scribbled in black and red paint. Mounds of debris are scattered across the floor and surfaces: cigarette butts, bottles, takeaway boxes, tissues and blankets.

Satori steps sideways through the open door.

Mark follows, looking around the room. There is no one here, but the wreckage defies all logic. Why would someone want to do this?

'Do you think they're still in the house?' Mark asks.

'Probably,' Satori answers.

The two of them cross the kitchen and open the door to the hallway. Mark shakes his head. The hallway looks untouched other than by dust. There aren't even any footsteps on the dust-powdered floor.

'What?' Mark asks.

'I don't know.'

'Why did they stop in the kitchen?'

'Maybe something scared them.'

'Lilith?' Mark asks.

'No,' Satori answers. 'Something else.'

175

Chapter 36

'Fuck me,' Star breathes into Ivan's ear.

He pulls her top over her breasts and strokes the soft pale skin of her stomach. He returns to their kiss. She breathes with his lungs. Their hearts beat together. She strokes his cheek. He purrs into her mouth. It makes her smile and she moves away just a few inches to look into his cool blue eyes. There is no judgement in those clear eyes, no expectation.

He lifts her arms and slides her t-shirt over her head.

Her breasts swell beneath the black lace of her bra. He traces her cleavage with his finger tip. She shivers. Every cell in her body is alive with excitement and anticipation.

'I love you,' she tells him.

'I know,' he answers.

Her ears strain to hear him declare his love for her. He does love her. She is sure of it. He worships every inch of her body. He will spend hours kissing and caressing her even after sex, but never has he uttered those words. She wonders why she wants to hear them so desperately. If he told her he loved her it would be like telling her he wanted, no needed, part or all of her for him and him alone. It would be like sealing a contract with his declaration. It would mean he wanted more than she could give him. So why does she want to hear him say it? Why is it important? Is this simply another hangover from her lack of paternal approval and affection, or is it more than that? She wishes there was someone she could ask.

Ivan flicks her nipples with his thumb and index finger and Star's mind switches back to thoughts of burning desire. Her bra feels too tight as her breasts swell to his touch. She feels breathless. She wants to strip them both. Hold his naked body against her skin. Sit on his lap and feel his penis strain upwards to meet her lips. The urge to rush, to be penetrated and feel whole again, makes her body shake. She pushes the feeling aside. She wants to enjoy each moment with him. Satori is not coming home. They do not need to rush their play.

Ivan kisses her throat and Star moans. She strokes and tugs his hair. Her hands leave his hair and stroke his face, throat and finally his warm, silky, hairless chest. She grabs his top and pulls it off him. Pressing her lace covered chest against his naked one, she clings to him. Her arms encircle his powerful yet gentle shoulders. They kiss, lick and bite each other's skin. At last he frees her of her bra and her hard nipples reach out to him. She crushes her breasts against the muscles of his chest. The words "I love you" rise in her again but she swallows them. *What does it matter anyway?*

'Ivan.' His name feels like a prayer in her mouth.

He kisses her breasts, cupping both with his hands to push them towards his mouth. She moans again and feels wet between her thighs. Her underwear feels like a prison from which she needs to be free. She pulls away and tears off her panties then returns to his lap.

As he sucks on her breasts his fingers rub her clit and labia. Touching the outside of her vagina to gather moisture and massaging it over the rest of her swollen sex. She gasps at his insistent touch and unzips his jeans. She pushes her hand inside and pulls his hard cock between the cold teeth of his zip fly.

His fingers continue to work her clit as she pushes herself down on his cock. He fills her. She rises and falls with her steady heartbeat. Her hair bounces as she moves. Curls obscure her vision. Sight has become the least important of her senses. She can feel, taste, hear and smell him. He needs her as much as she needs him. When he is deep inside her they are both complete.

Chapter 37

Satori steps into the hallway. His footprints mark the dust like virgin snow. He looks around at the dark wood panelling, the grand staircase and dramatic portraits. It's hard to see Paul in the crushing décor. It looks like an old maid's house, not the abode of a vibrant magician and lover. He can more easily imagine Miss Haversham descending the staircase in her flaming wedding gown.

He feels Mark move behind him, forming new footprints in the dust.

'Wow!' the boy exclaims.

'I know, huh.'

Satori shakes his head to clear the fog-like dust motes in his eyes. He points to a door. 'That was always my favourite room. Paul's library. Star was there once.'

'Star?' Mark asks.

'Yes. Star. She was my world.' Satori sighs. His face softens and he smiles.

'Where is she?'

'Huh?' Satori steps towards the room.

Mark grabs Satori's shoulder. 'Star, where is she?'

Satori turns to look at the boy. His blood freezes. *Who are you?* Studying those green eyes and that soft mouth, his desire thaws him. He tries to shake the thoughts from his head, lust and suspicion. Mark's presence discomforts him. 'Do you know, Star?' *Do I know you?*

Mark looks away at the door. 'Shall we go and see if it's been damaged?' He walks towards the library door.

Satori follows. His eyes bore into the back of the teenager's head.

The library is untouched. Not even dust has marred its beauty. Other than the cold grate it is exactly how Satori remembers it. He can see Star touching the spines of Paul's paperbacks. 'Sit down.'

Mark does as he is told and settles himself in one of the two leather arm chairs. Satori sits on the one beside him.

Mark shivers. 'Do you think we could light the fire?'

Satori stands up and grabs pre-cut blocks of wood from the box beside the fire place. He sets them in the grate and looks for a bin in the room. Spotting one beside Paul's desk, he pulls a crumpled piece of paper from it. The paper is dry and lights easily. Satori drops it onto the logs and returns to the armchair.

'Who are you?' Satori asks.

'My name is Mark. I came here looking for someone, for Star. But this place is crazy. People have been chasing me ever since I arrived: those people in white, and others whose faces are always obscured by shadows, and now some guy called Garlow and his gang of thugs. I don't understand any of it, or why they all think I'm important.'

Satori's mind struggles to fit the pieces of the puzzle together. He is certain he remembers the white robes from his distant past: an argument, his father calling Marian a witch.

She laughs. *What else can I remember? Dad hits Mum and she falls onto the sofa, still laughing. Her laughter echoes around the room. I creep towards them. I remember. My body is filled with energy: anger and fear.*

Dad doesn't see me. He's too busy trying to stop Mum laughing. What did I do? I remember blood, so much blood. Dad staggers and falls, yes, onto the coffee table. Glass explodes beneath him. Red on white, his blood on Mum's white dress. I hold her and she trembles in my arms. Mum?

Mum and I alone, she is crying. Then the room fills with people. A woman takes me from Mum. I fight. I bust the woman's lip. Blood drips from her mouth. More red on white. I shake myself free and run to my room.

The next day the coffee table is gone. Mum makes me eggs. She smiles and tells me I was dreaming, but there's a bruise on her cheek. I wasn't dreaming, was I?

'The people in white, my mum, who are they?'

'I don't know. She called me a demon. She said they had a place for me. She didn't tell me anymore than that.

Satori narrows his eyes and stares at the boy. 'Are you a demon?'

'Of course not. Do I look like a demon?'

Satori shakes his head. 'No, not at the moment. Okay, let me think. Star, how do you know her and what do you want with her?'

'It's complicated.'

Complicated? Who is my mother? Is Dad dead? Who were the other people, the ones who came out of nowhere, the

181

woman I hit? Why did I forget it all until now? 'Complicated, how?'

Mark fidgets in his seat. 'It's so cold. Can we move closer to the fire?'

Satori rubs his hands together. 'It'll warm up. Tell me about Star.'

Mark wraps his arms around him and shivers. His teeth chatter theatrically. 'Okay. I was told if I found her she'd have the answers I need.'

'What answers?' *Answers…so many questions and so few answers. How does Star fit into this puzzle?*

'I'm sorry, but I'm not supposed to discuss it with anyone other than her. Can you take me to her?'

'I don't think so.'

'Why?'

'Because I want to protect her.' *I don't trust you. How can I trust anyone? Fuck! How can I even trust myself?*

Mark frowns. 'You think I'll hurt her?'

'I don't know what to think. You haven't told me anything yet. I know you're on the run. I know you felt drawn to me and that Mum wants to hurt you for some reason. I'd never seen those people in white before today and I've lived with Mum all my life. It just doesn't make sense to me.' *Wait…that's not true. Still, I don't need to tell him anything. Think, Satori, think.*

'Nor me.'

'Okay, Garlow, what about this man Garlow?' *How does he fit into all this?*

'He's this guy. I met him through a couple of violent yobs. He's given me some delivery jobs. I don't really know much about that either. I've just done what I was told. Ever since I got here I've been following someone's instructions.'

Is that what I've been doing? All those years of feeling unique and powerful, is it all a lie? No. Wait. What did Mum say? "Years ago you chose a path of your own." I have travelled my own path. What did she want for me? Why can't I remember? And how does this boy fit in? Is Mark the danger about which Mum warned? A demon? He doesn't feel like a demon. He feels human. Although there is a power deep inside of him. He holds it at bay, but it bubbles at his core, like Star's.

Mark fumbles in his pocket and pulls out an envelope. 'I had to drop a packet to a woman and she gave me two envelopes. I delivered one and I was supposed to hand this to Garlow, but I came to you instead. I guess the rest is history.'

'What's in it?'

'I don't know. Money probably.'

Satori leans forward and holds out his hand. 'Can I see?'

'Are you going to open it?' Mark blushes. He looks nervous.

'Yes.'

'I don't know if we should. What if I piss Garlow off? What if he finds me? He'd hurt me. He has the eyes of a shark. Yours is the first friendly face I've seen here.'

Satori keeps his hand, palm up, in the space between them. 'He won't find you here?'

'How can you be so sure?'

183

'I'm sure that, if you want me to trust you enough to take you to Star, you need to trust me enough to show me that envelope.'

Mark shrugs. 'I guess…'

He hands the envelope to Satori who turns it over in his hand. Apart from the letter G scribbled on the front it has no further information on the outside. He squeezes the paper. It does not feel like money inside. The envelope is too thin for a wad of notes and too stiff for a single note. 'I'm going to open it.'

Mark leans forwards as Satori tears open the envelope. He pulls a photograph out, turns it over and studies the image. He shows it to Mark then looks at it again more closely. *What can it mean?* It is a photo of a raven's head. The raven has a red ribbon tied around its beak. Satori looks in the envelope, but there is nothing else inside. He shows the empty envelope to Mark then passes both to the kid. *More questions and no new answers.* 'Any ideas?'

Mark looks at the photo and shakes his head. 'None. Do you think it's a warning?'

'Who gave it to you?'

'A woman.'

'What was she like?'

'Strange. She smelt odd. Her flat was dark and a bit insane to be honest. I thought she might be a witch.'

'Maybe it's a curse.' *Satori touches the raven's beak. A face nudges into his thoughts, pale and beautiful.*

'A curse on Garlow?'

'Or he ordered a curse from her for someone else and this is the proof that she's carried out his instructions.' *Raven? Can it be a coincidence? I need to be alone. I need to remember and understand.*

'I don't know. Garlow didn't seem...well, he's just this guy who has a load of skinheads doing who knows what for him. He's like a gangster or something, but he didn't seem spiritual in the slightest. I think he runs illegal boxing rings, probably money lending and that kind of thing, intimidation maybe, but he's got muscle for that. The photo, the raven, they don't make any sense to me.'

'Yeah. Raven and a ribbon. Raven and a red ribbon...'

'What?'

'It has nothing to do with this situation at all. It just reminds me of an old friend. Someone I should have treated better when I had the chance.' *One regret among thousands.*

Mark nods. 'Funny how that goes. No hope of a second chance?'

'I don't think so.'

'Shame. I reckon everyone needs a second chance.'

Satori frowns. His mind is full of the bird's image. He squeezes his eyelids tightly together then opens them again. 'I've already had mine. It didn't work out as I'd hoped.'

Mark rests his hands on his knees and leans forward. 'Tell me about it.'

'Sure sometime. What about you? Tell me about your second chance, Mark. What are you hoping to put right?'

'My life.' Mark laughs self-consciously.

'I see.'

185

They sit in silence. Mark stares at the photograph while Satori lets his eyes wander over the bookshelves recalling that first time when he was here in this room with Paul and Star and how different things had seemed, different but the same. *She didn't love me then, either. I just tried to convince myself of her devotion. I was a fool. Somehow it's all connected: Star, Mum, Mark, Raven, being here in Paul's house. I'm performing in a play, but I don't know the script. Think, Satori, think.*

Get some sleep and let my unconscious mind explore the puzzle. It's too much for my exhausted consciousness. 'It's getting late. Let's check the rest of the house and see if the bedrooms are usable. Are you going to be okay food wise? I doubt there's anything here, but I'd prefer to head out and buy some stuff tomorrow when things have, hopefully, died down a bit. Will you cope or are you hungry?'

'I'll be fine,' Mark says. 'I'm more tired than hungry.'

'Are you sure your head's okay? Do you feel sick as well as tired?'

'Honestly, I'll be fine. I've had worse. Let's go and check the house. Or we could curl up in these chairs in front of this lovely fire.'

'I won't be able to sleep until I know the house is empty. You can wait here if you want,' Satori says.

'No, I'm good. I'll come with you. I'd like to know where the bathroom is anyway.'

'Bathrooms,' Satori says.

'Ahhh, of course.'

'You've seen the kitchen,' Satori says. 'Or what's left of it.'

'Yes.'

'This is the living room.' Satori wanders into the large living room where he had once burned Paul's clothes. Shivers run up and down his spine as he remembers the ticking sounds of the scurrying scarab beetles that devoured his friend's remains.

The room, while slightly shabby, has not been affected by dust in the same way as Paul's hallway. The furniture still holds much of its sumptuous splendour. Most of the ornaments are missing. Perhaps they were removed as evidence by the police, or stolen by whoever broke through the French doors. His artwork remains, however, gracing the walls: huge oils and watercolours and original sketches including a uniquely disturbing framed picture by Crowley.

Satori moves the heavy curtains and opens the large cabinet aware that Mark is studying him. 'No one here,' he says. 'Dining room next.'

The dining room and downstairs bathroom are checked thoroughly for signs of human occupation. The bathroom looks unused and the dining room is still laid with plates and glassware as if awaiting dinner guests.

'I guess we should check the cellar as well,' Satori says. 'I hope the lights still work down there.'

Some of the light bulbs must have failed over the years, however there is still enough light to safely descend the narrow staircase and check the shadowy rooms for anyone who might be hiding there.

187

'Do you hear it?' Mark asks. 'What happened here?'

Satori stands still. Wind whistles through a gap in the tiny window frame at the top of the room. 'It's just the wind.'

'No, it isn't,' Mark answers.

Satori listens again. On the edge of his perception he hears the cries of children. He shivers as he remembers the remains he discovered here before. The bones of children had lain in this cellar, casualties of Paul's magical experiments and carnal lusts. The police must have removed those too. The flagstones are uneven where they were carelessly replaced after the raid.

'I don't hear anything except the wind.' Satori walks swiftly past Mark towards the stairs. He spots an upturned flashlight on a worktable and grabs it. It feels heavy in his hand, like a bludgeon. 'There's no one here. We'll check upstairs.'

Satori hovers in the doorway of Paul's bedroom. The rest of the house is empty and, other than the chill in the air, perfectly habitable. In the morning they would do well to clean bed linen and tidy the kitchen, but for tonight it will do. *Just this last room to check.*

He pushes the door further open. The curtains are drawn. He reaches for the light switch, but like many others around the house it doesn't work. He sweeps the beam of the borrowed flashlight around the furniture.

Mark shuffles about behind him. 'You okay?'

'Yes. Just...memories.'

'I can check it out.'

'Would you?' Satori asks.

'Sure. Hand me the torch.'

Satori moves back from the doorway and passes the torch to Mark. 'Thanks.'

'No problem.' Without hesitating further Mark steps into the room. The invisible barrier Satori felt in the doorway does not seem to bother Mark at all. The beam from the torch flashes around the room. 'It's fine. It's empty. Probably the best room in the house. If you don't want it, I'll take it.'

'Feel free. I'll take the room at the rear. In fact, I think I'm ready to try and get some sleep. See you in the morning, Mark.'

'Goodnight, Satori.'

Satori shrugs out of his clothes and collapses onto the meagre single bed. The blankets smell musty, but he pulls them around himself in spite of this. He looks around the shadow-filled room. In one corner stands a large wooden wardrobe still full of clothes. At the wall opposite his bed is a chimney breast with a guard in front of the fireplace. On the outside wall large, moth-eaten drapes attempt to cover the window. Beside these a full length oval mirror on a stand, thankfully, tilts away from the bed. Satori isn't afraid of many things but reflections in the night have always unnerved him.

Chapter 38

The safe house Satori proposes is too grandiose for Mark's taste. It has none of the elegant simplicity of Lilith's villa. Its dark stone fascia looks modern and pretentious. The gates are locked. Together, he and Satori traverse a neighbour's garden to access the grounds. Mark has no trouble subduing the dogs.

As they approach the building Mark feels cold. Like the witch's apartment this building reeks of evil. It is a uniquely human smell. Not the evil which amoral gods might inflict without thought. This has a purpose, a driving force and a conscious wickedness unique to this world and these people.

Shattered glass from the forced French doors covers the kitchen floor. It cracks under his feet as the crosses the room. The walls and floor remind him of painted hideouts he frequented, as a homeless youth, when he first arrived on Earth, confused and disorientated. The same confusion mixed with impotent anger radiates from the graffiti and destruction. Spoiling beautiful things seems a human reaction to lack of power, purpose and possessions. Perhaps these vandals simply want the things others take for granted. He can understand that. The absence of his mother is a constant hole in his chest. As he watched Lilith form spirit into flesh in

Binah, he often wished he could regain the parental bonds they would soon receive.

'Lilith,' Satori says.

The name seems out of context. Mark pauses before answering. He struggles to recall the conversation which led to this naming. He chastises himself for allowing his focus to wander. *Of course, he's telling me which demon killed the owner – Lilith. Good for her.*

'Nobody important then?' Mark laughs at the irony of this statement. *Lilith – guardian, teacher, lover - the second most important person in my existence.*

Satori keeps talking. He fills the heavy stillness with questions about magic as if eager to bond. Mark answers without processing the questions fully. His mind is on other things. His ears capture the sound of terrible suffering beyond the kitchen door. Dozens of screams fill his mind.

The hallway beckons. They walk towards it. The wooden floor wears a shroud of dust, undisturbed by footprints. The dust looks more than a few years old. It looks as though some deity laid it here in remembrance and reverence, a way of marking this place as sacred and untouchable: a psychic "do not disturb" sign.

Satori takes the first step into the hallway, disturbing the stillness. Behind Satori's back, Mark shakes his head at the man's irreverence. It is as though Satori feels he has the right to use or despoil whatever he chooses. Mark's bitterness towards the man who stole his mother away turns into a simmering hatred of everything Satori is and stands for.

191

He watches the back of Satori's head as the man strides across the floor, arrogant and uncaring, oblivious to the suffering that happened here. Mark's fists shake as he fights the desire to push this arrogant fool to the ground and smash his skull open, repairing the damaged dust of shed skin with Satori's blood.

He pushes his rage into his stomach and promises to savour it later. The protective spell on the hallway is broken. The wails of agony and despair are silenced, at least for the moment. Mark breathes deeply and takes a step out of the kitchen and into character.

'Wow!' he exclaims.

Mark's reaction seems to please Satori and he is rewarded with a smile. The man starts talking again, asking questions Mark does not wish to answer. The boy is led into a room, a library. Together they sit while Satori drills him for information. He answers each question obliquely.

He remembers the envelope in his pocket and uses it to distract Satori's attention. The man is intrigued. He wants to know what's inside and the more Mark protests the more eager Satori becomes. The flimsy envelope becomes a prize beyond value. Satori's eyes darken; he will not be denied. He is used to getting what he wants. Mark gains pleasure from Satori's suffering and discomfort. To be denied knowledge or experience is more than some men can bear.

With a shrug, Mark hands the envelope to Satori. The man's hand shakes as his fingers make contact with the paper. He tears it open and pulls out a photograph.

Mark studies the picture, confused for a moment as to what it might mean. A raven with a ribbon tied around its beak. *Raven! That's how I will purge the board of knight and bishop. Raven.*

Satori suggests they search the rest of the house before retiring for the evening. As they open the cellar door and descend into the half-light, the tortured screams return. Mark feels punched back by the force of the spirits' rage and despair. 'Do you hear it?'

Satori claims it is only the wind yet the man shivers with discomfort.

The shadow of a man rises from the flagstones. A child hangs limply from his outstretched arms. The man's hands squeeze the boy's throat, but the child does not fight back. Perhaps he is already dead.

Entrails spiral out across the floor. The shadow-man studies the bloody gore, nodding as if with some new insight. Flames leap around the man. He laughs. Laughter morphs into screams as hands reach through the flames, dragging him downwards.

'We'll check upstairs.' Satori tramples through the spectral flames.

Mark blinks the vision from his eyes before following in his father's footsteps.

Chapter 39

Sleep comes quickly. In his dream Satori sees his tower, the one he created before his journey across the planes of existence. He cranes his neck to see the narrow windows and peak of the building. He wants to climb the cairn and walk inside but his staircase is missing. He tries climbing the hill, anyway. It is steep and every time he pushes himself upwards he slips back down to the base.

He turns around, expecting to see the forest that used to surround this cairn and tower. Instead of trees, he sees an endless bleak desert, full of dirty mustard-coloured sand.

Slowly, he turns back to the tower. The mound has levelled. His tower remains, but its foundations now rest on the same sand he sees in every direction.

He takes a step towards the building. He imagines the warmth inside: the library, chair and whisky. A low rumble echoes around the desert. He stops walking and stares at the tower. The sand ahead crumbles and parts. A shape moves upwards between Satori and his tower. Black curls and a pale oval face – Star. She rises higher. She holds her arms out on either side. In each hand she holds a terracotta jug. She rises further and her torso lifts above the sand. She is defiled and ruined. Her body, like it was in Binah, is broken. The gaping cavern in her stomach reveals bloodied entrails. Heart and lungs, still pulsing, frame the horrifying void. Below this her legs are covered in the black scales of a giant wyrm's head.

She stops moving upwards and tips her head to look at Satori.

'Star,' he mumbles.

She nods and twists her wrists to tip the jugs at forty-five degree angles. From her left a thick red liquid drips from the jug. From her right flows a white liquid. Behind her the tower shudders.

'What are you doing?' he asks her.

'Nothing,' she answers. 'You're doing it. Let it all disintegrate. You don't need it any longer.'

He shakes his head. 'Why?'

She holds his stare, but keeps her mouth tightly closed. The corners of her lips turn up a little, but the smile, if indeed it can be called a smile, is cold and humourless. The tower shakes. Stones detach themselves from the top and bounce off the sides as they fall to the ground. More follow, shaken by the blows from other stones; the speed increases and more of the building crumbles and falls.

Satori wants to run towards it, demand that it rebuild itself for him, but he is rooted to the spot, unable to move. Everything is wrong, nothing is stable and he doesn't understand any of it. He holds his ears and closes his eyes.

'Satori...Satori, wake up, Darling.'

Satori opens his eyes and stares at the shadowy ceiling above him. He removes his hands from his ears and looks around the empty room. His eyes settle on the oval mirror. A soft glow comes from it. He stands up slowly and takes a step towards the mirror. Unsure of whether he is awake or asleep, he holds his breath. Terror fills him. He doesn't know what he will see in the mirror but he is convinced he will not like it.

He steps closer again. He can see part of the room reflected. The room looks similar to the one in which he stands, although the lighting is different. He steps forwards again and stands directly in front of the mirror. The room is reflected back at him. Daylight streams through the window in the mirror-room. The furniture is the same. The bed he just left is reflected back at him, covers creased where he pushed them from his body. Everything seems the same but different. Everything is present, but the light makes objects clearer and easier to see. He can see tree tops framed by the window beside him. He can see everything other than his own face and body. He has no reflection.

'Satori. Satori, Darling, wake up.'

He knows that voice. He turns to look over his shoulder. 'Raven?'

Something hits his chest. The sudden blow forces him backwards and he falls. His body drops, sinks and plunges. He does not hit the floor. The floor has gone. He falls into a void. All is darkness. He cannot see if there are walls around him. All he can see is an oval far above, glowing with golden light that gets smaller and smaller until it disappears completely, and still he falls.

Chapter 40

Mark wakes suddenly. He sits up straight and looks around him. *What woke me?* Beyond the tapestry curtains drawn around the huge four-poster the room is dark. The house is silent. Did he imagine a noise? Was it a dream?

He lies back on his pillow. His body feels restless. Adrenaline pumps through his veins. He knows he will not sleep again until he checks the house for intruders. Anyone could have wandered through the open back door. *We did.*

He stands up. Goose bumps instantly rise on his flesh. He feels around for his jumper. When he finds it the fibres feel damp and colder than his skin. He decides to wear it anyway, hoping symbiosis will warm both garment and body.

He stumbles across the dark floor and reaches for the door handle. The landing is quiet and still. Mark decides to check Satori's room first. As he opens the door he sees the man flat on his back in the middle of the floor. He rushes across and lifts Satori's head. 'Satori. What happened? Are you okay?'

Satori doesn't open his eyes or reply. Mark puts his ear to Satori's chest and hears a steady heartbeat. Checking the back of the man's skull for blood, he cups his hand around Satori's hair. Satori's head feels dry and when he checks his hand it comes back clean. He shakes Satori's shoulders. 'Wake up, Satori. It's Mark.'

There is no response. Mark puts his hands under his father's shoulders and half-carries, half-drags the heavy body towards the bed.

He lifts head, shoulders and torso onto the bed then swings Satori's legs from the floor. Satisfied that Satori is safe from falling, Mark replaces the blanket over the unconscious form. He kneels beside the bed and speaks again, close to Satori's ear. His breath makes Satori's ear-rings shudder, but it does not rouse him from his slumber. Mark gives up and decides to check the rest of the house.

He checks the bathrooms, the third, fourth and fifth bedrooms then heads towards the large and desolate upstairs room they checked earlier. As he looks around at empty display cabinets and bare bookshelves he wonders what this room was for. He strides closer to the centre of the square room. His skin tingles. A shadow deeper than the rest lurks at the centre, and his flashlight refuses to define or dispel the shape. The shape moves, uncurling before his eyes. It grows upwards, stretching until it stands a foot taller than Mark. The torch shakes in his hand as he watches in awe. Two limbs, arms perhaps, separate from the bulk and rise above what looks like the shadow's head. The right shadow-limb is longer than the other and ends with a curved narrow point, a blade. Both arms are held aloft, reaching towards the ceiling. The black shape of the blade draws energy from above. Sparks, like lightning bolts, spread between ceiling and knife. Bright blue and vivid green arcs of energy crackle. The room flashes with their light, but the silhouette remains dark and unformed.

Mark clutches his torch like an insufficient weapon, not caring any longer which part of the room the beam hits. Lightning flashes illuminate everything around him, everything apart from the shadow, man or demon, who stands in the centre, drawing light and power into him. Mark shakes where he stands. Part of him wants to approach the figure, understand its nature; the other half wants to flee from the room and try once more to wake the sleeping Satori. Adrenaline floods his body. His limbs scream for movement in one direction or the other, but his mind is in chaos.

'Who are you?' His voice trembles as he speaks.

The silhouette changes. Mark sees a nose and chin protrude from the dark face as it turns around. Then the shape returns to its less-defined state. The creature faces him now, or so Mark presumes. It is aware of his presence in the room. Running is pointless. The urge to fight grows from his adrenaline-fuelled instincts, but to fight he must first understand.

He takes a step towards the lightning rod, entranced by the beautiful light and the mysterious darkness. All thoughts other than the need to understand leave him. Another step closer and he is chilled by the freezing air that rotates around the figure. He stretches his right arm towards the shadow, almost touching it. Another step and he will know how it feels. He hovers, breathing heavily before taking that final step. What he touches feels like slime: cold, moving, sucking slime. He pushes forwards, eyes focused on the black void which looks like a torso.

The figure falls away. It topples backwards, like a body pushed from the top of the stairs or the edge of the building. The wind around the shadow whistles painfully in Mark's ears. The room is dark, the lightning gone. Mark sweeps the beam of torchlight to where the shadow once stood, watching it tumble backwards to the floor, through the floor, vanishing without a trace.

Chapter 41

"Life and death is an entering and leaving of different dream worlds,

and reality is where we find or make it." Austin Osman Spare.

Satori falls through darkness. Arms and limbs flail as his body panics. Terrified he stares upwards. His mind tumbles with him. He grasps at memories as though they are straws to a drowning man: the mirror, the voice, the fall. *I'm dreaming.* He tries to wake up, but the pull downwards is irresistible. Burying his fear, he concentrates on his breath. The process calms him and his panic subsides. He stills his body, straightens his limbs and puts his hands either side of his hips, palms down. Opening his eyes, he searches for meaning in the darkness. *What is the dream showing me? What must I understand?* When his eyes adjust, he sees bright specks, like dust motes, fall around him. As he studies them they become brighter and brighter until he is afraid the power of their glow will burn his retinas. In the thick darkness, it is as though thousands of stars fall with him.

He feels like Alice, tumbling down the rabbit hole. His progress feels gentle. The air doesn't rush past his body as he falls. Instead he seems to float, feather-like, but without the horizontal rocking movement a feather might make as it is carried upon a breeze or updraft of air. Something damp hits his cheek. Another wets the palm of his hand. The brightness of stars fade and he sees millions of bubbles; some are as small as the pupils of his eyes and others as large as his entire head. They float upwards as he falls downwards, some pop against his skin and others float past into the darkness above.

The darkness shifts again. A black circle, somehow deeper than the absolute darkness around it, imposes itself on the gloom above. Around the circle a ring of red appears then grows brighter until its glow looks like flames around the silhouette of a black moon. The crimson halo moves like water, expanding and contracting around the black circle. Bright red spots break off and drip downwards. Falling through the bubbles and stars, they change shape as they fall. Sometimes they are perfect spheres, other times they look like beans and splatters. They fall faster than him, racing towards Satori through the darkness, colliding with bubbles in explosions of violent pink spray.

The first drip, to hit Satori, splatters against his face, the second, the back of his hand. Redness spreads across his skin, thick and sticky, like blood. The red rain continues to fall. It covers his skin and clothes. It feels warm as it soaks him, this blood from the black moon or black sun, covering him in warm slime, like an embryo in a womb. It hits his mouth and seeps between his lips. It tastes bitter and metallic, crawling across his tongue and into his throat, too thick to swallow. He tries to cough it up, bending his body double as he does so.

Air whistles past his ears as he falls faster. Blood no longer reaches him but falls back steadily, beyond his reach, lighting the sky above like fireflies. He keeps coughing and gagging until a sphere of crimson is pushed from his throat back onto his tongue then out into the air around him. It explodes like a firework, lighting the sky. In the flash he sees a ladder bolted to the wall a few metres from his hand. He kicks his legs and tries to move against the air like a swimmer. As he flattens his body his descent slows and the blood drops gain on him again. He keeps kicking towards the wall of the cavern and the ladder he hopes is still there. His fingers stretch. Trying to touch something solid, he kicks again and again.

Bubbles pop against his back and legs, blood drips onto his face and chest. He keeps reaching, kicking and pushing himself to where he hopes the ladder hangs. At last his hand touches something cold and smooth. Another fierce kick and he wraps his fingers around a metal bar. His feet keep falling but his hand clings to the ladder. As his body becomes vertical his calves knock against metal and stone. He searches with his heel for a rung and finds one. He clings to the ladder as blood falls onto his head and shoulders. His hands are slippery and he is terrified he might lose his hold. He just hangs there, clinging to invisible metal while blood covers him. He shakes his head and blinks, trying to see through the crimson film that covers his eyes.

The vicious rain ceases. One moment it is as heavy as ever, drenching him, and the next it stops falling. He looks up and can no longer see the black sun or the red ring of bloodfire, which surrounded it. Bubbles glow as they drift upwards through starlight, reflecting the silver light back as they float towards an unknown destination.

Carefully, he turns his body so he faces the wall. Fists wrapped tightly around the rung of the iron ladder, he wonders whether he should climb upwards in pursuit of the bubbles or downwards to search for their source. He considers both options while remaining still. If he wishes to descend he can let himself fall. If he climbs a while and finds nothing, he can choose the fall again. Continuing downwards is a passive gesture, accepting what will be. If that was the only option the ladder would not exist. To find this here, to reach it and be able to cling to it in spite of the slippery deluge, must surely mean he is meant to climb upwards.

He moves one hand to the rung above and moves his foot upwards as well. He continues in this way. In time the blood is rubbed from his hands and his grip becomes firmer, his progress swifter as he climbs towards whatever he might find.

Satori follows the bubbles upwards and reaches a ledge at the top of the ladder. He crawls from the pit. He dare not walk in case the ground vanishes beneath his feet again. He hears laughter to his left, its source unseen in the dark. He keeps moving away from the pit, trying to ignore the mocking laughter.

The sound follows him as he moves on hands and knees across the rock. Blood soaks his hands again, this time it is his blood, cut on jagged pieces of stone. Slipping and sliding he continues forwards. Darkness blinds him. Hopelessness settles in his chest. *I will never find my way.*

What if I can make my own light?

He unfurls his body and stands proud. Breathing deeply, he calms his mind and body. He reminds himself that like all realities and dreams this one is within his mind and he can alter it. Closing his eyes, he tries to draw light and energy into his body. Instead of bright light, he feels darkness pushing through his open chakras and closes them again. *Okay,* he thinks. He concentrates on a light inside him, love, burning in his stomach and chest. The light grows and warms him. Opening his eyes, he detects shapes in the gloom. The ground below him is solid as far as he can see. He walks within his self-made spotlight and marvels at how quickly his vision adjusts until he is barely aware of the viscous, pulsing darkness surrounding him, held at bay by his love.

Satori is in a large, wide tunnel. The walls look organic rather than man-made, perhaps hewn by water or a giant worm. Shapes move against the walls, they appear sentient but do not approach him and he has no desire to study them closer.

The air ahead glows red. He keeps walking. There is a bend in the tunnel and as he rounds it he sees something which steals his breath. Two great obelisks reach beyond the limits of the tunnel. One pillar is white, the other black and between them a crimson sun hovers. He looks left and right. There are no alternative routes to take. He keeps walking towards these twin towers, the dark and the light in balance, with the sun setting between them.

Hot air stifles him. Satori pulls at the t-shirt around his neck. His face and body drip sweat. A dog howls. Something low and heavy approaches him from behind. Afraid to turn and look at his pursuer, Satori hurries. He sprints forwards, between the pillars. Energy hits him and every molecule in his body spasms. He feels new connections form in his brain and nervous system. A wide grin spreads across his face. The feeling is wonderful. The balance between his spirit and his body has never felt more intact. Reluctantly he steps forwards and leaves the obelisks behind. The dying sun falls below the tunnel floor and reveals a chamber beyond. He strides towards it, energised.

Chapter 42

Freya pads down the stairs of her family home. As she enters the living room, she sees her mother cradling Jasmine, a look of pure love on her face.

'Morning, Mum.'

'Good morning, Darling. Did you sleep well? I'm sorry, I heard Jasmine wake up and thought I'd let you sleep longer. Is that okay?'

Freya shrugs. 'Sure.'

'Do you want breakfast?' Lorraine asks.

Freya watches the sleeping infant, secure and surrounded by love, in Lorraine's arms. She smiles, but inside her chest a maggot of jealousy wriggles. 'I can sort myself out. I remember where everything is. Want a cuppa?'

'And have to put this little cutie to one side while I drink it? ... Oh I'm sorry, Freya. Here do you want her?'

Freya considers the question for a moment then shakes her head. 'I'm fine, Mum. She seems settled where she is. Wasn't she hungry when she woke, though?'

'No, she just needed a cuddle.'

'She'll be hungry soon.' Freya's breasts are heavy with milk. They ache to be emptied.

'Can I make up her bottle? Please, Freya.'

'Mum, I breastfeed her.' Freya scowls. She pushes her anger back down and it lurks in the shadows of her heart, waiting for the moment she can release it.

'Oh yes, of course. Well, she's okay for the moment. We'll just cuddle while you get yourself something to eat. You need to keep up your strength, after all you're feeding two.'

Freya sighs and turns to leave the room. 'Yes, Mum.'

'Freya.'

Freya glances back at her mother. 'Yes.'

Lorraine smiles serenely. Her eyes shine with joy. 'It's great to have you home. Stay as long as you want.'

'Thanks, Mum.'

Freya fetches some toast and a mug of coffee from the kitchen and returns to the living room.

'Is that all you're having?' Lorraine asks.

Freya laughs. 'For now, Mum. Where are Dad and Ivan?'

'Your Dad had to work an extra shift today. He should be home around three. Ivan's gone to see Sarah.'

'Sarah?'

'Yes.' Lorraine nods.

'As in Star?'

Lorraine's lips tremble behind the smile. Her eyes darken. 'That's right.'

'Why?'

Lorraine plants a kiss on Jasmine's forehead. 'Well, maybe it would be better if he told you. It's kind of complicated.'

'In what way, complicated?' Freya's stomach churns.

Lorraine stares at the baby while she speaks. 'They are sort of dating.'

'What! But she's with Satori.'

'Not so much.'

'They live together, don't they?' Freya's skin crawls. She scratches her scalp and frowns.

'They've been having problems for a while. As I understand it, Satori moved out.'

'Because she is having an affair with…Ivan?'

Lorraine shakes her head. 'Sarah's okay.'

'What do you mean, Sarah's okay? You mean she's good enough for your only son? You mean she's good enough for my…brother?'

Lorraine coos at the baby. 'Shhh, Darling. You'll wake Jasmine.'

Freya ignores her mother's request. Her voice is loud and shrill. 'I don't believe this, Mum. How long has he been seeing her?'

'They've been close for years.' Lorraine's voice remains calm and low. She doesn't look up at Freya as if worried that eye contact will provoke her daughter further.

'Close? What does that mean? Don't you know she's a murderess?' Freya stops suddenly and looks at her hands. She shivers remembering Dave and the way she punctured his chest with her ambition. She thinks of Rob, wings of blood spread around his corpse in their bed. *Was that me too?*

'She's not a murderess. All that nonsense was dropped years ago.'

'It was?'

'Yes. There was no evidence to prove anything. You've met her. Can you imagine that shy, sweet little girl killing anyone? I mean really, Freya, it's like saying you're a murderess. It's nonsense.'

Freya nods. 'So he's with her now?'

'He's staying there a few days while she gets herself sorted.'

Freya stands up. 'Maybe I should go over there and see if I can help.'

'They'll be okay. Leave them too it.'

'What's the address, Mum?'

Lorraine lifts her face and stares at Freya. Her eyes harden and she slowly shakes her head. 'I said leave it, Freya.'

Jasmine kicks her legs and starts murmuring.

'Shhh, sleep Sweetheart,' Lorraine croons.

The murmurs get louder until they become a whimper then a scream.

'Let me take her, Mum. She'll be hungry.' Freya walks across to her mother and holds out her arms.

'But you haven't had your breakfast yet,' Lorraine says.

'I'll have it later. Give me my baby please, Mum.'

Lorraine looks at the red screaming face and agitated body cradled in her arms and passes the baby to Freya. Freya snatches Jasmine and hurries with her to the sofa. She lifts her pyjama top and lets the baby latch on greedily.

'She's beautiful,' Lorraine says.

'Yes she is,' Freya agrees.

'She reminds me of you.'

Freya studies the baby in her arms and tries to see Rob in her puffy cheeks and button nose. He isn't there. She can only see herself in those soft blue eyes and shell-like ears. There is nothing masculine about her. Even her wispy hair is white-blonde like Freya's, not strawberry like Rob's. She could just as easily be any man's daughter, Ivan's daughter, except that is impossible. She hasn't had sex with Ivan, magical or otherwise, for four years.

The thought that Jasmine belongs to her alone fills Freya with pride and dread. She strokes the baby's downy hair and sings softly. Lorraine watches from the other side of the room. Jasmine reaches a tiny hand towards Freya's face and Freya bends to kiss her fingers. The baby takes its mouth from Freya's breast and smiles at her mother. The smile is warm and pure and honest. The infant remains untainted by fear and hate, for that Freya envies her.

As Jasmine falls asleep again Freya turns her face towards her own mother who smiles at the tender exchange. 'Want her back?'

Lorraine grins. 'Of course. Are you going somewhere?'

Freya passes Jasmine between Lorraine's open arms. 'Just in the garden for some fresh air.'

Lorraine cradles the baby. Her face is peaceful. 'It's cold out there. Wrap up warm.'

Freya steps out of the kitchen door into the garden. The garden where she was caught spying on her brother and where her midnight dance was interrupted by her father who feared for her sanity. The branches of Ivan's tree are decorated with ribbons he attached years ago. The once

211

vibrant colours have faded. Now drab rags hang from the branches. It looks as though nothing new has been tied there for years. Freya wonders whether he has lost his faith. *Did I steal it from him?*

Star. Why? What is so special about Star? Why is Star always at the centre of everybody's world? She's no prettier than I am. She's vulnerable and weak, always sad, always moaning about something or someone. I'm sharp and funny. I have power. What has she got: red hair which she hides with black dye, and a downturned mouth? Why are all the heroines sad and pitiful? When does the clever, sassy girl get her turn? When will I be adored?

Rob adored me. He worshipped me. He never wanted to leave the apartment or me to go to work. Then Jasmine came along. He still loved me. He held me in his arms with fierce pride and joy in his eyes, and smile. He watched me while I fussed with her, fed her or bathed her, but it was as if he was too awed. He saw me as a life-creating goddess and when we made love it was as if he was praying. My pedestal became too high and wobbled. It was only a matter of time before I came crashing down, but did I kill him? No. I couldn't. I wouldn't. I loved him.

She touches a damp ribbon. It is the shade of mother of pearl. She tries to imagine what the original colour would have been. *Red perhaps?* Its vibrancy and energy faded over the years. It faded like her relationship with Rob had faded. It became mediocre and inconsequential, lost in a crowd of other loves, other ribbons.

She sits under the tree. The dampness of the grass penetrates through the denim of her jeans. *Ivan and Star! How the fuck did that happen?* She digs her heel into the soft earth and kicks. A clump of earth and grass bounces across the lawn away from her. *Fucking Star! Fucking privileged Princess! Everyone's fucking favourite, even Lilith's.*

She remembers Donna weeping about Star's absence, burning herself when the heat of her passion went unanswered. She remembers Raven's broken body being carried from the club, simply because she dared to touch Star's cast-offs. She remembers how Satori rejected Freya, *after he'd fucked me of course. You couldn't expect that reptile to be a gentleman. He told me he loved Star, would always love Star. So why did he leave, unless Star broke his heart - broke his heart by sleeping with MY fucking brother?*

Fucking Star! Fucking Ivan! I hate them both. How dare they do this to me, laughing at me while I watch their performance from the wings of the stage? Always the understudy, never the star. If I let her, she'll destroy Ivan. She'll destroy him like she destroyed Donna and Raven and Satori. She's poison. I have to stop her. There's only one way.

Then Ivan can come home and we'll be a family again: Dad, Mum, Ivan, me and Jasmine. We can be whole. We can heal the wound of my sister's death and we can move on at last, together.

213

Chapter 43

The chamber looks like the interior of a cathedral. Walls sweep upwards in a wide oval arch, so high Satori cannot see the apex. To his left rock outcrops make a huge altar with a ledge above it. On the ledge, two vultures crouch. One stretches its wings, the other follows Satori's movements with its head.

He walks towards the altar. Water flows from a fissure onto and over it like a moving altar-cloth. The water looks and smells fresh. A sudden movement makes him jump and a bright green frog leaps through the waterfall towards Satori. Moving his feet, he lets it hop past unobstructed. It moves away, towards the opposite end of the room and three figures. The trio stand close to the opposite wall, around thirty metres from Satori. Naked, they dance with each other, slowly, as if in a trance. He walks towards them, checking the floor to ensure he does not tread on the frog.

As he approaches, he recognises one of the figures. Star bends over with her hand between her thighs. She masturbates. Her eyes are full of lust and her throat emits bestial grunts. The other two figures are male. They watch Star play with her genitals. Satori sees the appreciation in their faces and massive, swollen cocks.

One of the men, a blond Adonis, moves behind Star. He wraps his arms around her body and tugs and squeezes her breasts. Star unfolds her body and leans her head against the man's chest, sighing in pleasure.

Satori watches open-mouthed as the man penetrates Star. Satori's head spins. It can't be Star yet he feels jealous. At the same time, his jeans feel tighter as he grows hard with excitement.

The other man has deep bronze skin. His jet black hair moves around the nape of his neck. Star kisses him while he wraps his arms around her and squeezes her ass cheeks. His cock presses against her stomach. He bends his back and angles his hips so that it slides between her legs then he too pushes inside the woman. The three of them grope, kiss and fuck each other. Star's body bounces between the two men as she rides them both with an almost grotesque look of ecstasy on her face. Her mouth hangs open and her tongue lolls from its cavern. Her face is flushed. Her eyes, glazed with lust, turn towards Satori, but she seems oblivious to his presence.

The man behind her, eagerly fucking her ass, squeezes her breasts so hard that they redden and bruise. Her nipples swell beneath the pressure. Milk sprays from them and hits the darker man's face.

A third man, no boy, approaches the group. Satori gasps. The kid looks like Mark. Mark at least does seem to sense Satori's presence. He turns and nods politely before joining the orgy. One delicate hand grabs each of the men's buttocks while Mark's mouth opens to catch the spray of breast milk.

215

Satori wants to run away, but is unable to move from the spot. He watches, both aroused and horrified. He hits his temple with his left fist while opening his jeans and pulling his erect penis from them with his right hand.

He hates himself for his excitement. It makes him feel perverted and wicked. It humbles him, the same way he felt when he had ached for Lilith. But he cannot stop. The punches to his face do nothing to dull his lust. He squeezes his cock tightly in his right fist and tugs, back and forth, back and forth until he explodes in blessed relief.

His semen spurts into the air before him. The cathedral breathes life into each squirt. He watches mesmerised as his ejaculated sperm floats and moves before him, changing shape continuously, becoming a figure, a face, a beast then a gargoyle with a huge tongue and horns. Horrors move before him more terrible than the scene of base lust beyond.

The separate horrors created by Satori's expended seed press together. A white translucent face grows in the air. Its eyes are huge, its nose flat and wide. It opens its toothless mouth in a soundless scream. White insects drop from its lolling tongue onto Satori's hair and shoulders. He brushes them off and steps back, shaking.

A female form with a solitary leg, which twists like witch hazel, grows from the ground. Her body sways. Her breasts swell and shrink as if pushed outwards by an internal hand then released. She reaches towards him. The claws at the end of her slender fingers are as twisted and misshapen as her leg.

An albino wolf shakes itself and splashes of the semen that created it scatter on the ground. Each grows into a new wolf

216

until a pack of hundreds of lupines snarl at Satori. They squat on their haunches, ready to pounce. Hungry eyes like stars fill his vision. His head spins and pain spreads from his frontal lobe to the back of his skull. His head pulses with the rhythm of his heart. He covers his eyes with his hands, trying to shut out the light. The eyes get closer. He sees them through his eyelashes and the cracks between his fingers. They press against him. Their moisture presses into his ears and nose. Pulling his hands from his eyes, he tries to beat them away. Screaming, he falls to his knees and rocks his body back and forth.

The horrors keep changing. Eyeballs become rats which make him jump back to his feet. The rats grow tattered wings like bats with rope tails. They push him back. His brain swims. He cannot think. The world splits before him and horrors crawl up from the bowels of hell to consume his soul.

Chapter 44

Mark dives through the empty floor after the shadow. His feet hit stone and he flexes his knees to soften his landing. He stands in the shadowy corner of a cavern. In the centre stands Satori. Mark watches his father's face twist in pain and disgust, and smiles. *How easily humans can be manipulated by their petty jealousies and insecurities.*

Between Mark and his father, there is an orgy of sorts. At its centre stands a shadow figure, Star.

He watches, neither aroused nor disgusted by the fornicating spectres. His mother's face has a strange beauty that only sex or pain can reveal. Her cheeks look flushed. Her eyes hooded and her mouth opens and closes in the parody of a kiss.

Satori shakes as he watches the scene.

How ironic it is that a person as sexually free as Satori, a man who has manipulated others' emotions without guilt, should view this scene as something obscene. Perhaps it is jealousy rooted in possessiveness or perhaps, for once, it's because he is not the centre of attention.

Mark steps out of the shadow.

Satori does not turn towards him. The man's attention does not waver from the trio before him. The squeezing of milk filled breasts, the eager fucking of Star's holes and her face transformed by obscene pleasure, perhaps Satori is disturbed that he has never seen his beloved look at him in that way? Perhaps he feels that he has never been enough?

Instead of approaching his father, Mark strides towards the lust-filled trio. He smiles as he faces away from Satori wondering what new torment he might inflict on the trembling man. Shadow-Star's breasts drip with milk. The stimulation of the blond man's fingers on her left breast increases the flow until her milk becomes a fountain, a jet of white, life-supporting fluid. Mark feels Satori's recognition as he steps into his father's blinkered view and turns to nod in acknowledgement. Bending his knees, Mark stands before the shadow-woman and catches her milk in his mouth. Some spills over his chin. It is warm and sweet.

He stretches out his arms and caresses the firm buttocks of both men. Although he feels aroused, he cannot tear his thoughts away from the observer. The thought of Satori watching the display makes him want to cry out with laughter. To stifle this desire Mark bends towards Star, filling his mouth with her breast. His lips surround her nipple.

On the edge of his hearing, beyond the lust-filled pants and moans, he is aware of sounds emanating from Satori. The man makes deep, low noises. His grunts suggest that he is masturbating as he watches, but these sounds are choked by fear, shame and horror. They intrigue Mark and he wants to tear himself away from the orgy to experience in full the distress and confusion his performance is causing. He grins and bites the shadow-woman's breast and her groans become louder. He stretches her nipple between his teeth turning his head just enough to catch glimpses of the scene beyond.

A fountain of semen fills the air. Each drop takes form. Mark forgets the orgy and disentangles himself from the embrace. He watches Satori. His father's face is a mask of terror. No longer watching the sexual display, Satori's arms flail through the air in front of his face as if trying to push away monsters which Mark is unable to see.

Satori's screams echo around the chamber as he falls to his knees, holding his arms above him in protection against an unseen assailant. Tears roll down the man's face and his body shakes.

Enough! Mark strides across to Satori. The man does not see him. His mind is full of the horror against which he protects himself. Gently, he taps Satori's shoulder. His father turns towards him and looks up with fearful eyes. It seems to take a moment for Satori to see him. Mark extends his hand towards the quivering man.

'Come on,' Mark says.

He leads his father to the chamber where the sleeping woman lays waiting. He smiles as he reunites the lovers and completes Satori's separation from Star.

***

Mark draws air into his lungs as his body pushes back, through the wooden floor and into the empty room. He lies on the floor, laughing. Sitting up, he claps his hands. He checks his mental chess board, the bishop has fallen. Mark runs from the empty room, repeating Satori's name over and over. Laughing and crying, he rushes into his father's room and kneels by his bed. Mark tests Satori's pulse. It is strong. The man is merely unconscious.

He goes back to his own room and dresses. He shivers deliciously as energy pulses through his body. *So close now!* Grabbing the photo of the raven and the empty envelope, he takes both downstairs. He searches the bureau in Paul's library and finds new envelopes and a pen. As accurately as possible Mark duplicates the writing from the first envelope onto a fresh one, places the photo inside, seals it and slips it into his jacket pocket.

Mark returns to Kevin's flat, determined to complete his mission and free himself from his obligation to Garlow.

'What the fuck, kid? We thought you'd run off. Garlow is fucking furious.'

'I'm sorry, Kev. I was attacked.' Mark moves his hair back so Kevin can see the deep purple and red bruise on his forehead.

'You been to hospital?' he asks.

'No. I was out cold for a while then I came back here.'

'Did they rob you?'

'I did the delivery to that woman. She gave me two envelopes. I dropped one off before I got battered. The other's still here in my pocket.' Mark draws the envelope from inside his jacket.

'I'll phone Garlow now. Let him know what's happened. He can call off the dogs.'

'The dogs?'

'Figuratively speaking. Well, you didn't think we'd just let you disappear, did you?'

'I guess not. I'm sorry, Kev.'

'You're alright and nought's stolen. Don't stress it. All will be forgiven.'

'Hey, it's me, Kevin...yeah...yeah I found him...Garlow there? ... Good morning, sir. Yep I've got him here. Says he did two deliveries and he has an envelope for you here...Says he was attacked...Yeah, he's got a golf ball on his forehead. Looks like someone took a piece out of him...yeah, it's okay. I've seen it. The envelope's here...Okay...Yeah, we can make it in ten.'

'Right, Mark,' Kevin says moving his phone from his ear. 'We'd better get a move on. Boss wants to see you.'

When they arrive at the bar, Garlow sits in the same corner as before. Mark goes to approach him, but Kevin grabs the sleeve of his jacket and jerks him back. 'Wait.'

Mark shakes his arm free of Kevin's grip. 'For what?'

'To be invited, you ill-mannered twat.'

Mark shuffles about impatiently, but waits beside Kevin until Garlow beckons them over.

'Hey, Kid. We thought you went AWOL.'

'No, sir. Sorry. I did the first delivery. The woman, she gave me two envelopes and an address. I dropped the first off, no bother, but then it all went weird. I'm sorry, Mr Garlow.'

'Kevin says you got knocked out.'

Mark nods and pushes his hair back from his forehead.

Garlow inhales noisily. 'Looks nasty, Kid. You feeling okay?'

'I'm fine.' Mark frowns. He wonders how much time he will have to waste here.

Garlow smiles. 'Kev's right. You are a tough one.'

'I've got the envelope for you.' Mark passes it to Garlow.

Garlow takes it, studies the envelope and writing then tears it open. He glances at the photograph, nods and places it back in the envelope and on the table.

Mark is desperate to ask what it means, but remains silent, studying the man's calm face. 'Sir?'

'Yes, Kid.'

'I've found someone who knows where my mum is.'

'Is that right?'

Mark nods.

'Is that how you got that bruise?'

Mark nods again. 'I'm kinda eager to go back there, if you know what I mean. I don't want to be rude, Mr Garlow, but do you think we're finished here?'

'No worries, Kid. Take Kevin and Simon. They'll get the information for you.'

'That's not necessary, sir. I just wanted to let you know I won't be back.'

Garlow creases his brow and frowns. 'What do you mean, you won't be back?'

'I'm gonna find my mum.' Mark feels weighed down by Garlow's scrutiny. He fidgets again.

'Hang on, Kid.'

'Yes, sir?'

'Take Kevin and Simon.'

Mark shakes his head. 'I don't need…'

'I'm giving you time to find your Ma, but this isn't goodbye.'

Mark grits his teeth. 'I did what you wanted. I followed your instructions. It's time to let me go.'

Garlow laughs.

Mark turns to walk away. Bristling with the threat of violence, Kevin blocks his way. Mark looks around the room. Everyone is standing, watching. He turns to face Garlow. 'What do you want?'

Garlow picks up a beer mat from the table and taps its edge against the wood. He studies Mark's face, staring at his green eyes as if deep in thought. 'I've taken an interest in you, Kid. You intrigue me. I only want the best for you. You must understand that. Take Kevin and Simon with you to see this man.'

Mark sighs. 'Thank you, Mr Garlow.'

'Just remember you owe me big time for this, Kid.'

Mark nods.

'Kevin,' Garlow calls.

'Yes, Mr Garlow.'

'Take Simon and go with the kid. There's someone who needs to be convinced to talk.'

'No problem.' Kevin nods at Mark. 'You ready to go?'

'Yes,' Mark replies. 'I'm ready.' *Are you?*

Chapter 45

The spectres change again. This time they rise above Satori, a serpent with three heads and three gaping, vicious jaws. Their fangs drip venom as they prepare to strike. Satori lifts his arms above his head to protect himself from their attack. The heads descend, flashing through the air towards him. His knees give way and he falls to the ground, weeping. His hands flail above him trying to ward off the horror.

Something touches his shoulder. It isn't the strike of attack but a gentle and affectionate pat. He looks up. Mark stands in front of him, smiling.

'Come on.' Mark extends his hand towards the whimpering ball that is Satori.

Satori grasps his hand and allows the boy to pull him to his feet. He stands unsteadily looking at the teenager. Remnants of breast milk glisten on Mark's chin. 'Is it you?'

Mark doesn't answer.

Satori stares at Mark's nakedness. He has a wiry strength and his body is beautifully toned, almost sculpted in places, far stronger than Satori feels any teenage body has the right to look. He feels aroused again, but banishes the feeling. *I am holding the hand of a child not a man,* he reminds himself.

Mark leads Satori away from the spectres. When they try to follow Mark growls at them and they shrink back as if in fear. Satori studies the boy's face. Mark's jaw is fixed with determination, but his lips are soft and generous; his skin has a warm olive glow and his eyes are the brightest green Satori has ever seen. They shine with an intense beauty. They remind him of Lilith.

Hand in hand, Mark and Satori walk towards a low archway. Both have to bend a little to pass safely through. As Satori's head and shoulders enter an anti-chamber he hears the whoosh of a bird in flight. Black wings beat against his face. He waves his free arm to scare the raven away. The bird is as large as a cat with a vicious looking beak. It squawks at Satori and flies out of reach.

'She's waiting for you.' Mark squeezes then releases Satori's hand.

Mark steps toward a sleeping woman. She rests upon an outcrop of rock. The curves of her body strain through a black chiffon dress. Ebony hair rests, like a veil, obscuring her face. Satori knows that body, those generous breasts and hips. He has kissed them, held them and admired them, a long time ago, before she died.

'Raven.' Satori strokes her hair and pulls it gently away from her face. Her eyes are closed but her mouth hangs wide open. Her jaw smashed, bloody and bruised from the violence which killed her four years ago. He turns away and searches Mark's face for an answer.

'You need to wake her with your wand. To wake the dead, the magician must place a wand inside the corpse's mouth.'

Satori shakes his head. 'I don't have a wand.' He faces Raven again and stares, mesmerised by her fearful mouth.

226

Mark's voice is faint. 'You have the one you used to summon Lilith.'

Angry hisses fill the room. Satori turns around. Mark has vanished and where he stood moments before, two snakes writhe on the ground. Their bodies are intertwined. One is white, the other black. Satori backs away. His hand touches the ledge on which Raven rests, waiting for him to wake her. The snakes rear up. He has no weapons, but he knows he must get rid of them. Edging away, he looks around the room for something, anything he could use to frighten the serpents. There is nothing.

He looks at his trembling hands and focuses on his pale skin. Black letters rise across his skin like a tattoo. The black letters he used in Binah to kill the wyrm. The terrible wailing and the stench of burning flesh from that wyrm echoes through his mind as the two snakes move towards him. *I have no choice.* He opens his eyes and utters the magical sounds, directing the power in his fingertips towards the snakes. Lightning rips through the air and pins the snakes to the ground. He watches as they jerk and twist in pain. Their scales melt and meld together, becoming one mass of disintegrating puss. Satori holds his ears to shield himself from the sounds of their agony. He pulls back the lightning. For a moment, the melted horror that had once been two snakes lies motionless. With a blinding flash it implodes and a pebble of black glass, no larger than the palm of Satori's hand, clatters to the floor.

Satori looks back at Raven. His body shakes with energy and fear. *What did I use to summon Lilith?* He had summoned the goddess twice, once to his bedroom to negotiate Star's release and once into Chaos, but he does not remember a wand. The first time replays in his head.

I stood within a circle and called "Lilith, succubus, serpent, temptress of Eve, first wife of Adam, dark mother." I jerked off. As I called to her I used my semen as a tribute and she came. My hand clutched my penis and I rubbed it back and forth as I called to her... My cock is my wand.

He stares at Raven's grotesque mouth. Her lips are drawn back exposing blood covered teeth on one side and on the other stumps where teeth were severed from their roots. Her jaw is a strange triangle, almost normal on one side. Stretching into a wide leer on the other where upper and lower jaw are smashed and hang disconnected from her skull. Satori shudders at the thought of what he must do if he wishes to wake her then wonders whether he should wake her at all.

'We could have been good together if I had only seen it earlier, Raven. I remember how you flirted with me when we first met. How bold and dominant you seemed. I never saw past the paint and armour. I never knew, until the moment Star left with Lilith and I slept beside your cooling body, that I could love you. Even then I was so wrapped up in my obsession for Star I chased her and left you behind. I'm sorry, Raven. I should have been better for you. Maybe then we would both be happy. To wake you I must place my wand, fuck it let's be honest here, my cock in your mouth, but I'm scared, Raven.'

She does not respond. He tries to see beyond her wounds, but his eyes are drawn back to her crushed cheek and smashed jaw. 'I don't think I can do this.'

He tries to place his lips on hers to wake her with a fairy tale kiss. The congealed blood in her mouth smells sour and rotten. His stomach churns and forces him away. He paces up and down the room like an expectant father, deathly afraid and excited about the prospect of new life. *Coward! You owe this to her. Stick it in her fucking mouth. You weren't too proud to do that before.*

He bends down to pick up the glass pebble from the floor. He turns it over again and again. There is something inside. It looks at first like a fault line, but it twists and moves as he watches. He tries to think back to all his readings. *What does it mean? Is the stone important? Can it help me?*

'It can't help you, but it can help her, afterwards.'

Satori turns and sees Mark leaning against the archway. The boy's grin looks treacherous.

'I thought you had gone?'

'I came back. It looks like you need my help.'

'Are you really Mark?' Satori asks.

'Are you really Satori?' Mark replies.

Satori shrugs and blushes. 'I don't know.'

Mark nods. 'So what are you going to do about our sleeping beauty?'

'I don't know that either. I think I'm supposed to put my dick in her mouth, but…'

'But what?'

'I don't think I can.'

229

Mark laughs. 'A man of the world like you, Satori? Tut tut.'

Satori shakes. 'Have you seen her face? Have you smelt her breath?'

'And whose fault is that?'

Satori sighs. 'Star's.'

Mark shakes his head.

Satori inhales. 'Lilith's.'

'Try again.'

'Mine. Yes, everything that has happened has happened because of me and my selfish obsession. It has cost me everything.'

'It cost you less than it cost her.' Mark points at Raven's corpse.

Satori sighs again. 'Okay, I'll do it, but please...don't watch me.'

'I'll be outside if you need me.' Mark ducks through the archway into the huge chamber beyond.

'Raven...' Satori sighs. He stares at her broken face. 'Oh god, I'm sorry... W-what I'm about to do...' He shakes his head. 'I can't. It feels wrong, even by my standards, but I guess it's what I'm supposed to do, what I have to do, if either of us is going to get out of here.'

He unzips his trousers and pulls out his flaccid penis. It tries to hide among his pubes, but he finds it and drags it into the stagnant air of the tomb. 'I guess you don't have to be hard for this,' he says.

Gently he turns Raven's head so she faces him. Her face looks more terrifying than ever. There is a chasm where her ear used to be. He wipes his fingers on his jeans and tries to control his nausea. He holds his penis between forefinger and thumb and directs it towards Raven's gaping mouth. Swallowing hard, he bends his knees and shuffles forwards until he holds that small yet dominant part of himself between her withered lips.

She opens her eyes.

He jumps back, startled, pushing himself back into his jeans and zipping them. 'Raven.'

'Satori.' As she speaks Satori watches her wounds heal. Her mouth reforms into the same soft and generous lips that had often smiled at him. Her cheek bone reknits and fills her perfectly pale face. She pushes herself upwards and sits looking at him. 'How?'

'Magic,' he answers.

She smiles.

'I believe you might need this.' He passes the black pebble to her.

'Yes.' She swallows the stone. Her throat swells for a moment as it is forced downwards then she looks normal again, beautiful.

She stands up and takes Satori's hand in hers. 'Let's go home.'

A single step takes them back to the spare room in Paul's house. Satori lies above the covers while he watches Raven move around the room. He frowns. 'You're fading,' he says.

Raven's skin and hair, even her dress becomes translucent. She becomes a part of the air. A narrow halo of light traces the edges of her body. She looks at her arms and shrugs. 'I'm not real. I'm still dead.'

'What was all that for, then?' he asks.

She steps towards him and strokes his face. Her fingers are deliciously cool. He reaches for her hand and draws it to his mouth, kissing each finger in turn.

'This is what it's for,' she answers. 'Now we can be together, as we always should have been.'

She slides beside him on the single bed and wraps her arms around his body. Her breasts press against his chest and he feels his penis, so shy before, harden in response.

'I love you,' she tells him.

He answers her with a kiss.

Chapter 46

Ivan lifts Star by the waist and carries her to the bedroom. She falls back onto the mattress and laughs. Her arms reach for him and he comes to her.

They kiss again and she spreads her legs. His fingers move against her sex, stroking rubbing, squeezing and flicking her labia and clitoris. She gasps. He uses her moisture to further inflame her desire, teasing her, never probing deeper than the entrance of her vagina.

She clings to him, willing him to penetrate her, yet enjoying every moment of his attention. Her tongue flicks inside his mouth as she grinds herself against his hand. As their passion builds, the noises they make become more frantic.

At last, his fingers plunge deep inside her. She opens her eyes, smiles and gently squeezes his bottom lip between her teeth.

'Fuck me,' she whispers.

His hand withdraws. The warm, firm pressure of his cock between her legs makes her gasp again.

'Yes.' She sighs.

Then he is inside, pushing deeper, filling her, pulling out and plunging within. Pushing inside her again and again and again, his heartbeat matches hers. Their souls reach to one another, communicating joy, gratitude and a world beyond the confines of earth and physics.

Shuddering, Star screams out in ecstasy. She digs her fingernails into his shoulders and tightens her thighs around his hips. His moans grow more frantic, his eyes roll and sweat washes his brow. He pants and grunts and matches her shudder as he fills her body with semen.

For a moment they stay there entwined then he kisses her forehead and rolls to one side. She places her cheek on his chest. His heartbeat vibrates against her ear drum. She closes her eyes and, with his arms around her waist, falls into a deep sleep.

The room is dark when she wakes screaming.

Ivan sits up and holds her shaking body. 'What is it?'

'A dream, I think.' She shakes her head trying to clear the images.

'What did you dream?'

'It was horrible. Satori was there. He was frightened and angry. I was…' She sits, staring at the wall, unable to say any more.

Ivan tries to coax her from her silence. 'It was just a dream. You can tell me. It might mean something.'

Her breath is ragged. Her arms shake and she wraps them around her. For a moment she is still then her entire body shivers. Tears gather in her eyes as she stares at Ivan. She looks away from him before speaking. 'I was being fucked. He was watching.'

Ivan loosens his grip on her and shrinks back. 'Was he watching us?' He looks around the room as if expecting an audience.

'Not you. You weren't there. Two men and a boy, a teenager, I didn't know any of them. They fucked me while Satori watched.'

'Shhh, it's just guilt, about the situation and us and everything. You don't want to hurt him.'

Star nods. 'I don't. I can't get it out of my head though. It feels too real to be just a guilt induced dream.'

'Do you want to call him? Make sure he's okay?' Ivan asks.

Star shakes her head. 'No. It's late. Let's try to get back to sleep.'

Ivan lies back and Star rests her head on his chest again. She does not close her eyes. Instead she watches his stomach rise and fall. Each time she attempts to push the images of the dream aside they force themselves back into her consciousness. *If it is only a dream what is it trying to tell me?*

The dark room is like a cave. Maybe it is the cave in the mountains, where Satori tried to bring me back to him as we made love. No, that doesn't feel right. In the dream Satori watches from afar. He grieves for, and is repulsed by, me. Perhaps the repulsion is my own? It isn't easy, struggling with these terrible desires. Could the three lovers represent my insatiable sex-drive and Satori powerless to do anything but watch?

*Caves and caverns represent the vagina, don't they?
Could the dream just mean I'm ashamed that I invite more
than my fair share of people into my body? I am ashamed.
This isn't me: these feelings, trying desperately to cling onto
self-control. The fire inside me, is it a remnant of Binah, of
Lilith? Or does it come from the same place as my bubbling,
hissing vortex? Is Satori right, after all? Do all my problems
stem from my determination to suppress my own self? Are
magic and sexuality one and the same?*

Thoughts spiral inwards. Star feels them condense and
settle in the centre of her mind. The weight of them puts
pressure on her skull. Her ears hiss like a kettle that's starting
to boil. Ivan is asleep beside her. She could wake him, but
she doubts he can help. Her thoughts reach out to Satori.
Black hair obscures a face. Fingers push the silky veil aside.
Milky eyes open. Raven grins. Star pulls away. She shivers in
Ivan's loose embrace. Her eyes sting but tears do not fill
them. It feels as though her soul has been scooped from her
body. She is empty.

When the apricot tint of sunrise casts its blush across the
room, she gets up and makes coffee for them both.

Chapter 47

As Satori's hands trace the lines of Raven's body he remembers the time she came to him in his room. Star had run off with Lilith and Raven offered to comfort him. Her passion for him was real then. He wonders whether it can be now. *Can a ghost love?*

As she looks at him her smile reaches her eyes. She nods as if reading his thoughts. Her face blurs as she moves to kiss his mouth. Her hair shields them both, a safe place in which they can hide from the world. Even if she is not real, her love is. Satori realises that he loves her too.

They kiss and caress each other. Like before, she rides him. Her soft and generous breasts bounce above him as she moves. Being inside her feels cold, but her muscles embrace him and the sensation is wonderful. He does not imagine she is Star. He imagines she is alive and that they never separated after that glorious day in his bedroom. That they are home and the world is good and filled with love. He will never feel lonely or unwanted again.

Raven does not tire. She bounces as energetically as before. Satori is surprised he has not come. He wonders whether they could do this all day and never grow tired. Beyond her beautiful face and thick black hair, a strange

237

shadow moves across the wall. His body tenses, but she does not seem to notice the change in him.

Satori focuses his vision, away from Raven's lovely features, to the wall beyond. A strip of wallpaper hangs away from the plaster. It seems to move, although perhaps it is simply his perspective as he moves beneath Raven. He looks at the strip of wallpaper beside it. As he watches this too curls down and peels away from the wall. The one on the other side does the same. The flesh pink plaster beneath puckers into boils which grow larger and angrier. The boils burst. Darkness flows from them, consuming the plaster, the wallpaper and the wall. The room vanishes into darkness and all that remains is his single bed and his body ridden unceasingly by his dead lover.

With a strangled cry, he ejaculates.

Chapter 48

When they reach the gates of the Snuff Hills mansion Mark tries again to open them.

'How do we get in?' Kevin asks.

'Last time we wrestled three Rottweilers and climbed over the wall at the back.'

'Hmm,' Simon says. 'I reckon I could pick it easy enough.'

'Have you got your gear with you, Si?' Kevin asks.

'You're kidding, right. Where else would I have it?' Simon answers.

'Go for it.' Kevin nods. 'Posh neighbourhood like this, someone might call the cops. Have a wander up and down the road, Kid. See if there's anyone about. I'll keep watch here.'

'No need,' Simon says. 'Done it.'

'Already?' Kevin asks.

'Course.'

Kevin pushes the gate open. After years of standing guard, it groans in protest and shudders on its hinges. The three walk through and close it behind them.

'Should we bring the car up the drive?' Simon asks.

Kevin glances over his shoulder. 'Nah, better where it is. Just in case.'

Simon nods in agreement.

'In case of what?' Mark asks.

'Just in case a curtain-twitcher phones the pigs and we have to leave by another route.'

'Oh,' Mark says.

The two skinheads nod and smile. 'Yup.'

Mark hasn't seen the house from this angle before. In spite of the time it has spent empty, its glamour dazzles him. He thinks of the shadowy rooms within and shivers. The huge doorway and the mock Tudor windows jealously protect the house's secrets.

'Shall I pick it?' Simon asks as they approach the front door.

'It's already open at the back,' Mark answers.

The trio skirt around the building.

'Look guys, do you think you could wait here while I pop in and see him?' Mark asks.

Kevin looks through the broken French doors and whistles. 'Shame. Fucking vandals.'

'Where is he?' Simon squeezes through the doorway.

'He might still be upstairs,' Mark answers. 'Look…'

'Come on then,' Kevin urges, 'Let's see what this tosser has to say for himself.'

Mark sighs and follows them inside.

Simon steps into the dusty hallway ahead of the others. 'Now that's fucking creepy.'

'What?' Kevin asks.

'Come and look.'

Kevin steps through, inhales deeply then turns around to face Mark. 'What's this about?'

'It confused us too. Maybe it's haunted?' Mark suggests.

Simon spins around like a ballerina looking at all the paintings and rugs. 'It's a fucking Aladdin's cave, Kev. We need to come back with the van.'

Mark passes them and mounts the stairs. The two men follow. They gasp each time they spot a new treasure. Mark leads them to the bedroom in which he left Satori a few hours before. He nods. 'In here. Look, can you…'

Kevin shoulders past and opens the door.

It takes Mark a moment to register the change when he steps into the room. No longer on his back, Satori lies peacefully on his side; between his naked body and the wall of the room is a sleeping woman.

The female figure rises first and looks straight at Mark. Her snow-white hair dazzles him. A fragile looking white dress barely covers her ebony skin. As she moves, Mark realises he can see through her to the pattern on the wallpaper behind.

'Who are you?' he asks.

She doesn't answer.

Kevin grunts and wanders over to poke Satori's arm. 'You mean this ain't the bloke you told Garlow about?'

'Huh?' Mark asks.

'Is this or is this not the bloke who knows where your mam is?'

Mark nods. 'But…'

Kevin pulls Satori from the bed to the floor. Shock registers in Satori's eyes as he bounces against the floorboards. Kevin grabs a fist full of hair and drags his head off the floor. 'Hey, girly boy. We got a couple of questions to ask you.'

Satori tries to shake his head free. His eyes dart around the room.

'Look at me,' Kevin growls.

Satori seems unable to keep his head still. He watches the walls. His head keeps turning and the skin beneath his eyes twitches. His face is full of terror yet he seems oblivious to Kevin's presence.

Mark looks from Satori to the woman. The woman snarls. Her fists are balls and her muscles twitch with anger. Neither of the skinheads notices she is there.

'Tell him where he can find his mam, you cunt!' Kevin spits into Satori's face.

Satori's eyes turn toward Kevin. His expression is blank, his eyes dark with confusion as if he wonders where he is and what he's doing on the floor.

'Raven,' he says.

The woman's head and neck twist to face Satori.

'It's so dark.' Satori groans.

'Satori,' Mark calls.

Satori looks across the room at Mark. Kevin lets go of his hair and Satori's head drops to the floor with a thud. Simon kicks Satori's waist, making him gasp and cough. Satori's eyes do not waver from Mark's. Mark stares at him in silence then looks back to the bed. The woman's hair floats around her face. Her mouth is open as if she screams in silent fury. Both arms in front of her, she pounces from the bed and tears at Kevin and Simon's cheeks. The two men howl and shrink away from Satori.

'How the fuck!' Simon yells.

The woman rushes towards the skinheads again. Her nails dig into their faces. Their deep wounds pour with blood. They face Mark terrified.

'We should go,' Simon stammers.

Mark nods.

'Kid, come with us. Get out of here. There's some kind of fucking ghost in this house, Mate. We'll find your mam another way.'

The two almost fall through the doorway and down the stairs in their haste. Mark stands still, watching Satori. The female figure sits beside the magician, stroking his hair.

'Can you see it too?' Satori's wide eyes focus on Raven's face.

She continues stroking his hair. Her mouth moves as if she might be singing a lullaby.

'Who is she?' Mark asks.

'Raven,' Satori answers. 'Can you see it? Can you see the darkness in the walls?'

Mark shakes his head. 'No, the room is light. Is she dead?'

'Kind of,' Satori says. 'Above you, there.' He points to the corner of the room.

Mark looks where he is directed. There is a faint brown tint to the wallpaper as if discoloured by mildew.

Satori scratches his arms. His face looks pale. 'Did I dream it or did a couple of men just attack me?'

'Yeah, I'm sorry about that,' Mark answers.

243

'They said you're looking for your mum, right?'

Mark nods.

'And you think I know where she is.' Satori stops scratching his arms and stands up to face Mark. Raven floats in circles around Satori caressing his waist and his head, pouting with a kiss on her lips.

Mark nods again.

Satori closes his eyes, breathes deeply then opens them again. Mark feels the man's careful study of his face, the dark hair, warm skin and the bright green eyes. 'And you can't see the darkness around you?'

'No sorry. I can't,' Mark replies.

Satori shrugs and frowns. He cocks his head to one side. 'Who is your Mum?'

Mark stares at Satori. Raven disentangles herself from Satori and floats towards Mark. She traces the lines of his face with her cool finger tips. She frowns and shakes her head then returns to Satori and whispers theatrically into his ear behind her cupped hand.

'Who is your mum, Mark?' Satori asks again.

Mark swallows hard. 'Star.'

Tears gather in Satori's eyes. He stares at Mark, his son, and shakes his head. 'You're much older than I expected.'

'Where is she?' Mark asks.

'So that's why all those people were chasing you.'

'Where is Star?'

'My mum, her friends, they must have known. How did she know?'

'They want to steal my power,' Mark says.

Satori sneers. His back straightens and he seems to grow taller. 'Your power? What power do you have worth stealing?'

Mark lowers his eyes. 'Just tell me where she is.'

'No,' Satori replies.

'What?'

'I am not telling you where she is. You can run back to Lilith and tell her I told you to fuck off.'

'Dad, don't.'

Raven turns and stares at Mark again. She smiles and mouths the word "Dad".

'Fuck off!' Satori shouts. 'It's the end of it. We've left those places for good, even if the darkness wants me back, I'm staying here and so is she.'

'Really? You weren't there while you were sleeping, plucking that woman from death's embrace?' Mark points at Raven who smiles.

'I don't have to justify myself to you. I've faced enough challenges and won them all. Just go.'

'I'm not going and I really don't want to hurt you.'

Raven snarls at Mark and raises her claws in warning.

'Go,' Satori says. He holds his hands against his temples. His eyes try to focus on Mark, but the pupils keep drifting towards the walls.

Mark raises his right arm and steps forward. 'Where is Star?'

Satori whispers under his breath. Words, whose meanings are long forgotten, draw energy from the room.

A ball of flame grows in the palm of Mark's hand. 'You know who I am. You don't want to fight.'

Satori keeps whispering and draws his hands apart, energy crackles between his palms. Raven moves between the challengers, scratching Mark's face and caressing Satori's arm. Neither stands down.

'Dad, I really don't want to hurt you. Just tell me where I can find her…'

Satori turns his palms to face his son. Lightning bolts hit Mark and send him flying through the air. The boy hits a wall and falls to the floor. He gets back up, his face dark with shadows. Mark breathes into the palm of his hand and makes a fist. As if throwing a ball to Satori he pulls back his arm and releases a sphere of fire.

Satori's hair catches first. It burns like a halo around his face. He screams. Flames rush downwards, choking the sound of screams, and burning through the man's flesh. Satori's screams of pain rush through Mark's veins giving him strength. The fear and horror his father feels fill Mark with energy that makes his organs crackle and his skin tingle. Satori's body blackens as the inferno engulfs him. Within seconds his father is no more than a twisted and withered set of charred, human remains on the floor of the room, but the fire keeps spreading. It moves outwards from the corpse. A ring of fire consumes furniture, curtains and wallpaper. As it reaches Mark, it splits to move around him. The fire burns out as it reaches the door to the upstairs landing. The tendrils of flame do not reach beyond the doorframe. Mark looks at Raven. Draping her body over Satori's corpse, she weeps.

246

'You should have just told me,' Mark says. 'Fuck it! I know anyway. This is pointless. Why didn't you just let her go? Why must you always be the protector?'

Raven turns and looks at Mark. The female spirit's features shift. Her eyes grow huge and fierce, narrow at the edges, bulging at the centre. Her nose flattens and widens, her nostrils flare. Her mouth opens so wide she looks as though she could swallow Mark's head whole. Inside teeth like daggers are revealed as she screams her silent yet terrible scream of rage.

White hair floats around her black shoulders. She pounces at him. Claws dig into his skin. Her tears of anger scald his skin. She loves this man: Mark's father. She loves him beyond reason and now she wants to kill his murderer.

The force of her blows sends Mark running from the room. She chases him down the stairs. Her wails waken other restless spirits in the house: dead children, mutilated by the previous owner in his quest to horde power. With Raven as their leader, the desperate children surround Mark eager to have their revenge on someone, anyone. Their suffering in life poisons their sleep. They cannot rest. They must destroy and make others suffer in the way they suffered. While Raven pulls his hair, scratches his face and rips his cheek with her teeth, the children gather around him, prodding him, punching him, kicking him. They tear at his clothes and use their fists and arms to debase him in the many ways they had been debased before they died.

Mark cannot think. The pain and anger which surround him confuse his senses. He shakes his head. He is greater than this. These ghosts cannot hurt him and yet they do. Their humiliation and rage infect him. He sways with their blows. He screams as they invade his body. He sees in Raven's bulging eyes a complete surrender to her rage, to the point of insanity, and he feels sorry for her. Tears of regret for the harm he has caused flood from his eyes and the pores in his skin. His tattered clothing is soaked in misery.

'I'm sorry,' he says. 'This should never have happened.'

The ghosts take a step back and study him. His skin looks purple and green from the bruises they have inflicted. A puddle of tears and sweat spread from him across the floor. His face hangs with sadness and shame. The ghosts cry too. They share his guilt and they pity him.

He watches their distress for a moment and walks away out of the hallway, through the kitchen and into the garden. He keeps walking. Ignoring his torn clothing, he tries to separate himself from the hall of death as quickly as possible. As he moves away his soul repairs the damage. It stops the infection spreading. He feels stronger with every step he takes. By the time he reaches the driveway a smile spreads across his face and he starts to whistle.

A cold hand on his shoulder makes him jump. He turns around to face the ghost of Raven. Outside the house her colours have changed. Her skin is white and her hair black. Her features have quietened and her face, while strong and unique, is no longer an object of terror.

'Well done,' she says.

He shivers. He had thought she was mute. Her voice pours into him like freezing mercury, gripping his heart and lungs.

'I'm sorry.' He tries in vain to mimic the shame and sadness which had affected the ghosts so profoundly before.

Raven appears unconvinced by his display. She frowns. 'You took away the man I love. He saved me from death only yesterday. We were going to spend his life together and you killed him.'

'In that case, technically...'

Raven screams. Mark covers his ears.

'I want revenge,' she tells him.

He shakes his head. 'You can't hurt me.'

'Oh yes I can,' she tells him. 'I know who you are looking for.'

Mark shakes her hand from his shoulder and takes a step back.

'And I know how to kill her.'

'I'm sorry. You can't kill anyone. You're a ghost. You're dead.'

'Wait and see.' Raven laughs, waves and disappears.

Mark stares at the space left by Raven's absence. In it he sees her plan: the girl, Freya, a knife, and sees the flaw. Freya will not kill Star. She will try and fail and, in so doing, complete the plan he set in motion when he brought Freya here.

Chapter 49

Freya wanders back into the house.

'Do you want me to take Jasmine out in the pram?' her Mum asks.

'So you can show her off to your friends?'

Lorraine blushes and laughs.

Freya squeezes the fingers of her left hand and forces a smile. 'Sure, Mum.'

'You'll be here when we get back,' Lorraine says.

'Yeah,' Freya answers. 'I'll watch TV or read or something.'

Lorraine takes Jasmine into the hallway and places her gently in the pram. 'Could you get me Jasmine's blanket?'

'I'll get her coat as well,' Freya says.

Jasmine doesn't wake as the women prepare her for the great outdoors. Lorraine leaves Freya with a peck on the cheek and wheels her granddaughter out of the house. 'See you later.'

Freya waves goodbye then returns to the living room and sits on the settee with her head in her hands. Her brain aches. She feels dull and heavy. She cannot get the image of Ivan and Star out of her head. Maybe she could drink herself into oblivion.

As she stands up to fix herself a drink her arms prickle and her hair stands up on end. She looks around her, but the room is empty. The temperature plummets as a cold breeze fills the room. Wondering whether she left a door open, she checks first the front and then the kitchen door. The kitchen door is ajar. She peers outside and sees ribbons jostle in the branches of Ivan's tree. 'Ivan.' She closes the door.

'Star will take him from you.'

Freya spins around. The room is empty. The voice must be inside her. She nods sadly.

'You can stop it.'

Freya's eyes narrow. She is certain the voice is external. It doesn't sound like her voice. Deya is not taunting her into action. *So who?*

Blinds rattle against the kitchen window. Cupboard doors open and close. The light flickers on then off again.

'What?' Freya asks. 'Who are you?'

'It doesn't matter,' the voice replies. It sounds familiar. 'She's hurt us both. If you want to save Ivan you must stop her.'

'Stop her?' Freya asks.

'Kill her.'

'Kill her...kill Star...save Ivan...' Freya shakes her head again. 'Ivan isn't in danger.'

'Satori was killed because of Star.' The voice hisses in Freya's ear.

Freya turns toward the voice. Freezing air rushes at her face. She closes her eyes against the cold assault. 'Satori's dead?'

'Yes. It's Star's fault and Ivan will be next if you don't save him.'

'How? Who are you and where are they?' Freya asks.

'An old friend. Now grab a pen and paper.'

Freya's hands shake as she transcribes the address. Staring at the piece of paper, she imagines walking in on the couple as they make love. Bile rises in her throat. Her mind recalls another time she watched Ivan with a woman.

'Raven?'

Laughter fills the room.

Freya spins around trying to see some change in the air, any indication that this is not another aural hallucination. 'Is it you? Why now? Why didn't you come and see me before?'

'Star is a worthless slut!'

Freya nods. *Fuck it! Raven is right.* 'What do they see in her?'

'She's damaged, vulnerable and needs someone to complete and take care of her.' The voice grows stronger as if rage gives it power.

'Yes.' Freya sighs. She leans across the work surface, afraid she might faint.

'Men have never outgrown the desire to be knights in shining armour.'

'And Satori's dead?' Freya hopes he is, yet a tiny part of her realises she will miss him. He may have treated her shamefully, but he did understand her. Perhaps he was the only person who ever did.

'A boy killed him. Killed him to reach Star. He'll kill Ivan too if you don't stop it.'

'Raven?'

'Yes.'

'Tell me about my brother.'

The air warms. Freya can feel affection and love wrap around her. 'He's too good for Star.'

'Is it wrong that I'm in love with him?'

'Of course not. Go, save him. Be the hero.'

Freya puts the scribbled address in her pocket and heads for the hallway. Shrugging into her coat, she remembers her own knight. *Rob used to hold my coat for me. Now he's dead. If I can kill the man I love, finishing Star should be easy.*

Chapter 50

'There's someone at the door,' Ivan calls.

'Can you answer it? I'm just finishing on the toilet.'

Ivan steps towards the front door then stops. 'What if it's Satori?'

'If it was he'd use his key.'

Star listens to Ivan's movements through the bathroom door. She hears the front door open and close then low voices. 'I'll just be a minute,' she calls.

'It's okay, Star. It's Freya.'

'Oh. Hi, Freya,' Star shouts over the whooshing sound of the flush.

She doesn't hear Freya's reply.

'Can I make you a cuppa, Freya or do you fancy coffee?' Star walks from the hallway into the living room.

Ivan hurries over to Star and holds her back. Star stares at the back of Freya's head. The woman sits motionless on the settee, facing away from them. Only her hair and the ribbons twisted through it are visible.

'Freya?' Star says. She cocks her head and looks askance at Ivan. Silently she mouths the word 'what?'

'Star.' Freya replies not turning to face her.

'Are you okay?' Star tries to step forwards, but Ivan keeps hold of her arm and holds her back. 'What is it?' she whispers.

'Something's wrong,' Ivan answers.

Star wrestles free of his grip and strides towards the settee. Ivan follows beside her.

'Freya?' Star looks at the woman's profile.

Freya scowls. She turns her face to look at Star, snarls and pounces.

Ivan rushes between the two women. He grunts and falls. A deep red puddle spreads from beneath him across the carpet. Freya screams and falls to her knees beside Ivan. Star backs away, grabs the phone from the wall and runs to her bedroom. She pushes her dresser in front of her door and sits on her bed, staring at the blocked door and listening to the frenzied cries beyond. She remembers the phone in her hand and dials 999.

'Emergency services. What is the nature of your emergency?'

'Help. My friend's been stabbed.'

'Are they breathing?'

'I don't know. The attacker's still in my house.' Star stares at the barricaded door. Ivan's blood spreads across her vision. She rocks herself back and forth.

The voice on the telephone sounds distant as though from a half remembered dream. 'Where do you live, ma'am?'

Star hears a scream of rage beyond the door and quickly relays her address to the operator. 'Please hurry.'

The bedroom door judders. The heavy thuds of a shoulder battering against wood, crash around the room. The wooden panels shake with the impact.

'Freya,' Star says. 'Is Ivan okay?'

Another scream and three more thuds.

'The police are on their way, Freya,' Star shouts.

The wood cracks. Star pushes herself backwards across the bed until her trembling body rattles the headboard. Another crack, wood splinters and the tip of a knife breaks through the door.

Star feels like the victim in a horror film. Curled against her headboard, she tries to put as much space as possible between herself and the door. Fear paralyses her. Ivan is hurt, perhaps dead and his sister is trying to carve a hole in the door to reach Star.

The knife is withdrawn and Freya grunts with effort as the slams the blade back through the door panel.

Star shivers. *All I've survived, why am I afraid, now?* 'Freya. Go home. Let me see to Ivan. The police are on their way.'

Freya laughs. 'You won't take him from me.'

'I'm not trying to,' Star shouts back.

The knife hacks through the panel again. Fingers push through the jagged gap to drag out a large splinter of wood. Star glimpses fragments of Freya's movements through the split. The headboard rattles against the wall as she shivers with fear and adrenaline. Sirens wail in the distance. The sound grows louder. Freya slams the knife into the slit and forces the blade left and right, trying to prise the panel apart.

256

'Freya,' Star says. 'Is Ivan still alive?'

Freya withdraws the knife again. The sirens are close now. Freya places her eye next to the gap. 'Star.'

'Yes, Freya.'

'Raven says "fuck you" and wants you to know Satori is dead.'

Freya jerks away from the door. Footsteps retreat along the hallway towards the kitchen. The kitchen door opens and closes. There are loud knocks and shouts at the front door. Star gets up from the bed and moves the dresser away from the broken bedroom door. With a crash, the front door explodes inwards.

Star reaches Ivan's body as the police swarm into the room. One grabs her arm and pulls her back.

'Freya, she stabbed him. She's gone... that way.' Star points at the open kitchen door.

The police officer holds Star's arm. 'We caught her. Let the paramedics to their jobs.'

'Is he alive?' Star asks.

'Is there somewhere we can sit so I can take a statement from you?' the officer asks, turning Star gently so she can no long see Ivan's body.

'Umm, the bedroom, I guess,' Star answers.

Star and the police officer walk along the hallway. As they sit on the end of her bed the officer removes her hat.

'What happened?' the officer asks.

'I don't know. It was his sister. I think she was trying to stab me.' Star feels numb. Her body shakes, her muscles are

257

beyond her power to control. Her body feels like something distant and alien. She tries to stand up.

The officer grabs her arm and guides her gently back to seating position. 'Do you know why?'

'She said I was taking her brother away from her. She also told me. Look, I don't know whether this is true, but she told me Steve Michaels is dead.

The officer flicks back as few pages of her notebook and whitens. 'This is 26, Brook Lane, isn't it?' she asks.

'Yes,' Star answers.

'We were coming to see you when we got your emergency call. There was an incident, a fire.'

'And Steve?'

'We aren't sure yet. We need to…we think we might have found his body in the fire.'

Star doubles over and weeps into her hands. 'And Ivan?'

'The man in your living room?' the officer asks.

'Yes, the man in my living room.' Star's voice grows shrill. Darkness fills her mind. *Dead. All dead.*

'I'm sorry,' the officer says.

'Oh fuck!' Star screams.

'I'm afraid we'll need you to come to the station with us.'

Star rubs the tears from her eyes. Her mouth tingles and her tongue feels too large. She swallows metallic tasting saliva and coughs. 'Yes, of course. Does Marian, Steve's Mum, know yet?'

'Give me her details and if she hasn't been contacted already we'll make sure she is.'

Star nods. She grabs handfuls of her hair and stares blankly at the knife wound in her door. Tightening her grip, she tugs at her scalp.

***

'Marian,' Star says, running across to Satori's mother.

Marian looks up. Her face is red with tears and her shoulders shake violently.

'I'm so sorry,' Star says, sitting beside the grieving woman.

'They just told me. They've identified him. My son is dead.'

Star puts her arm around Marian's shoulders. The woman shrugs away. Star drops her arm and sits with both hands on her lap staring at the floor.

'What happened?' Star asks.

'Don't you know?' Marian spits in reply.

Star shakes her head slowly. 'They haven't told me anything yet.'

'He died at Paul's, in a fire. He was trying to save your son.'

'My son?'

'We found him. The other followers and I, we were going to secure him. Keep him away, safely. We knew...we knew how dangerous.'

'My son? Satori's son? Have you seen him? Is he here?'

Marian shakes her head. 'I don't know where he is now.'

'Look, Marian. I – I've got to go. I need to find out what…tell them I'll be back…later…and I am so sorry. I'll find out what happened to Satori.'

Star glances across at the glazed door that leads to the front desk. She looks around the lobby where she and Marian are seated. No police officers linger on this side of the desk. With each fist tugging at locks of her hair, she stands up and hurries out of the police station door, remembering the last time she fled from this building, naked, hand in hand with Satori. *Satori, I'm sorry.*

Chapter 51

Mark walks between the iron gates and out of Paul's garden. The two skinheads Kevin and Simon wait for him outside. They stand there, comical almost, like Tweedle Dum and Tweedle Dee, smoking and fidgeting. Their nervous eyes scan the empty street.

'Mark,' Kevin says as he turns and sees him. 'What happened in there?'

'I guess we were attacked by the same ghost that stopped anyone getting past the kitchen, huh?' Simon adds, looking to Mark with wide eyes as if expecting the answers to one thousand unspoken questions.

Mark shrugs.

'So, Kid. Did you find out where your mam is?'

Mark shakes his head.

'And that guy up there, do you think he will talk to us if we get him outside?'

'He's dead,' Mark answers.

'Fuck!' Simon shouts. 'Ghost kill him?'

'No.'

Kevin walks over to Mark and offers him a cigarette. 'What happened, mate?'

***

'I got angry,' Mark replies.

The two men nod their heads, knowingly.

'We'll find her,' Kevin tells him. 'Look, we'll go and see Garlow. He always knows what to do. Come on. Let's get out of here.'

Mark nods and they walk together to the car.

'These neighbours aren't nosey at all,' Simon says as they walk. 'Would be an easy job to rip this place off.'

'Yup,' Kevin answers. 'But first things first. Let's get Mark sorted.'

Garlow is in his usual spot when they return to the bar. Mark waits patiently until he is summoned, wondering whether the boss has a home. He feels empty.

Kevin touches Mark's shoulder and the boy jumps.

'Come on, cheer up, Kid. Garlow's ready to see you.'

He walks over to the table and Garlow gestures for him to sit on the chair opposite.

'What happened?' Garlow asks.

'He wouldn't help me,' Mark answers.

'Pity,' Garlow replies. 'Family is important. They're the most important things in the world to me. I'd do anything to protect them and if one of them was lost, I'd kill to recover them.'

Mark doesn't answer.

'Did you kill the man?' Garlow asks.

Mark nods.

'But you still don't know where or who she is?'

'Her name's Star,' Mark answers.

262

Garlow nods thoughtfully. 'Sounds like a stage name. Is she an actress?'

'No, I don't think so.'

'Kevin tells me there was something else in the room with you. Is that right?'

'Yeah. It scratched Kevin's face and Simon.'

'What was it?'

Mark shrugs.

'A ghost?'

Mark looks up and snorts. 'Do you believe in ghosts?'

'Of course, don't you? I believe in all sorts of things, Kid: ghosts, magic, demons, demi-gods and the anti-Christ.'

Mark shivers.

'I believe in you,' Garlow continues.

'Me?'

'Yes. I knew there was something different about you when I met you.'

Mark turns away and scans the room. About a dozen men sit around drinking and smoking, a few play cards and others play pool. He knows that they are also watching this exchange. They are Garlow's protectors and enforcers.

'Something in those bright green eyes, an unnatural arrogance, I suppose.'

Goosebumps rise across Mark's arms. 'You think I'm unnatural?'

'I know who you are and I know who you met. I also know why people are chasing you.'

'How?'

'That woman, the one I had a package for, tell me about her,' Garlow says.

'She was…is she a friend of yours?'

'You won't offend me. Tell me what you thought of her.'

'She smelled funny. Her flat was creepy. I thought she could see through me into my soul.'

'She could. She did. What do you think she saw there?'

Mark shakes his head and swallows hard. 'What?'

'Darkness and power. How did you kill the magician, Kid?'

'I set him on fire.'

'How?'

Mark swallows hard. His eyes darken. 'With my mind.'

Garlow nods. 'What do you know about your mother and father?'

My mother's called Star and my father's dead.'

'Is that all?'

'Yes.'

Garlow nods thoughtfully. 'Where did you grow up?'

Mark stiffens and begins to stand up.

'Don't,' Garlow tells him.

'If you know so much you must know I can leave any time I want,' Mark answers.

'And go where? Continue to be chased by those followers of Sith? They're just the first of many. You must realise that. Others will realise you are here – the anti-Christ.'

'What do you want?'

'To protect you and help you grow to be a man. We can change the world, Mark.'

'No,' Mark replies. 'That isn't my name. I just use it here.'

'What is your name, Kid?'

'Edensun. But I'm not the anti-Christ.'

'That's what they'll call you. If enough people believe a thing it becomes real. So who do you think you are?'

'Nothing.'

'You are the destroyer, Edensun.'

'No,' Edensun says. 'I'm just looking for my mother. I want to know why.'

'Why what?'

'Why she left me there.'

'The envelope you delivered to me. You opened it, didn't you?'

Edensun nods.

Garlow leans across the table towards the boy, Mark - the demon, Edensun. His breath smells of mint. 'Do you remember what was inside?'

'A bird.'

'Yes. It was a raven with a broken beak.'

'And?'

'That's how you'll find her. Use the raven with the broken beak.'

'Raven. That was the ghost's name.'

'The ghost at the mansion? The one who scratched my boys?'

Edensun nods. 'Yes, that's what Father called her – Raven.'

'Then you know where to start looking, Edensun. Take Kevin and Simon in case there's trouble. That man you killed, Satori, his mother is a follower of Sith. She's looking for you.'

'What does she want with me?'

'Could be one of three things: to worship you…'

'That wasn't the impression they gave me.'

'To harness your power for their own purposes or to kill you. Now you've killed her son, it's probably the latter.'

Edensun snorts. 'Yeah, mothers are funny like that.'

'It's family, son. Nothing in the world is more important than family.'

'If that were true my mother wouldn't have left.'

Garlow pats Edensun's arm and frowns. 'Perhaps she had her reasons. Find her and ask her.'

Edensun nods. 'I will. Thank you.'

'And then come back to me. We have plans to make – you and I.'

Edensun smiles. 'Your family are lucky, Mr Garlow.'

'I'm the lucky one,' Garlow replies.

Chapter 52

Freya wriggles on the mattress. She pulls against the restraints which hold her wrists and ankles to the bed and looks around the room. No one else is there. Her mouth feels dry and her mind heavy with sedatives.

'What happened?' Freya asks.

We killed our brother.

'Why?'

It was an accident. We were trying to protect him from her.

'From Star?'

Yes. The bitch enchanted him. She was going to take him away from us. We would have lost him.

'And now he's dead?'

Yes.

'Did we kill, Rob?'

Who's Rob?

'Don't tell me you've forgotten Rob. We lived with him for four years. He's Jasmine's dad. He was our saviour. He took us away from all...'

All what?

'This insanity, this crazy obsession, it's wrong.'

There is no shame in love, only completion.

'Those are Lilith's words, not ours.'

We can share them.

'But she's wrong. It is shameful to love your brother. It is shameful to kill a man, who worships the ground you walk on, just to be close to Ivan again. There is no goodness in us, no completion.'

We tried our best.

'No we didn't. What's going to happen to Jasmine now, and Dad? He'll never forgive us.'

Jasmine will be fine. Mum and Dad will take care of her until we're well.

'We'll never be well, Deya.'

Of course we will, sister. You just have to let go. I'll take over. You rest.

'No.'

You will. When you can no longer cope with what you've done you'll leave me to clean up your mess again. Like before.

Freya tugs harder at her restraints. 'Leave me alone.'

You know I can't do that.

'Then kill me. Put me out of my misery. This isn't our body anyway. We only borrowed it. We should leave and give it back.'

That's ridiculous. There's no one to give it back to.

'Dave.'

He's gone. You killed him.

'I didn't. I just wanted to borrow his body, for insurance.'

You killed him.

'No.'

You killed them all: Dave, Rob and Ivan, all to hold onto something that was never yours.

'No.'

When did you start to unravel, Freya?

'I don't remember.'

Was it when your sister died?

'No. Later, I think.'

When you found the book?

'Lilith's book?'

Yes. Remember your excitement, the way you trembled when you first turned those pages and realised you could be powerful? You weren't the baby any more, were you? You weren't a victim?

'I remember.'

Would you do things differently if you had your time again?

'I wouldn't kill Ivan.'

Maybe we can still go back.

'How?'

I don't know yet.

'It was Raven's fault.'

What?

'That we killed Ivan.'

She wanted revenge?

'Yes.'

Because Star killed her.

'Yes.'

Star killed her because of Lilith.

'Did she?'

Yes, don't you remember?

'No.'

She changed when she met Lilith.

'So did we.'

It's Lilith's fault.

'Yes.'

How can we put things right?

'We can't.'

If we'd never gone into that cave. If we'd never brought her here.

'But we did. If we hadn't we wouldn't have had that night with Ivan either. Raven and Ivan would still be fucking in the park and we'd still lose him.'

Is there nothing we can do?

'There's always something.'

We just have to figure out what.

'Exactly.'

Should we go back?

'Where?'

To our willow tree.

'It started before then.'

To the park?

'Yes, the park. Now help me get out of here.'

Chapter 53

Star runs along the street. It's a long way, but she can make it there on foot if she keeps moving. She checks bus stops and looks for taxis, but her mind will not let her wait, she must keep moving, running. *What if he's still there, my son?*

Tears blur her sight. *Satori, dead. Ivan, dead. Who else will I lose? I have nothing left. All gone.*

'Lilith,' she says. *That was where it started, my dream and then those musty old books in Satori's bedroom.* She remembers the way they smelled and the strange writing within them – Hebrew. She recalls how the letters clung to her fingers, calling Lilith to her. *The passion I felt in Lilith's arms, was it real? Is that why I never loved, really loved, Satori. Did I yearn for someone else?* 'Lilith?'

Now my son, our son, is here. He's somewhere in the city. Perhaps he's looking for me. 'I'm sorry I left you. I never should have. I could have stayed and watched you grow. Perhaps I might even have been happy.'

People turn to face her as Star jogs along the pavement. Perhaps they overhear snippets of her conversation with herself. She does not care. Nothing matters to her now, except finding the son she thought she had lost for ever.

She sees a bus ahead. It waits at a stop to allow travellers to filter on and off. She joins the queue and asks whether it is heading towards Snuff Mills. The driver shakes his head. 'You want the number forty,' he tells her. She jumps back off and checks the timetable and her watch. The bus isn't due for twenty minutes. She knows she will not be able to stand still for that long.

As she runs through suburbs, houses grow bigger and the streets quieter. There are very few people to stare at her now. Tiredness weighs down on her shoulders and limbs but she keeps pushing herself, breathing heavily. *Not much further.*

She turns a corner and sees the street. The houses here are large and detached. Paul's gates stand ajar and she slips through the gap into his driveway. She remembers the times she walked here before. The first time with Satori, he was excited to show her his wonderful friend. Star shudders as she remembers Paul's coldness. He hated her. He saw her as a rival in love. He wanted Satori for himself, but it had seemed more than that, as if he sensed something inside of her, something terrible. He had been right. *I am wicked. I can shine as brightly as any star and yet I have never lit anyone's way, let alone my own. All I have ever done is burned those around me. Only Lilith knew the potential of my power.*

She tries the front door but it is locked. She wonders whether to ring the bell, but decides to walk around the house instead. She enters the kitchen through broken doors and shivers. She feels cold with fear. She is not alone. There is something or someone left in this house. She considers leaving. Turning around, she sees a woman. The figure darts behind the summerhouse and out of sight. Star steps outside and scans the garden. *Who is it? Should I go and check? No. It's female and adult. It is not my son.*

She passes again between the French doors and across the kitchen. The hallway beyond is dusty and there are a jumble of footprints across the floor, at least four different sets, all of them too large to belong to her infant son.

She sighs and decides to check upstairs for clues. She follows the footprints to the foot of the stairs. Sat three steps from the bottom is a teenage boy. He looks up at her as she approaches. His bright green eyes shine and his lips curl into a warm smile.

'Hi,' she says.

'Hey,' he answers.

'Is anyone upstairs?'

'Who are you looking for?' he asks.

'I – I was hoping…' She opens and closes her mouth. She realises that she has no plan. She just needs to see where it happened, to understand. She wants to know if she's to blame for Satori's death. She shakes her head and her curls slap her cheeks. She sits beside the boy on the stairs. 'What happened here?'

'There was a fire upstairs. My friends are looking to see what happened.'

'Your friends?'

'Just two guys who look out for me.'

She stares at his face. His eyes are vibrant and full of intelligence. He hardly looks like a child from this distance. 'Do I know you?' she asks.

273

'I think so,' he answers. 'Did you come looking for Satori?'

'Not really. The police…they said…' She looks at the floor. 'The truth is I'm not at all sure what I'm doing here. Satori and I used to live together. I thought I owed it to him to…'

'Mum?' Edensun asks.

'What?'

'You're Star.' His face glows and his eyes shine with joy.

She studies his face, her brow creased in consternation. 'Yes. I'm sorry I don't…'

'Yes you do. You just can't remember. You left and I grew up.'

'Son?'

Edensun embraces her. She jolts out of his arms, stands up and backs away from the stairs. 'But…'

'Did you think time would be the same, there?'

Star shakes her head.

'I am Edensun, your son. I was born in Binah. Lilith took care of me when you left. I came to find you.'

'Edensun…'

'Yes, or Mark.'

'Edensun. Is that what Lilith called you?'

'Siloth, chose the name.'

She takes a step closer. Her fingers press against her lips. Slowly, as if approaching a dangerous animal, she extends her arm and places the tips of her fingers on his cheek. 'You're my son?'

274

He nods. Tears fall from Star's eyes, but she smiles. He eagerly returns her smile. They stand there in silence, staring at each other. She bends her knees slightly and squeezes the palms of her hands against her cheeks then repeats the action on Edensun's face. She shakes her head. Her eyes widen and her pupils dilate.

'Oh baby. I've missed you so much. How are you? I'm sorry I left. I never should have. I didn't know how to go back and find you. Now you've found me. We…' Star sees a movement on the other side of the hallway. A female figure steps out from the shadows.

'Marian?' Star asks. 'What are you doing here?'

Five white robed figures step through the kitchen door behind Marian.

'Thank you, Star,' Marian says. 'We can take it from here.'

Star frowns.

'Mum?' Edensun asks.

Star shakes her head. 'I guess she followed me. I'm sorry.'

Edensun reaches for Star's hand. 'Come on.' He pulls her behind him as he runs up the stairs. Star looks over the bannister and watches the others swarm through the hallway behind them. The robed figures reach the bottom of the staircase as they reach the top.

'Kevin, Simon,' Edensun calls. Men rush out through a doorway and run across the hall. Mother and son press themselves to one side so the skinheads can dart past them onto the stairs.

Star hears a roar of rage as they leave the fighters behind and run into an empty room. She looks around. There are no exit routes, only a small skylight in the ceiling too high to reach. 'Why here?'

'Do you trust me?' Edensun asks.

Chapter 54

'Where are we?'

Edensun looks at his mother. She shines in the darkness. She catches his eye and smiles.

'We're in between,' he answers.

He watches as Star turns slowly around, taking in the enormity of nothingness.

'Are you okay?' he asks.

'There's nothing here,' she says.

'We are,' he answers.

'Yes. What now?'

'We're safe here. We can step back into your world whenever we wish. I thought, perhaps, we might talk and then…'

'Then?'

'Well, after we've talked you'll have a decision to make.'

'What sort of decision?'

'You're jumping ahead.' Edensun holds both his hands out to Star and she takes them. 'It's good to see you again, Mum. Tell me all about yourself, about when I was born, and why you left.'

Star blushes. 'I – I…'

'No guilt, Mum. I just want to know where I come from.'

'I'll try,' she says. 'What do you want to know?'

'Tell me everything. Time doesn't exist here. We literally have all the time in the world.'

'About my parents?'

'My grandparents, yes, tell me.' His skin prickles with excitement. *At last!*

'I was an only child. Both my parents were older and very religious. Dad was a preacher and Mum would never question a thing he said. I suppose you could say, it was hard to fit in. They were used to being childless. I think they often resented having to take care of me.' She blushes. 'Is this the kind of thing you want to hear?'

'Anything. Everything.'

'Okay. I loved art, still do. It's the only thing that really makes sense to me. I would paint and sculpt with whatever materials I could find. I created things from my imagination. My parents were afraid of what I imagined. They thought I was wrong and Dad punished me. He made me feel like I was evil. They sent me to therapists, psychiatrists and even tried to exorcise me.

'I left home when I could. I escaped to University. I met a friend, Donna, and she introduced me to the rest of them: Satori - your father, Raven and Freya. We were close friends, the closest I've ever had. I fell in love with Satori.

'He brought things out in me, stuff I had buried, things which scared me, darkness. I started to think Dad might be right. Maybe I was evil. I tried to bury the ways in which I was changing, hide them from everyone including myself, but they always resurfaced. In the end I left Satori.

'He didn't want to accept it was over. That's when he brought Lilith here, to win me back for him. I think he felt he owned me. He couldn't stand the thought that I could walk away.

'Lilith didn't follow his instructions either. I think she frightened and confused him even more than I did. I'm not saying your father was a bad man, but he was self-centred. He had this idea that the world owed him everything he craved.

'Lilith enchanted me. When we danced it was as though my soul was pure and fresh and clean. I thought I loved her. She's your parent too. Between the three of us you were conceived.'

'Satori, Lilith and you are my parents?' Edensun asks.

'Yes. I can't explain it better than that. I guess it was part of Lilith's magic.'

Edensun nods. 'How did you feel?'

'When?'

'When you knew you were pregnant.'

'You have to understand a few things first. I killed my friend, a woman called Raven. I'm not sure why I did it. When I later realised I was pregnant, I blamed you or my hormones, but now, when I look back I only see betrayal – her betrayal. I thought we were friends and she revelled in putting me down, making me feel small. I think she probably hated me. The same with my father, I guess. She wanted to hurt me, keep me under her power.

'I murdered Raven. I did it in a nightclub bathroom. I saw red. Since then I keep seeing red. Except now, it isn't anger.

It's regret for the pain I've caused, the deaths I'm responsible for. I guess I'm still jumping ahead.

'I ran off with Lilith. I didn't even know that she wasn't human. Things got more and more violent. I was stuck in a nightmare and I was scared. When she told me…when she said I was carrying her baby…I thought I was going mad.

'I started imagining that I was carrying the anti-Christ, like Rosemary's Baby, have you seen that film?'

Edensun shakes his head.

Star blushes. 'No, of course not. Well, before I could even think straight about what was happening, Lilith was gone and Satori was dragging me back to civilisation. I couldn't cope. Everything confused me. I was terrified. So…'

Star pauses and Edensun squeezes her hand.

She smiles at him, but there are tears in her eyes. 'I'm sorry.'

'Don't be. What happened?'

'I stabbed myself. I was trying to kill us both. I didn't know. Please forgive me.'

Edensun swallows hard then pulls her trembling hand towards his lips and kisses her fingers. 'I understand. The world, your world, terrifies me too.'

'Yet you came here…'

'To find you, yes.'

'And you did. We found each other.'

Edensun nods. His mother's words are painful. Some things he simply understands and others Lilith told him, but some things are new. He now realises how difficult Star's childhood had been, more difficult than his own. Lilith, at least, loves him and her handmaidens tend to his every need, but there is a hole he needs to fill and Star can help him. He will wait to hear everything she has to say. Her tiny movements enchant him. The way her mouth changes shape, the way she stares at her feet when recalling a painful memory and the way she twists her hands when she worries about hurting his feelings. 'What happened after you stabbed yourself?'

'I woke up. Lilith had taken me to Binah and you'd already been born. I don't remember your birth at all, I'm sorry.'

'When you saw me, did you love me?'

Star wrings her hands. 'I – I…'

'What was I like?'

'You didn't look human.'

'Ahh. I scared you. This.' He grins and passes a theatrical sweep of his hand in front of him. 'I had to learn, over time, how to…pass.'

'Pass?'

'As human.'

Star nods and wipes her eyes. 'How do you really look?'

'Do you really want to know?'

Star sighs. 'I've seen many things. More than a mind should be able to process in one lifetime and I'm still standing, somehow. Yes. I want to know how my son really looks.'

Edensun nods. The change happens slowly and gradually. Edensun's eyes become a brighter green. They stretch and protrude from his face. He grows taller, until he towers above

Star, almost twice her height. His hair thins then disappears. His ears grow smaller until they are simply holes in either side of his elongated face. His nose widens and flattens and his warm, brown skin fades to a pale grey. The texture of his skin changes; it crisps like bark and splits into small, rough scales.

His face ceases altering and he watches as Star's eyes drop to his body. His clothes no longer cover him. Her vision glides across the grey scales which decorate his torso. His body is gaunt. His ribs protrude and his stomach dips below them, as though he is emaciated. His arms have the same scales. His upper arms are huge and powerful, they taper below the elbows and each ends in a single vicious sting-like claw. These claws rest on the floor with a third slightly larger claw between them from the end of his single, tail-like lower appendage. Framing all this horrifying magnificence, huge black, leathery wings unfold from his shoulder blades and spread out behind him. He stands like a tripod, holding his body motionless so as to not frighten her more, but when she looks up at his face again she shakes with fear.

Edensun feels tears swell in his saucer-like eyes. He opens his mouth to speak, remembers his razor-sharp teeth and closes it again.

Star nods. 'Edensun.' Her voice is full of awe. 'My son.'

He changes back to his human form and takes a step towards her. They are the same height and he wraps his arms around her and rests his chin on her shoulder. 'This is who I am.'

He feels Star's arms circle his waist. She hugs him tightly.

'You are beautiful,' she tells him.

'So, why did you leave me?' His tears drop onto her shoulder. His voice trembles. He feels as though a hole in his chest will swallow him at any moment.

'Satori came for me,' she answers. 'And I felt I had to leave. There wasn't a day that passed when I didn't wonder whether I made the wrong decision. I should have stayed or brought you with me. I'm sorry.'

'You thought of me?'

'Always. I hoped I might see you again and you might forgive me.'

'Oh, Mummy. I forgive you.'

He feels Star's body shake in his arms. Her tears soak his skin. He pulls away and looks at her beautiful face. 'We can be together now, if that's what you want.'

'Of course it is,' she answers and wipes her face with her sleeve.

Edensun nods. 'But I have to give you the choice. There are rules.'

'I've made my choice,' she answers. Her face is lit with joy and love.

'It isn't that simple. Things have happened through your life. I have the power to change them. I can take you back to any point. Think of a time you might want to change and I can place you there. You might be able to have a better relationship with your parents. You might choose a different university, in which to study, and never meet Donna or Satori. You might stay with Satori and he might never have opened the door for Lilith.'

'But if those things changed you wouldn't exist.'

'I know,' Edensun says. 'But Ivan, Raven and Satori would still be alive. That is the choice you must make.'

'Between you and the others?'

'Yes.'

Star sits down. 'You're asking me to decide whether my friends live or die?'

'I am. I can't make the choice for you. It's yours and yours alone.'

'Why?'

'It's a balance, death and life. One cannot exist without the other.'

'But why must it be my choice?'

'It just is.'

Star nods. 'It isn't fair, but I know, more than most, I guess, that life is not fair. So I can return to any point in my past, but if I do I will lose you?'

'That's right.'

'What if I return to Binah, when you were just an infant, before I left with Satori?'

'He will still come for you.'

'But if I refuse to leave?'

'He would stay too and Lilith would kill him or he would kill me, perhaps both. Satori and I cannot exist together. You must choose.'

'If I stay here?'

'Then together we can go anywhere we want, but your friends will be dead.'

Star nods. 'I understand. I've made my choice.'

284

Edensun kisses her cheek. 'Tell me, please.'
'I choose you.'

Chapter 55

'It's good to see you, Daddy.' Freya grasps her father's fingers and squeezes.

She ignores the distractions around the room as best she can: the coughing nurse and the watchful orderly who appears to be suffering from an itchy forearm. Her father has come to see her and that is all she cares about.

He looks sad and older than she remembers him. She wonders how long she has stayed within these walls. It doesn't feel longer than a week, but her mind is always full of chemically induced fog and it's hard to remember.

'It's good to see you, Freya,' he answers.

'How's Mum? How's…' She swallows back tears. *Ivan is dead. They told me yesterday and the day before. How could I forget?* 'How's Mum?'

Mike sniffs, squeezes her hand gently and shakes his head. 'Are they treating you well?'

Freya has never considered the question before. She doesn't feel hungry and she has not been beaten. They make books available to her. She frowns. 'I guess so.'

'The funeral is tomorrow,' he tells her. 'I'll say goodbye for you.'

Her heart races and her forehead sweats. She starts to pant and the nurse moves to stand. 'I didn't mean to…' Her huge eyes plead for forgiveness.

The nurse touches Freya's shoulder.

Freya flinches at the unexpected contact. 'I'm okay now.'

The nurse nods and returns to her chair at the edge of the room.

'They're always watching,' Freya whispers. 'Eyes everywhere.'

A tear rolls down her father's cheek and he sniffs. The sound is ragged and wet. 'They want to keep you safe.'

Freya shudders. Her father is sad. He's sad because she killed his son. But she didn't mean to. He can't be sad. He needs to be strong. He is the mortar that holds everyone together. Panic rises from her chest to her throat. She tries to turn from his tears, but cannot. Their glistening wetness draws her eyes. She feels herself drown in the saline and tries to swim against the current of his sadness.

She frowns at him. She is the cause of his suffering, but this time he does not want to save her. His ashen face is hard and determined. His resentment cuts her like ice. She wants to remind him that she is his and he belongs to her, always. 'What will they do with me, Daddy? What will happen to my baby?'

Mike straightens himself and leans back. He allows Freya's hand to slip from his fingers. 'Your mother and I…' He narrows his eyes and breathes deeply. 'Your mother and I plan to adopt Jasmine.'

287

Freya shakes her head. Voices scream between her ears. Pressing her palms against her earlobes she tries to focus. *Are you rejecting me, Daddy?* Her voice rises in panic. 'No,' she says. 'You can't. She's mine, not yours.' She rises to her feet, hands clenched.

Mike backs away. The orderly catches Freya mid-lunge. Her hands never reach her father's throat. A sound somewhere between a scream and a gurgle bursts from her open jaws. The nurse makes soft cooing sounds as she presses a needle into Freya's arm. Freya's eyelids feel heavy. She wants to say goodbye. She wants to ask her father to come back and see her again. She wants to ask him to bring her daughter next time, but her mouth will not obey her instructions. Her lips feel swollen and her eyes fill with impotent tears.

'I think it's probably best if...' The nurse says before Freya loses her grip on consciousness.

Chapter 56

'Can we go home?' Star asks.

'Which one?' Mark replies.

'Earth, Malkuth, my house…no the park, the one near Raven's old flat. We can walk together and talk.' She giggles. 'I can push my son on the swings.'

'Mum!' he says.

She laughs louder and is delighted when he laughs too.

'Okay,' he says. 'The park. Hold my hand and jump.'

They land together on brittle grass. The frost filled air steals Star's breath, but the sun is shining. She takes her son's hand and starts to walk.

'You can live with me. We'll have to get you into the local school. I'm not sure how to go about registering you. Do you even exist?'

He laughs and grabs her, lifting her into the air and swinging her round as though she is the child. 'You find out you have a demonic son and you want to know whether you can register him in the local school? You are completely insane. You know that, right?'

She playfully beats her hands against his chest. 'Put me down this instant, young man. Show your mother some respect.'

He pulls a face at her and she laughs.

She turns away giggling and notices a crowd of people staring at them. 'Umm, we appear to be drawing a lot of attention to ourselves, Edensun. Maybe we should try to blend in?'

He puts her down gently. The crowd of spectators thickens. They no longer watch in amusement or confusion. Their faces twist into angry masks.

'What's going on?' Star asks.

Mark shakes his head. 'I don't know…but…run.'

He grabs her hand and pulls her away. Her shoulder burns from the sudden jolt. They run together as fast as she can manage. She glances back at her pursuers. The group is growing in numbers. 'What do they want?'

'I don't know,' he tells her.

They keep running. They dash through the park gate and on to the street. Star sees more people as they turn the corner. A few wear the same long white robes as worn by the worshippers who followed her to Paul's house, but most are dressed normally. All of them look enraged.

Mark sees them too. He spins around and pulls Star in the opposite direction. They dart across the road. Tyres screech as a van tries to brake. With a thud, the swerving vehicle pushes Star upwards. She lets go of Mark's hand and flies through the air. For a moment she drifts. It feels like freedom. Her body is weightless. The air embraces her as she soars. Silence surrounds her. Then she falls, bouncing heavily on the road. The peaceful silence breaks as her bones shatter. Noise punches her eardrums and her vision turns red. She sees feet and legs surround her. Voices rise and become roars of manic excitement.

'I'm here,' Mark tells her, a calm centre within the storm.

She focuses only on him. As he holds her hand, the crowd thickens around them. Fists and feet dart towards them. She feels echoes of the blows Mark receives. 'Get us out of here,' she whispers.

Chapter 57

Edensun strokes his mother's hair. He rocks her in his arms as if she were his child. Perhaps she is, for now he has the chance to help her grow, discover anew what makes her special. He knows she will make him proud.

Star opens her eyes, looks around and gasps. Edensun watches as she fills her fists with damp soil. He frowns, confused for a moment then continues to stroke her hair, trying to calm her. He feels her shudder in his lap.

'Welcome home, Star,' Lilith says. The goddess strides towards them. She touches Edensun's shoulder. 'You did it.'

'Yes,' he nods. 'Welcome home, Mum.'

The giant wyrm slithers behind his mistress.

'Lilith, Siloth, Edensun, I'm home.' Star's voice shakes. She pushes herself from Edensun's lap and sits up. 'Somehow, I knew I'd end up here.'

'Does that make you sad?' Lilith asks.

Star turns her head. She looks towards the great Siloth, Lilith and at last at Edensun. He feels himself absorbed by her hungry stare. As if after all these years she can know him simply by looking into his eyes. He shudders and wonders whether in fact she can.

'No,' she answers simply. 'It's where I belong.'

Lilith smiles and Edensun tightens his grip around her. Siloth nods his blind head in agreement.

'What now?' Star asks after a few moments of silence.

'That's up to you,' Lilith answers. 'It always was.'

Star turns to face Edensun again. 'A second chance, to do things right. I want to know you. I want to make up for my years of absence.'

Edensun smiles. Warmth spreads through his body. This scene is more perfect than any he could imagine. His mother is here and she loves him. There is nothing he cannot do with her by his side, watching him in admiration.

He stands and gently pulls Star to her feet with him. 'I can give you a tour. Do you want to see where I was born?'

She nods slowly.

The four of them move together. They do not rush. Star seems unsure of her footing. Edensun holds her arm. Every few steps he feels her falter and shake.

'Are you ready for this?' he asks her. 'It can wait.'

Star shakes her head. 'I've wasted too much time already. Show me, please.'

The distant villa is their destination. As they approach its outer walls it shimmers, becoming less rather than more defined. Plant colours bleed into each other. The place does not appear solid, but rather an impression created by light, like a painting by Monet.

Edensun feels Star's grip on his arm tighten as she pushes herself against his body. He wonders whether it is fear or awe she feels. He has lived here most of his life. However, the villa still confuses his senses. It is a place and yet it is not a place. It is an idea of a place projected by Lilith's mind. It changes with the goddess's mood. Today it is sunny and bright, full of excitement.

'It's okay,' he whispers in his mother's ear.

Lilith pushes open the shifting, shimmering door with a gentle touch. Inside white marble shines like moonlight. Every surface glows. 'This is where I work.' Lilith smiles at Star.

'The columns of mist?' Star asks.

Lilith nods. 'Everything is created by The One. Potential and energy are filtered through Binah in these columns you see. That energy is boundless. It carries within it everything than can be achieved. The energy is anarchic, fluid, borderless and limitless. I give it limits. I mould the energy, the pure thought, into flesh. Then it is ready for its journey towards birth and Malkuth - Earth. I made you and I made Edensun. By tying energy to flesh I give it both life and death. Energy does not die, but flesh does. I am the terrible mother. I give life and bind each new life to its own mortality - to death.'

'And Edensun?'

'If Edensun were to live on earth as human, his form would age and die eventually. It is the nature of things.'

'But here?'

Edensun grips Star's hands and turns her to face him. 'I am not human, Mother. You have seen my true form. I am the god of In Between, the god of nowhere and everywhere. Outside the tree of life, I am free to make my own rules. I reign in the darkness, the places beyond.'

'And here?' Star stares into his green eyes.

'Here, like you, I am Lilith's guest, but we are welcome guests and no harm will come to us.'

Star embraces her son and looks at Lilith. 'Can we die here?'

Lilith laughs.

Star shudders.

Edensun catches hold of fragments of Star's memories as they flood into her skull. She bled here. Her stomach was open and her organs exposed, yet she did not die.

'That depends on my will,' Lilith answers.

He realises the pain and torment he caused his mother. His infant fangs had torn her flesh. He had terrified her. He holds her tightly until she stops shaking. 'I'm sorry, Mum.'

Star steps back a pace and stares at Edensun. 'Sorry for what?'

'Hurting you.'

'You are my son, my only son. When my body healed, a void was left, an ache that was constant. When I left Binah part of me was left behind. I'm the one who should be sorry.'

'You're here now.' He squeezes her fingers.

A loving smile lights up her face. 'Yes. Forgive me, Edensun.'

'There is nothing to forgive.'

Her eyes glaze and darken at his words.

He searches his memory for the source of her pain, but cannot find it. 'What did I say?'

'Someone else said that to me many years ago, as I lay dying.'

'I'm sorry.'

'Don't be. I should never forget. In spite of everything, he really did love me.' Star turns away. Her shoulders rise and fall. She sniffs and rubs her forearm across her face. When she turns around again her eyes glisten with tears. 'I am a terrible person.'

Edensun shakes his head.

Lilith steps closer and pats Star's shoulder. 'We are all selfish, one way or another. The flesh, which separates us, makes us so. Perhaps you should forgive yourself?'

Chapter 58

'Come,' Lilith says. 'A celebratory feast has been prepared.'

Edensun rises from the couch and Star follows. Star's eyes lift to look at Lilith's face and she blushes. Lilith smiles.

'There is no need for shyness, Star. We're old friends.'

Star nods and blushes more deeply. Lilith laughs lightly.

'I'm sorry, Lilith,' Star says. 'It's just a little... overwhelming.'

'You'll get used to it.' Edensun squeezes his mother's hand.

Lilith leads them to a great dining hall where Magenta, Violet and Sapphire are already seated. They rise as Lilith enters the room. Lilith waves her hand and they sit once more before their empty plates.

'It's incredible,' Star says. She sounds breathless.

It isn't the most impressive feast Lilith has hosted. The meats and fruits at the centre of the table, while vibrant in colour and tempting in odour, are limited in variety. However, she is delighted to have thrilled her guest.

'Come, taste...' Lilith says.

Lilith sits at the head of the table. Edensun and Star sit beside each other opposite the handmaidens. She smiles at how politely everyone waits, hands in their laps. Lilith reaches to spoon some food onto her plate. As she raises her silverware to eat, the others follow suit.

'It's delicious,' Star says after swallowing her first mouthful.

Lilith nods. 'That's good to hear.'

Star avoids the meats, but piles her plate with fruit and vegetables the likes of which she has probably never seen before.

'You don't like the meat, Mother?' Edensun asks.

'I'm vegetarian,' Star answers.

'Why?' Magenta asks. 'I-I'm sorry, that was rude of me.'

'No, not at all,' Star replies. 'I just don't think we should eat animals.'

Lilith cocks her head. She looks at each face around the table in turn. Edensun and the handmaidens look puzzled. Star looks as though she wishes the ground might open up and swallow her. *Be careful what you wish for*, Lilith thinks. She laughs and the others join her laughter until the tension is broken.

'Do you think we farm animals here, Darling?' Lilith asks before filling her mouth with succulent meats.

Star looks at her. Lilith watches as her blue eyes glisten for a moment then dull with her passing thought. 'I don't know.'

'Well, we don't. No animals were hurt in any way in the preparation of this feast.'

'I don't understand,' Star stammers.

'Why should you? There are many things about your world I do not understand. Cruelty to animals is only one of them. I create food as I create life - from magic.'

Star nods. 'I'm sorry, Lilith. I didn't mean...'

'Shhh, there's no need to apologise. Your world is wrong. It's good that you want to change it.'

Star's eyes make contact with Lilith's. Lilith feels the woman try to probe her thoughts. Star quickly gives up and her body relaxes back into her chair.

'All in good time,' Lilith tells her.

Lilith empties her plate and leaves the table. She moves into an antechamber which she fills with music with a click of her fingers. One by one the others follow her. Edensun arrives last, following his mother.

Lilith lounges on a pile of silk and velvet cushions. She watches the others as they lower themselves to the floor, trying to mimic her grace, but missing the mark. She does not try to suppress a self-satisfied grin.

'What do you think of our home?' Lilith asks.

'It's lovely,' Star answers.

'Will you stay?'

'I want to be with my son.' Star turns from Lilith and smiles at Edensun. 'Yes, I'll stay for as long as I am welcome.'

'That's good. A boy needs his mother.'

'Lilith,' Edensun says. His voice has an edge of sharpness. It makes Lilith bristle.

'Star understands, Edensun. She knows I am right. I am always right.'

Star nods. 'It seems that way, now.'

Lilith laughs. Her laugh is infectious and the others laugh too. They laugh long and hard, pushing their bodies back into the cushions and staring at the painted ceiling.

'Star?' Lilith asks as the laughter fades.

'Yes Lilith,' Star answers.

'Will you share my bed tonight?'

Star turns to look at Edensun for a moment. When she faces Lilith again she is frowning. 'I…'

'Too soon?' Lilith asks.

'I lost Satori and Ivan today.'

Lilith nods. 'I know.'

'It's just…'

'You think it shows more respect to the memory of your two lovers if you sleep alone tonight?'

Star sighs. 'I wouldn't have said it quite that way, but yes, perhaps that's it.'

'If you change your mind, dream of me and I'll come to you.'

'If I dream of you, you'll come?' Star shudders.

'Yes.'

'My dreams aren't private here?' Star asks.

'Your dreams aren't private anywhere, dear child. Did you think otherwise?'

'Yes, I did.'

Lilith laughs again. This time she laughs alone.

Chapter 59

Star doesn't remember her dream, but when she wakes she is not by Lilith's side. She lies alone on the softest mattress she has ever had the pleasure to sink into. Closing her eyes, she imagines floating on a cloud. She swallows hard. *Are there clouds in the sky above Binah?*

Smiling, she visualises Edensun's bright eyes. Nothing else matters. She will not miss the world she left behind or the people she sacrificed to be with her son. She realises how selfish this makes her, but chooses not to care. It is her second chance at happiness, or is it her third or fourth chance? Whatever, this time she won't fuck up.

She stretches remnants of sleep from her body and gets out of bed. The clothes she removed the previous night are no longer draped over the chair where she left them. She wonders whether nudity is acceptable within the villa's dress code then decides that it would be uncomfortable and confusing to be naked in her teenage son's presence.

A set of double doors lead to a walk-in wardrobe. The vibrancy of the colours held within its belly astounds her: silks with more shades than the fruit and vegetables she consumed at dinner. The dresses are beautiful. Exquisitely cut, she suspects each will fit her like the proverbial glove.

However, she cannot find a single black garment within the mix.

Cursing the choices beneath her breath, she pulls a few of the deeper shades from their hangers. Gowns in jewel tones of sapphire, emerald, ruby and amethyst she carries from the wardrobe to the foot of her bed.

She hears a knock at her door and turns toward the sound.

'Who is it?' she asks.

'Violet. Do you need any help dressing?'

'Umm, maybe, but…'

The door opens and Violet sweeps into the room.

Star shakes her head and frowns. 'There's no black.'

Violet studies the garments on Star's bed then walks towards the open wardrobe. 'No black,' she says. 'Is that important?'

'I always wear black.' Star blushes, acutely aware of how peevish she sounds complaining about the magnificence of her wardrobe.

Violet nods. 'You don't like change?'

'Change?' Star's voice grows shrill. Hysteria threatens to engulf her. She breathes deeply, trying to stay calm. 'I've travelled between worlds and left everyone I know. I'd say that constitutes a huge change, wouldn't you?'

Violet smiles, patiently. 'I agree and it makes you uncomfortable.'

Star slumps onto the bed and sighs. Silk crushes beneath her. 'No, it's not the change. I'm always uncomfortable.'

Violet nods. 'Lilith tells it differently. She tells us stories of your becoming.'

'My becoming? Is that what she calls it?'

'When you transformed and became the sun. When you gave her back what she lost aeons ago. Yes, she calls that your becoming, although I suspect she feels it changed her as much as it changed you.'

'I changed back.'

'What do you mean?' Violet asks.

Star shakes her head. 'I'm not a hero.'

'Lilith thinks you are.'

'Lilith's wrong. I'm a weak little girl who has never gotten over the fact that her parents didn't love her.'

'Aren't we all?' Violet answers. 'Isn't that exactly how Lilith felt before you taught her the value of forgiveness?'

'Is that really what she says?'

'Sometimes, when she's drunk and happy.'

'What about when she's unhappy?'

'Then she beats the shit out of one of us until she's smiling again.' Violet laughs.

Star wonders whether the woman is joking and decides a smile would be the safest response.

'Have you decided what you'll wear?' Violet asks.

Star gets off the bed and looks at the creased gowns. 'I've wrecked them.'

'Not at all,' Violet answers shaking the clothes and patting out the wrinkles.

'You choose for me,' Star says.

'Are you sure?'

'Go for it. I can't decide.'

Violet grins. 'What if I choose yellow?'

'You wouldn't. Nobody could be that cruel.'

'I don't know, with your colouring and bright blue eyes...'
Violet giggles. 'No, just fucking with you.'

She hangs the darker gowns back in the wardrobe and
shows Star a diaphanous silver dress with a low neckline and
no sleeves. 'This one.'

'Are you sure?'

'Absolutely. I insist you try it.'

Star shrugs and pulls the dress over her head. The soft
material caresses her naked body like a cool breath. It
whispers sweet secrets to her as she spins and watches the
skirt fan out around her legs.

'Beautiful,' Violet assures her.

Star looks in the mirror and nods. 'Yes.'

'Well, shall we?' Violet asks.

'What?'

'Go and meet your adoring fans and your beautiful son.'

Star pulls a face. 'Lead the way.'

Walking, Star enjoys the dress more than ever. She feels
like a goddess. Perhaps she is. *Does the mother of a god get
an automatic promotion?*

Chapter 60

Edensun gasps as Star steps through the doorway. 'Mum!'

She blushes and looks at her feet.

'You look beautiful, Star,' Lilith says, striding across the room and grasping both Star's hands in her own.

'Thank you,' Star replies. 'Not my usual colour, but...'

'It suits you.' Edensun feels his chest swell as he looks at her.

'Lilith, do you think you might be able to add some black clothes to my wardrobe?'

'Why? You don't need to hide here,' Lilith replies.

'It's...it's not about hiding, Lilith,' Star says.

'Are you sure of that?'

Lilith and Star stare into each other's eyes for a moment before Star breaks away and looks towards Edensun. Her eyes implore him to help.

He sighs and shrugs. 'Mum?'

Star turns back to face Lilith. 'You know me, Lilith. Wearing black isn't about hiding.'

'Why is it so important to you, Darling?' Lilith's tone is light, but her face is set.

Star shrugs. She opens her hands, but Lilith does not let go. When Star steps back one pace, Lilith steps forwards.

'It's me.' Star's voice shakes. 'I thought you wanted me to be true to myself.'

'Black is for mourning. We do not need your sadness here. Whatever makes us sad we simply change,' Lilith says.

'Okay.' Star nods to acknowledge her defeat. 'So I should be me, but I should be happy?'

'Exactly!' Lilith exclaims. 'When you left us you were happy. You saw potential in everything including yourself. When Edensun found you, you had already lost that spark of joy. Why?'

'Satori and Ivan, I loved them and they're dead.'

'Before then, dear Star, you were unhappy before then.'

Star shifts uncomfortably on her feet and hangs her head. Edensun wants to rush to her, embrace her and make it all better. He remains still, Lilith's audience. He knows he must not interfere with the lesson.

'I didn't feel worthy of love.'

'Because your parents didn't love you? That's a pile of bullshit and you know it. I love you. Satori loved you. You were and are worthy. There is no way that you can have fallen this far again without wanting to.'

'You left your taint on me.'

'My taint?' Lilith spits the word. 'My taint! What the fuck do you mean, Star?'

Star's body shakes violently. 'I wanted...I needed...oh fuck, Lilith, you made me into a nymphomaniac.'

Lilith laughs. 'Excuse me? I did no such thing, and don't try to pathologise your sexuality here.'

'What do you mean?'

'Nymphomania is a muzzle created by men who wanted to control women.'

Star shakes her head. 'No. I couldn't control myself. It was terrifying.'

'You wanted to have more sex, and you thought that made you a slut, so you pretended you were mentally ill instead.'

Star shakes harder. Edensun worries she might fall.

'Let me go,' Star says.

'No, you need to face this, Star,' Lilith answers.

'I felt evil. I was a predator.'

'We are strong. We are whole. If the weak call us predators, that doesn't make it true. Look at your son, Star.'

Star turns to face Edensun. Tears shine in her eyes and roll down her cheeks.

He swallows hard. 'Do we need to do this, Lilith?'

Lilith throws him a terrifying look which silences him.

'He's a boy, right? A child. In your world if he were to enjoy physical pleasure with Magenta, Violet or Sapphire, or all three of them at the same time, it would be a crime.'

Star nods.

'Does that make it wrong?' Lilith asks.

'I-I don't know.' Star's voice is weak.

Lilith draws Star towards her and holds her tight. She strokes her hair. 'You are not wrong, Darling. I did not make you wrong. You made yourself whole. To be whole takes courage. It isn't easy to do what others will not. Here, you will never be judged for how you feel or what you want. Here, you will only be loved.' She kisses Star's tear-soaked lips and releases her hold.

Star staggers and Edensun rushes to help her to a chair.

'Are you okay?' he asks her.

Star's face looks paler than normal and her eyes are rimmed with red. Her lips tremble and her body shakes. She looks around the room. Her gaze rests on each woman and then returns to his face. She smiles. 'I am,' she answers. 'Do you think I could have a drink?'

He grins and jumps up. 'Of course you can, Mother.'

Chapter 61

The drink calms her. Star sips it slowly, giving herself a break from the social interaction she will undoubtedly be expected to resume the moment her glass is empty. She looks up from her glass expecting all eyes to be on her, but they aren't. Edensun and the four women are interacting with each other at some level. Watching them is like watching contemporary ballet. They communicate without the need for words, moving around the room elegantly and silently with nods and twists of limbs which appear to be a form of language.

'I'm ready to try and justify my love of black clothing,' Star says as the last drop of liquid falls onto her tongue.

'Oh, darling.' Lilith's voice is soft and melodious. 'You don't have to justify anything to me. You've been trying to justify it to yourself.'

'Hey, that's not fair,' Star answers. 'I asked you for black clothes and you started on about hiding and mourning, not me.'

Lilith laughs and moves across the room towards Star. She touches the crown of Star's head in a way that makes her entire body shake. Lilith stands there for a moment then sits beside Star.

'Violet, do you think we can get something to drink over here?' Lilith calls.

Violet hurries over with a second glass and the decanter. She fills both glasses and leaves the decanter beside them.

'Okay, Star, I'm listening.'

Star nods. 'In my world women have become decorative objects. I wear black to challenge that. I want to show that who I am and how I look are not one and the same.'

Lilith smiles.

'Fashion is a huge industry. Animals are slaughtered for their skins and people exploited to make throw away clothes for consumers. By wearing only black I do not need to update my wardrobe each season and I can afford to buy what I want from reputable makers.'

Lilith's smile grows wider.

'In my world it is not acceptable to be unhappy. People are medicated and coerced into smiling. Women in particular are challenged by strangers if they do not have a smile permanently plastered across their faces.'

Lilith nods. Her smile maintains its brightness.

'Goths challenge the idea that we should all be happy. We see beauty where others do not even choose to look because it makes them feel uncomfortable. We know that beauty can be chaotic or sinister.'

'I see,' Lilith answers. 'Black clothes are a statement of how much better you are than those around you?'

'Not better, different.'

'Different, how?'

'Because I don't need people to like and admire me.'

'Do you have friends?'

'Yes.'

'Do you care if they like and admire you?'

'Yes.'

'Do they also wear black?'

Star nods.

'So rather than being different, you are identifying as part of a group by way of a uniform?'

'Yes, but...'

Lilith cocks her head. 'You're an artist, Star. Do you only ever use black paint?'

'No.'

'Why?'

'Because sometimes I want to paint things as I see them and other times I want to paint them as I feel them. When I paint feelings I use a lot of black and sometimes red and blue.'

'So black represents your feelings when you feel unable to share them another way.'

'I guess so. Do you think that's a bad thing?'

'No. Why would I? I'm just trying to understand.'

'It feels as though I'm being cross-examined.' Star looks away. Her head feels heavy and her eyes sting.

'Does that make you uncomfortable?'

'A little.'

Lilith strokes Star's cheek. 'Why?'

'I'm not sure.'

'Are you afraid of revealing too much?' Lilith asks.

'Too much of myself?'

311

'Yes. Is there something inside you that you don't want others to see?'

'There is.'

'What is it?'

Star looks towards Edensun for advice. He smiles at her, but doesn't speak or move closer. He appears entranced by the conversation. *What is it? That's a good question. It used to be the vortex: that little hub of power inside me of which I always felt ashamed. I felt I must be evil to have such chaos inside me. Now I know that the power doesn't have to be chaotic, it can be focused and useful. It can be as bright as the sun. It saved me and Satori. It healed Lilith. Is that what I am still ashamed of?*

She looks at Lilith who sits patiently waiting for Star to find her answer. She looks at Edensun, the boy who grew up without a mother. *Is that what I'm ashamed of? Leaving my son when he needed me most, but he was a monster. We didn't bond and he hurt me. I can forgive myself for leaving and he has already forgiven me. What then?*

She looks into her lap, past the deep cleavage exposed by the cut of the dress between her breasts. 'I'm ashamed that I'm a woman,' she answers.

'What?' Edensun cries.

Lilith holds the palm of her hand towards him to silence his outburst.

'Eve's shame,' Lilith whispers.

Star nods.

'The human race hasn't evolved much in thousands of years.' Lilith sighs. 'Do you believe it when they tell you you're inferior, a temptress, evil and shallow?'

'I don't feel I'm good enough.'

'Good enough for whom?'

Star shakes her head.

'Every day I make flesh for new spirits, some are male and some are female. The spirits within both are infinite until I make that arbitrary choice as to how to shape their flesh. Each is limited by their new shell. Their bodies separate them from each other, organising the spirits into logical patterns which conform, with varying success, to the rules which cage them. Do you follow?'

'I think so.'

'Rules such as you can no longer fly; you can no longer expand into your environment; you can no longer merge completely and seamlessly with another; one day you will die and your spirit will return to the source. These are the rules of being bound into flesh and they are the same for male and female forms. Everything you have been taught since you were pushed from your screaming mother, other than these rules, is bullshit. New limits which humans have imposed upon themselves, and each other, are not real. They hold no profound truth about yourself or the human condition. You are neither inferior nor superior to the billions of other spirits caged in flesh which roam the earth.'

'If that's true what is the purpose of life?'

'Purpose?'

'What should be our goals?'

313

'Should?' Lilith grins.

'Lilith!'

'The purpose of life is to find your own purpose and your goal is death.'

'That's ridiculous!' Star shakes her head.

'Why?'

'If death is our goal why do we live at all?' Star's eyes are wide, pleading almost.

'To discover, to learn, to have fun.'

'We don't do those things.'

'Some do. Others have become confused and in their confusion they look for answers to the wrong questions.'

'Why is the world so unfair and unequal?' Star glances at Lilith whose face is hazy through the veil of tears.

'Because people make it so.'

'So there is no purpose?' Star looks down and squeezes her fingers.

'Do you need there to be?'

'Yes.'

'Then make your own purpose.'

Star stares at her hands. 'My own?'

Lilith's voice grows sharp. 'Why are you so infuriatingly stupid and blind, Star?'

Star frowns. She bites her bottom lip and pinches the back of her hands between her fingernails, stretching skin from bone. 'I'm afraid to fail.'

'Fail at what? How can you fail at living for a while then dying?' Lilith gesticulates wildly, losing all semblance of calm.

'It isn't that simple.'

'Of course it is.' Lilith's voice heightens in frustration.

'But all the other people…'

'What of them?'

'You don't live there. There's a hierarchy, societal pressure. It isn't just five people in a room chatting.'

Lilith's voice softens again. A soft smile plays on her lips. 'Or more accurately two chatting and the other three listening.'

Star looks up and catches Magenta's eye. Magenta blushes and looks away.

'Maybe they should talk too?' Star says.

'That's up to them. This is freedom. They are neither obliged to talk or to stay silent.'

'They aren't free, Lilith. They're your servants.'

'They help me. I do my job willingly as do they. If I stopped making people God wouldn't soar through that veil and tell me to start again. I have simply decided my purpose and I fulfil it.'

'How did you start?'

'You know my beginnings.'

'In the Garden?'

'No, before then. I was the light of the moon. I was cast out and I fell to earth. I was born demon from the womb of the moon. God made me human, but the price was too high. After The Fall, not my fall, but The Fall of humankind from the Garden, he asked for my help. I ensured I made the right demands this time. I discovered quickly what I value most highly. I am free to do whatever I please and most of the time

I am pleased to manage this factory of human creation. It amuses me, imagining the potential of each new spirit to change everything around them. While it's rare, some spirits do shine more brightly and do change things.'

'For the worse and for the better.'

'You still don't understand. The lives of humans are of no concern to us. We do not guide them. I am simply entertained by change.'

'I wish I had changed more,' Star says.

'What would you change?'

'I'd abolish animal farming and inequalities of wealth. I'd make sure everyone had enough for survival but not a glut of resources. I'd stop war and I'd stop the sexualisation of women.'

'Big changes,' Lilith says, nodding.

'Yes, too big. I didn't have the power to change any of them.'

'You didn't use the power you had,' Lilith says.

Star looks at her empty glass and refills it from the decanter. 'That's true. I didn't.'

'It's not too late,' Lilith says.

'What do you mean?'

'For you to change things. Shake the world up a little. Why don't the three of us make a little visit to Malkuth? It could be fun.'

'I don't think so, Lilith.'

'Why not?'

'For a start, who am I to decide what other people do with their lives?'

'If you hate it, change it.'

'But it's not my place to do so.'

'Nonsense. It's everyone's place, everyone's responsibility to be the change they seek.'

'If you and I go to Malkuth, we'll have undue influence. We are too powerful.'

'Yet before you said you wished you had changed things, but you felt powerless. Which is it Star?'

Star bows her head. She sits silently, studying the lines on her hands and the creases of her silk dress. Slowly she raises her head and stares into Lilith's eyes. Her lips twitch. Her features slacken in resignation and she sighs. 'Both.'

Chapter 62

Lilith notices the tiny shiver across Star's skin. 'You don't really want to talk about all this heavy stuff, do you? Why not have some fun with us?'

Star smiles. The laugh she offers sounds hollow, sardonic almost. 'Lilith, you make my head spin. Okay, I'll bite. What do you do for fun?'

'Truthfully we mostly eat, drink and have sex, but if that's a little avant-garde for you, especially with your son present and all, we could go for a walk, play hide and seek, go swimming.'

'Children's games?'

'How do adults have fun?' Lilith asks.

Star shrugs. 'We talk, we drink, we dance…'

'Dancing! What a marvellous idea? It'll be just like the time we met in that club. What was it called?'

'Club Midian.'

'Sapphire, darling, play some music for us.' Lilith stands up and holds out her hands towards Star.

Shaking her head, Star blushes and giggles self-consciously. 'I-I…'

The moment the music starts Lilith moves with it, gliding with serpentine grace across the room, pulling Edensun, Magenta and Violet to their feet. They follow her lead.

Bodies weave around each other. Sometimes they dance so close that there is not a sliver of air between them. Lilith returns to Star's side and offers her hands again. Star's smile makes her tingle. This time the Goth stands up and allows Lilith to steer her towards the centre of the room.

As Lilith watches Star move, it is like gazing upon evolution. The timid, confused and often irritating little girl blossoms into a confident and beautiful woman. The lines of worry across her brow vanish and her soft mouth curls into a smile. Her hooded eyes scan the room. She looks mischievous, predatory and alive. Lilith almost forgets her own steps as she watches this angel of the dance floor.

Star weaves between the other dancers. Her hands move like falling leaves, sometimes hovering for a moment on the shoulder of another.

One by one the dancers fall away. Edensun and Magenta play a game of chess together and Violet returns to a piece of embroidery. Star appears as unaware of their absence as she had been of their presence. She is completely lost in the rhythms of the music.

Lilith watches patiently as the movements of Star's arms become smaller and the swaying of her body less random. When Star looks up from the floor, Lilith smiles at her.

'You're a wonderful dancer,' Lilith says. 'Motion is your medium. Perhaps you should be a dancer rather than a painter?'

Star shakes her head. 'I am not nearly talented enough and I don't like the feeling of being watched. I just enjoy dancing. It makes me feel...'

319

'Free?'

'Yes, exactly. I guess it's like meditation. The music shuts down my conscious mind and lets my subconscious surface. It feels like flying. Hey, Lilith, do you remember that time in the club when we floated above the dance floor? Oh no, wait, that was a dream.'

'Reality is a construct of your conscious mind. Dreams are constructs of your unconscious. Why put a higher value on the one while dismissing the other?'

'But, how could I expect you to remember if it's my dream?'

Lilith nods. 'I remember.'

Star looks pensive for a moment. 'What is this music?' she asks.

'Ancient, tribal songs from the desert updated with a mixture of traditional and modern instruments for the twenty-first century,' Lilith answers.

'It's beautiful.'

'Yes, it is.'

'Do you understand the words?' Star asks.

'This one, right now, it's comparing the desert sand to children, moulding and forming them then watching them blow away on the wind.'

Star closes her eyes and pictures the desert. The imagined sun warms her face and grit irritates her eyes. 'Will you take me to the desert, Lilith?'

'It's just beyond our garden wall, child.'

'No, the one where you wandered, before and after Eden.'

'As you wish. We can have a world tour, the three of us: all the pain, suffering, cruelty and hardship we can pack into two weeks.'

'It isn't that bad,' Star says.

Lilith frowns. 'Really? It is exactly that bad the way you tell it and it certainly is that bad in the land I used to call home.'

'I'm sorry.' Star reaches out and touches Lilith's hand.

Lilith looks at the pale skin covering her own deeper tones. She looks up from their hands and into the blue eyes of the woman before her.

'That was rude of me,' Star continues. 'Forgive me. Your land, is it a war zone now?'

Lilith nods. 'Enough talking, we either dance or we can take a walk outside in our own desert.'

Star's pupils dilate and her face glows. 'I'd like very much to walk with you, Lilith.'

'Shall we leave the children to their games?' Lilith nods towards Edensun, Magenta, Violet and Sapphire.

'Yes, they seem happy.' Star smiles.

'So do you, at last, my dear. So do you.' Lilith offers her arm and Star accepts it. Together they leave the villa grounds and step onto the soft yet barren earth.

'Does nothing grow here?' Star asks.

'Everything grows here,' Lilith answers. 'But I need space to think so I can do my work.'

'Do you ever get bored of the monotony?'

'No.'

'I think if it were my land I'd need more contrasts, more change.'

'I know, but it isn't your land and I already know who I am. I don't always strive to see what's waiting around the corner while ignoring the things that I already possess.'

'Do you think that's what I do?' Star turns and stares coldly at Lilith.

Lilith suppresses a smile, shakes her head and continues walking.

They walk in silence for a while.

'How large is this world?' Star asks.

'Large enough for our needs.'

'What about the geography?'

'What do you mean?'

'Is it all dirt and sand other than the villa?'

'Pretty much.'

'What about at the edges?'

'The edges? Do you mean the boundaries?'

'Yes.'

Lilith stops walking and points. 'Do you see that light in the distance?'

'Yes.'

'That comes from Samael's world. The spirits walk through the veil between his world and mine so I can mould them into flesh.'

'What is his world like?'

'Dark, crowded and chaotic. He enjoys having distractions around him.'

'Do you hate it?'

'I couldn't live there, but there are reasons enough to visit.'

Star catches Lilith's eye and coughs. 'How about in that direction?' She points away from the light.

'There's a lake. Satori crossed it to enter this world.'

'Can we see it?'

'I don't go there. I am certain Edensun would join you, if you wanted to make the journey.'

'Now?'

'There really is no peace inside of you, Star, and there will never be, unless you learn to be still.'

Star nods. 'Okay.' She sits down and Lilith sits next to her.

Sand caresses Lilith's toes. She smiles and turns toward Star. Star looks deep in thought, her eyes fixed on the horizon. The woman's skin shines like moonlight. Tiny hairs on her cheeks catch the light and glisten. The pores beneath them offer hours of exploration. Her top lip where it points downwards slightly in the middle quivers as she breathes. Beyond that Lilith can glimpse the whiteness of teeth and the pink curve of her tongue. Her nostrils flare each time she inhales. Dust, from the desert air, journeys in and out with her breath. Fine spider webs, of blue and red veins, decorate the internal walls of her nostrils.

Star turns to focus her eyes on Lilith. Her pupils widen. The pink tip of her tongue flicks across her lips, moistening them.

'I would like to kiss you,' Lilith tells her.

'I've never known you to ask before.' Star laughs.

'Things are different now. I'm different and so are you. We are equals. I won't kiss you unless you want it too.'

'I do,' Star replies.

The pale face and dark curls blur as Lilith moves closer and closer to Star's lips. She tastes like ocean spray and summer fruits. As they kiss Lilith's need grows. She pulls Star closer, touching her hair then her throat then her arms, filling Star's mouth with her tongue. Her excitement mounts as she feels Star's tongue push sensuously back.

They tug at each other's clothes. Discarding fine silks on the sand, they press flesh against flesh. Breasts squash against each other as legs and arms entangle. They roll across the sand letting it cover their heated bodies, completely unaware of everything but each other.

Lilith grips Star's breast. The woman moans with pleasure. Lilith licks sand and salt from Star's skin. Her fingers trace the curves of her lover's pale body. They stroke Star's soft rounded stomach, downy with fine blonde hairs, then explore the tangle of auburn curls below, before reaching her clitoris and squeezing the swollen mound between teasing fingers.

Star's body rises and falls over the crest of desire. The woman grips Lilith's hair and pulls her back from breast to mouth. Tongues dance as hands and fingers explore. The world beyond the confines of each other's flesh melts away. The universe becomes their hot yielding flesh and the pleasure they share. They dine on each other's sweat, saliva and the juices produced by their mutual ecstasy. They feast on pleasure, producing and consuming, greedily.

Chapter 63

Edensun looks up as Lilith and his mother enter the room. He concedes the game to Magenta; she would have beaten him soon anyway, and wanders over to pour drinks for the two women.

Both are covered in sand and Star's clothes are inside out. Edensun grins. His smile widens when his mother grins back. She places her hand on his shoulder and thanks him for the drink.

'Who won?' Lilith asks, nodding towards the chess board.

'Who do you think?'

'Tsk, you're too easily distracted, boy.'

Edensun pours himself a drink. 'And you're not?'

Star blushes and Lilith giggles.

'Recreation time is important,' Lilith says lightly. She strokes the tip of her index finger playfully across the back of Star's hand.

The two women look at each other and smile.

'Have you guys decided anything?' Edensun asks.

'About what?' Star says.

'Star's decided she wants to see the lake. I have no desire to take her. Why don't you two take a picnic and spend some time together?' Lilith says.

Violet appears within moments, bringing a hamper that she places on the table next to Star.

'Thank you, Violet,' Lilith says. 'I'm going to take a bath. You two enjoy your walk.'

Edensun and Star walk hand in hand. In his other hand Edensun carries their feast. Star's arm sways gently as she walks. Their clasped hands swing like a pendulum. Half of him wants to ask about Star's time with Lilith, today and long ago, before he was born, but the other half is perfectly content walking hand in hand with his mother towards the lake of sorrows.

Silence covers them like a blanket. It is not an uncomfortable silence, but rather a shared appreciation for the present. The twilight sky is softened by mist. The sand does not resist them. Their passage across the desert is effortless. Edensun's hand is warmed by the skin of his mother, as though the perfect pressure of her grip feeds him. He watches her face. When she looks ahead a gentle and wise smile plays across her lips and when she turns towards him that smile grows and her eyes shine with pure love. By her side, he feels ten feet tall. By her side, they could change the world if they wanted to. In this perfect moment, he does not wish to change a thing.

He knows things will change. Lilith wants to open Star's eyes to the evil natures of human beings so that Star will desire, and become a catalyst for, transformation. If their intervention makes the world a better place, Star will remain the happy self-confident person who walks with him now. If it changes for the worse, he might lose his mother forever.

'It's red!' Star exclaims as the lake comes into view.

Edensun turns to his mother. 'Are you okay?'

'It looks like blood.'

He laughs softly. 'It isn't blood. It isn't water either.' He walks behind her as she runs to the edge of the lake. 'I wouldn't…'

'It's so cold,' she says turning to face him. She cradles her fingers in her other hand. Her eyes are full of tears and her body trembles. 'What is this place?'

'The lake of sorrows,' he answers.

'I thought that was just a name.'

'Did you?'

She nods and drags a forearm across her face to dry her eyes.

'Do you still want to stay here for lunch?' Edensun asks.

She looks thoughtful. The way her brow creases towards her nose, as she ponders his question, enchants him. She nods, takes a few steps away from the edge of the lake and sits down.

He takes the picnic basket to her and opens it. Inside he finds a flask, two glasses and an array of sweet smelling and brightly coloured fruit. Star reaches in and grabs a handful of strawberries.

'Leave some for me.' Edensun laughs.

'So, how does it work, this lake of sorrows?'

'As far as I understand it the sufferings of humans are stored here when they're done with them. Energy cannot be destroyed blah, blah, blah. It has to go somewhere. It comes here.'

'So it's pain.'

'Pain, anger, guilt…'

'There's so much of it.'

'And it keeps growing.'

'What happens to the people who created it?' Star asks.

'For the most part they heal and forget.'

'I wonder how much of it is mine,' Star says.

Edensun places his hand against her jaw and rubs her cheek with his thumb. 'It's probably best not to think about it.'

Star sighs. 'Probably.'

His hand falls from her face and they eat together. Gradually, he feels his spirits lift again and notices Star is smiling.

'Have you met God?' Star asks.

Edensun coughs, trying to dislodge the food which halted in his throat with her sudden words. When the morsel is free to continue its journey towards his stomach he speaks. 'Which one?'

'The one who talks to Lilith.'

'Samael.' Edensun's mouth is full of food. Juice runs down his chin.

Star wipes the food from her son's face, grinning. 'No, not Samael, the one she calls God.'

Edensun swallows. 'How could I? He doesn't exist.'

'You mean he's all in Lilith's mind?' Star's voice quivers.

'Well, no.'

'What do you mean?'

'I'll try to explain, but it's complicated.' Edensun shrugs.

Star laughs. 'I've heard that before.'

'God doesn't exist in the way you and I exist, or even in the way the sky exists or this lake. Everything which exists originates from him, her, it, but God is nothing. He has no mass, no molecules and no kinetic energy; he is pure thought and those thoughts have the potential to think anything into existence. Everything which exists is God and yet God is nothing. Everything is one. Everything is nothing.'

'I don't understand.'

'Neither do I. If we understand, when we understand, we too will cease to exist and become one with the source again.'

'So even Lilith doesn't understand?'

'She accepts. That's the best she can offer. If you want to understand, the first step is to know that everything is one. It might take you several lifetimes to reach that point. From there you can start to understand that one equals none.' Edensun laughs. 'Your eyes are glazed. I've lost you. Here, brain food.' He passes her a mango.

'All is nothing. It sounds like a nihilist mantra.'

'It isn't.'

Star nods. 'I think we need to think of smaller topics for discussion. Tell me about your life for the past four years.'

Edensun nods and inhales, noisily. 'Wow! Okay... I guess that's fair.... After all, you told me about yourself. Let me think while we finish the food.'

The basket is emptied in silence. Star lifts her face to the sky. Edensun follows her eyes upwards and watches the billowing mist move purposefully above them. He shivers. The air feels cold. He moves closer to Star and wraps his arm around her shoulders. She plants a soft, warm kiss on his cheek.

'My first memory is curling up to sleep between your arm and your chest. You warmed me as your body lay still beside me. It felt natural. I guess it was all I knew. When you woke at last, it confused me. You tried to pull away. I didn't understand, but it hurt and I knew you didn't love me. But, I also remember the first day you held me in your arms. The memory is so clear in my mind. I can feel your arm supporting my tiny body, and hear your voice as soft as a whisper. When you left, I tried to follow.'

Star's eyes glisten with tears. 'I'm so sorry, Edensun.'

'No, please don't cry. You're back now. Look, it wasn't so bad. Violet, Magenta and Sapphire took care of me. I slept against their bodies instead of yours.'

Star's eyes darken and she shivers.

'Are you jealous?' Edensun asks.

Star blushes. 'A little.'

'Don't be. I never forgot you. I grew fast. I wandered ceaselessly. Lilith advised me to stand still, but I couldn't. I was a shark. I felt I would die if I stopped moving... I kept asking Lilith about you. She promised me, as soon as I was big and strong enough, she would let me search for you. I had lessons. I learned about God, the planes, humans, different religions and science and how they tried to explain existence. When my mind wandered through knowledge, I could keep my body still. I learned patience and began to plan.'

'Plan what?'

'How to bring you back to me.'

'Am I all you thought about?'

'You were always in my thoughts, but I wasn't miserable. I had hope.'

Star squeezes the hand draped across her shoulder. 'Were you happy?'

He smiles. 'I was strong, full of energy. The women around me loved me. I had as much physical affection as anyone could need. I had friends and advisors: Lilith and Siloth. Yes I was happy, but I wasn't content. Does that make sense?'

'Absolutely.' Star nods. 'I have never felt content. Perhaps you inherited that from me?'

'Are you content now?'

Star breathes deeply. Her eyes probe his face before darting around at the sky, lake and landscape. At last her eyes settle and she stares ahead. 'Almost.'

'I wonder…'

'What?'

'I think you carry too much of your sorrow. Maybe you should… you know… let it go. We're in the right place.'

Star looks across at the lake and shakes her head. 'I can't lose my memories of what I've lost or what I've done. Not yet.'

'Why?'

'Because I am my memories. Without them… I don't know who I would be.'

'Happy?'

'Again? Is that all you people care about?'

Edensun touches her arm. 'No, not all. But this burden… it doesn't make you who you are… it limits who you can be.'

'Don't!'

'Don't what?'

'Just leave it, okay. I'll change when I'm ready.'

Edensun nods. 'Of course. I'm sorry, Mum.'

Chapter 64

The dinner table is already set when Star and Edensun return to the villa. Star does not feel hungry, but the glorious fare enchants her and she fills her plate with pink and red-fleshed fish and green, yellow and purple vegetables.

Lilith sits at the head of the table again. Star glances across between every morsel she consumes. The goddess looks serene yet thoughtful. Her eyes fixed on her plate, and her auburn hair pulled from her face and braided, she reminds Star of a bronze statue, achingly beautiful.

Conversation is muted, yet the diners' silence is not uncomfortable. Bird-song floats through the open windows, filling the room with gentle chatter.

Star wants to reach across the table, grasp Lilith's hand and offer her a penny for her thoughts. Awe and respect prevent her. Instead, she keeps gazing at the woman, then her food, and the woman again. She forgets all else, even her son, in this tender enchantment.

When the plates are emptied, Violet gathers them and removes dirty crockery and cutlery from the room. Lilith stands, pushing her chair away from the table. Her face holds no expression. She seems unreachable.

Lilith's gaze sharpens, as if resurfacing from a dream or meditation. 'I'm going to my room. Enjoy your evening.'

Star's heart sinks from its own weight. She wonders what she might have done wrong, believing that only she could have such a profound effect on Lilith's mood.

'Goodnight,' they call after Lilith's retreating body.

Waking from her own trance, Star glances around the table at Edensun, Sapphire and Magenta. 'What's wrong?' she asks, rubbing her face.

'Nothing's wrong,' Edensun answers, squeezing Star's hand lightly.

'I should go to her,' Star says.

'Only if you wish to,' Edensun replies.

Star stares into her son's emerald irises, trying to unravel hidden meaning in his words. 'Do you think she'll be angry if I follow her?'

'No.'

'Do you think she wants me to follow?'

'She would have told you if she did, Mother. Relax, drink with us.'

Star shakes her head and looks towards the doorway. The air glimmers like steam above a sun-baked road. 'Okay.' She swallows hard and tries to push Lilith's siren-song from her mind.

'What would you like to drink, Star?' Magenta asks.

Star shivers. Her skin feels like ice. Her eyes ache and her mouth is hot and dry. 'Where's her room?'

'Lilith's?' Edensun asks.

Star nods.

'Follow me.'

Edensun stops at one end of a wide hallway. Statues hold sentry along both walls: marble imaginings of tree branches hung with fruit, and snakes displaying forked tongues, beautiful men and women with exaggerated genitals, holding the sun and moon in their hands. Edensun points to the double doors ahead. The doors shine like silver, padded with deep-pile velvet cushions, riveted to the panels by golden studs.

Star takes a step towards the doors. She turns back to Edensun for reassurance, but he is gone. Breathing deeply, she tip-toes towards the doorway and knocks gently. There is no reply. Star pushes her ear against the narrow gap between the doors. Soft music plays in the room. Perhaps Lilith did not hear her tentative knock?

Star sighs and considers returning to the dining room, but her feet refuse to carry her there. Her shaking fingers tighten into a fist and hover before the door. She exhales loudly then knocks.

Footsteps approach from beyond the door. Star looks around her. Every marble face stares at her. She frowns at the unwelcome audience and turns back to face the door at the moment it starts to open.

'Star?' Lilith's voice is a whisper, a gentle breeze that would make rose-petals tremble.

'I'm sorry to...'

'Don't be. Would you like to come in?'

Star nods and steps into Lilith's private suite. In the centre of the room is a sunken bathtub the size of a modest swimming pool. Turquoise and violet lights dance, reflected, on the ceiling above towering bubbles.

'The water's lovely,' Lilith promises. 'Would you care to join me?'

Star's expression must provide all the answer Lilith requires as the goddess starts to unzip Star's dress. She silk caresses her body as it slips from her shoulders. Glancing down at her nakedness she feels no shame. Star smiles and jumps into the soapy water with a satisfying splash.

The moment she resurfaces, between mountains of foam, Lilith's lips find hers. They sink together in a loving embrace. Body presses against body. Arms wrap around each other. They bob, sometimes floating, other times gracefully sinking, into the warm water.

Star's fingers wander down Lilith's silky back until they reach her high, supple buttocks. Lilith laughs as Star squeezes, teasing as if forming flesh from spirit. She wants to remake Lilith in her own image. She wants to be mother and lover to the goddess. With no need for words, she transmits her thoughts through tongue and fingers. Lilith's body clings to her, communicating everything Star needs to hear. They hold each other as the belly of the water holds them.

Lilith steps out of the bath. Star watches her limbs stretch and relax as she climbs the submerged staircase. She follows in Lilith's footsteps, wrapping her body around those elegant limbs and kissing her damp face.

Lilith smiles. She looks graceful, reaching for the largest towel Star has ever seen. Soft, cotton fibres wrap around them both, but they do not waste time drying themselves or each other. Wetness is welcome.

Star feels like a child in a blanket fort, surrounded by love and acceptance. Words bubble in her chest and tickle her throat. 'I still love you,' she whispers.

'That's a good thing.' Lilith kisses Star's eyelids and earlobes. 'Are you beginning to love yourself?'

Star opens her eyes. Lilith's face glows. Her expectant eyes are wide and warm.

'I am.' Star smiles, nervously.

'That's even better. Do you see yourself as I see you?'

'How is that?'

'Beautiful, wise and full of desire.'

Star grins. 'Is that really how you see me?'

'Yes, my darling.'

'I don't disappoint you?'

'Your head is full of questions. You search for answers and find only new questions, but you never stop looking. You love with every fibre of your being even when others hurt you. Star, my love, of all my creations you make me the most proud.'

Star clings to Lilith's shoulder for support. 'I feel dizzy.'

Lilith takes her hand and leads her to a deep pile rug. They sit together amid silken fur. It tickles Star's thighs in the most delicious ways. Star rests her head against Lilith's breast and the goddess wraps her arms around Star.

'This is wonderful,' Star whispers.

Lilith's hair bounces with a nod.

'I want to spend the rest of my life with you, Lilith, you and my son. I want to be your friend and your lover. I want to see the world with my hand in yours. With you, I believe, I can find all the answers I need.'

Lilith kisses Star's forehead.

'Will you take me to all the places I've never seen?'

'In Malkuth?'

'Everywhere!'

'Some places you must travel alone and only when you're ready, but we can explore your world tomorrow, if you wish.'

'Oh yes!'

'Perhaps you should get some sleep? Wake up fresh in your own bed. You feel a little feverish, my love.'

Star nods. She turns her face upwards, towards Lilith's and kisses her mouth. Eagerly, she strokes her pale hands across Lilith's olive skin. Her fingers slide between the goddess' legs.

Lilith sighs.

'A nightcap before bed?' Star pushes Lilith to the floor and buries her face between supple thighs. She glides her tongue between soft, generous labia, flicking the rose bud clitoris with her tongue before tasting the rich, sweet juices within.

Star's fingers, tongue and lips explore, tease and pleasure the sex of her goddess. Lilith's sharp, frantic cries of orgasm send shockwaves through every nerve in Star's body. The rush of energy brings Star to climax and she shudders between Lilith's thighs.

She nestles beside a very happy and contented goddess, kissing her shoulders and throat as her body becomes calm and her heartbeat returns to normal. Her flesh and mind relax and she finds sleep easily.

Star stands before a red lake. 'I don't need my pain anymore,' she says. Kneeling at the water's edge, she pushes two fingers into her throat and purges herself of sorrow.

Chapter 65

Star wakes and stretches the sleep from her body. She heads straight for the wardrobe and pulls a gorgeous red dress from the hanger. After slipping it on she hurries to the dining room for breakfast. Today Lilith has promised her a world tour: all the places on earth she has never seen, available for her exclusive viewing pleasure.

She is the first to arrive in the dining room. The table is clean, but not laden yet with breakfast. Star realises that she has never seen the kitchen and wonders in which direction she might find it.

She opens a doorway and steps into a room filled with light. The room is void of furniture. An open door leads to the desert. Spirits enter the room. Columns of mist fill the space, pulsing with thoughts, waiting for Lilith to mould them and send them on their way. Star wanders around the room, allowing curious spirits to touch her flesh. Their consciousness washes through her. She sees vortexes of potential in each mind she touches. Their thoughts are chaotic and limitless. They make her mind reel.

'Star.' Lilith's voice cuts through the room. 'What are you doing here?'

'I was looking for the kitchen.'

'Violet has already prepared breakfast, Darling, if you're hungry.'

'Are you working today?' Star asks.

'Not for long. I haven't forgotten our trip.'

'Can I watch you work?'

Lilith smiles. 'Of course.'

Lilith stands in the middle of the room and widens her arms. A consciousness narrows itself to fit between her hands. She cups her fingers and pushes the mist inwards as though she is working with clay rather than energy. The thoughts are pushed and pulled into order. A sphere the size of a rugby ball of sparkling light hovers before the goddess's face.

Lilith pushes her fingers into her stomach and sculpts flesh around the contained mind. From her own flesh, the goddess builds a mortal body for the spirit: a tiny form, an infant. It watches Star with sly intelligence.

Star recoils from the child's judging eyes. Her stomach growls. 'I'll see you after breakfast,' she tells Lilith and rushes out of the room.

The dining table is full of fruit and cakes. Star grabs the back of a chair. Her head swims and she feels unsteady on her feet.

'Are you okay?' Sapphire places a hand gently on Star's shoulder.

Star manages to nod.

'Here, sit down.' Sapphire helps Star into the chair. 'I feel the same way.'

'Huh?'

341

'Watching her work. It's dizzying. All that energy squashed into a tiny life.'

'Yes,' Star answers.

'Are you hungry?' Sapphire asks.

'I'm not sure.'

'Take a bit and see.'

Star reaches for a ripe papaya.

'I'll prepare it for you,' Sapphire places the sliced fruit onto a plate before Star. 'So you are going to see the world today?'

Star chews. Juice drips down her chin. She nods.

'What will you see?'

'I don't know. Wonders, perhaps?'

'There are wonders enough here,' Sapphire answers.

'That's true, but I couldn't turn down an opportunity to see new things.'

'Man's folly.' Sapphire sighs.

'What?'

'Always searching for the next experience.'

Star's hand hovers above her plate. 'You'd rather be static?'

'I like it here.'

'So do I, but there is so much more to know and understand. Amazing things to see.'

'If you say so.'

'I do. There are entire continents on which I have never set foot. I know so little of my world. I want to see its people and new places.'

Lilith steps out from her workroom. 'Where's Edensun?'

342

'With Magenta,' Sapphire answers.

'Go and get him, please. It's time we left.'

Lilith disappears through another door and comes back wearing different clothing: a dark, tailored suit that is cut perfectly to fit her body. She eats a few pieces of fruit in silence. Star watches her. Everything the woman does is graceful.

'Ready?' Edensun says as he walks into the room.

'We've been waiting for you,' Lilith says and places a kiss on his cheek. 'Magenta keeping you busy?'

'Nothing I can't handle.' Edensun laughs. 'So what exciting pleasures and experiences do we have in store for Mother?'

'I thought she might like to see the world as it really is rather than a sanitised version for tourists.'

Star shifts uncomfortably. She feels absent from the conversation. 'Sounds good to me.'

Lilith laughs. Her laugh sends shivers down Star's spine. It sounds cruel and hard. She wonders whether Sapphire is right. Maybe she should be content to stay here.

'Will it be safe?' Star asks.

'Of course. We are simply observers,' Lilith answers. 'Where first?'

'I don't know.'

'Asia, Africa, America?'

'Africa,' Star answers. 'I've always wanted to see lions.'

Lilith links arms with Star and Edensun. 'You know the drill,' she says. 'One little step.'

They arrive in a village. The ground is cracked, baked by the white sun that dominates the sky. Strewn across the dusty street are bodies. Their limbs twisted and their skulls broken. Flies cover the carnage. In the distance, Star hears gunfire and the laughter of children.

'What is this?' she cries.

'Africa,' Lilith answers.

'This isn't what I meant. You know that, Lilith. Take me somewhere else,' Star begs.

'Do you not want to understand?'

'No, I don't.'

'Very well.'

Star clings to Lilith's arm as they step forward.

They arrive in a pig farm. The stench overwhelms Star. Thousands of pigs crowd into a tiny area. The air is filled with their screams. The noise sounds human, but the smell is animal: sweat, faeces and fear. Pigs bump into each other. Their bodies covered in blood from bites and scratches.

'Stop it! Stop it! Stop it! I know what you're trying to do. But it won't work. This isn't my world,' Star cries.

'It is,' Lilith answers.

'This is the price pigs pay to feed American stomachs,' Edensun says.

'Is there anywhere you plan to take me that I will want to see?' Star asks.

The three step forwards again. They arrive in a large square filled with people and colour. At the edges, stone buildings loom above them. Star is reminded of a cage full to the brim with exotic birds. Women are singing. Star does not recognise the words, but the sound is mournful.

To the right, Star hears men's voices raised in anger. Women scream. The crowd jostles and pushes back. Gunfire fills Star's ears. The crowd pushes forwards again. More screaming. Colours move and blur. Everything is red then black. Star's scream joins the fearful chorus. 'Enough!'

'Already?' Lilith asks.

'Lilith. I'm not stupid. I know the world is full of pain and suffering, but this isn't all there is. This is cruel, Lilith. Why are you doing this?'

'She's not doing anything,' Edensun answers. 'We're simply watching what human's do.'

Star stamps her foot and shakes her head. 'We don't only destroy. We create as well.'

Lilith squeezes Star's arm and they step forward. Before them, anchored to snow and ice, stands an oil rig.

'You create an unsustainable need for energy,' Lilith says.

'This is nonsense.' Star shakes her head.

'This is truth,' Lilith answers. 'I could take you to a thousand places and in each one fear and oppression would reside. This is what you make of the life I give to you.'

'No, we make art and music.'

'Band aids for arterial wounds. They salve your guilt by escaping the reality that humans are evil parasites.'

'Not all of us. And you said you didn't care. You said people could do what they wanted. That it made no difference to you or God. That you felt nothing for our plight except amusement. What are you trying to prove, Lilith? You build me up one day with love and tenderness… then this. Do you want to make me crazy?'

'I just want you to see,' Lilith answers. 'Are you better than them?'

Star nods then shakes her head. 'No.'

'Remember when I asked you whether your friends should survive and you let them die so your guilt at leaving me could be absolved?' Edensun asks.

Pain tears at Star's chest. Edensun betrays her with his words. She steps back. Her eyes darken. His cruel words echo around her mind. Deep inside she knows he is right, but for a second that makes her hate him more. She pushes down her anger. This is her son. She must love him. Always, or what hope does she have? She nods. 'There must be a reason. How do we do it? How can humans be so selfish and cruel?'

'You forget. When you are cruel, when you cause pain or when you are hurt the energy is deflected. It is the only way you can continue,' Edensun says.

'The lake?' Star asks.

Lilith and Edensun nod.

'Take me there.'

'To the lake of sorrows?' Lilith asks.

'Yes.'

'What will you do?' Lilith asks.

Star feels the prickle of energy spark through her limbs. Her head itches as her hair stands on end. 'If we give humans back their pain, will they, we, behave differently?'

Lilith looks at Star askance.

'I would imagine so,' Edensun answers.

'Yes, perhaps,' Lilith says.

Star turns to face the oil rig and nods. 'We should.'

'What do you mean?' Edensun asks.

'Can we find a way of returning the waters of the lake to Earth?' Star asks.

Lilith faces Star and grasps both her hands. Her eyes shine and reflect the icy vista.

Star stares at those cold green eyes. 'You want to change things too, don't you? That's why you showed me this. Is it possible?'

'Everything is possible. I am the god of in between. I can make a funnel between the two worlds. We can make it rain,' Edensun says.

Lilith gasps and claps her hands. 'Anything could happen.'

'People might learn to be kind?' Star says.

'They might,' Edensun answers. His expression is unreadable.

Chapter 66

Lilith, Star and Edensun stand under the giant, pink flag of the Langham Hotel. Silk crackles above as agitated air whips the three flags which decorate the hotel's grand facade. Behind them sandstone glows like sunlight. In the road, synchronised amber spheres blink.

Dark clouds gather above. Lilith smiles and wonders whether Star is prepared for what they are about to unleash.

'Ready?' Edensun asks.

'I think so,' Star answers.

Star stands between the two gods. Lilith reaches for Star's hand and squeezes.

The rain starts to fall. It is red, just as it had been in the lake of sorrows. Huge drops fall from plum and black clouds, hitting the pavement and the faces of people walking along the street.

Someone screams. Another scream joins the first. A man, five feet from where Lilith watches, covers his eyes with stained hands and falls to his knees. He emits a strangled wail. His shoulders hunch over his knees. Moving his hands from his eyes, he forms two fists and begins punching himself in the face and upper body. More red liquid falls, soaking through his clothes and matting his hair. Others fall beside him. Some bend over the ground as if in Islamic prayer and hit their foreheads against paving stones until they lose consciousness. Women dig fingernails into their cheeks and tear the skin from their faces. Others use things they are carrying, bags and umbrellas to beat their backs and heads.

'What's happening?' Star asks.

'All that extra pain at once. Some of them are being driven mad with grief. They'll become accustomed to it.'

'But they're supposed to use their pain to change things. They aren't supposed to die.'

'They won't all die,' Lilith assures her.

Star steps out from under the shelter.

'Mum,' Edensun calls after her.

'I have to do something,' she says.

A woman kneels beside a pram. She takes a baby from under its covers and shakes it by the arms.

Star strides towards them. 'What's wrong?' she asks the woman.

The woman doesn't answer. She lifts the baby over her head and slams it with all her strength onto the pavement before her. The baby's head opens like an eggshell and its blood splatters Star's shins.

Star shakes her head until the motion makes her dizzy. 'What have you done?'

The woman does not seem to hear her. The mother's fingers rake at her own scalp, tearing her bleached-blonde hair out in clumps, throwing them on the ground. Star stares first at the dead baby then at the distraught woman. Grabbing the woman's arms, she tries to stop her. At last the woman's eyes seem to focus on Star. Star pleads with her to stop her madness. The woman growls. Bearing her teeth, she bites Star's wrist. Star screams and releases the woman who returns to scalping herself.

Waters from the lake of sorrows pour onto Malkuth soil. People run blindly as red liquid covers their faces, screaming in terror, agony and rage. Insanity reigns. People rip open their stomachs and eviscerate themselves. Bodies fall. Only a few remain standing, stronger than the rest. Survivors stare at the dead and dying, eyes wide with horror. The young fair better than the old.

'What have we done?' Star walks further away from Edensun and Lilith, scrambling over bodies, hugging weeping children.

Lilith approaches Star and places a hand on her trembling shoulder.

Star turns to face Lilith, her face smeared with pain and confusion.   'This isn't what I wanted.'

'Shhh, child. These people are fools. Others will behave as you hoped. They will overthrow oppression.'

'Where?'

'Everywhere. It's happening already. Can't you feel it?'

Star stares at Lilith. Her lips tremble. 'Please, take me to Parliament Square.'

The Houses of Parliament look black beyond the curtain of red rain. Lilith watches with satisfaction as crowds of people surge into the broken building. Fires burn all around them. Cars and buildings blacken in the heat. Anger fills the air and with it the potential to change things.

'This is the change,' Star says.

Lilith nods.

'What do you think will happen?' Edensun asks.

Star stands straight and proud. She gazes at the crowd, smiling. 'The people will take back the power which was stolen from them. Each will live out their lives in the ways which are natural to them. No longer cogs in a huge machine, but people. Not merely existing, but living.'

'You see all that in this violent mob?' Lilith asks.

'Yes.'

'How?' Edensun asks.

'Because I saw Lilith fashion those souls and each has the potential to change everything as long as they change themselves. This violence is focused. It has a purpose. They're overthrowing the old to bring in something new, something fairer.'

Star's eyes gleam. Her fanaticism borders on madness. Lilith wonders whether the woman's mind is broken from grief. The goddess looks at Edensun who frowns at his mother. His face creases with worry.

Helicopters buzz overhead like angry wasps. Missiles hit the ground. The crowd screams. Some keep pushing into the iconic building. Others scatter and run towards alternative shelter.

'Why aren't the soldiers affected by the rain?' Star asks.

Lilith shrugs. 'They probably are. Each soul has its own direction to travel.'

'Will they win?' Star asks.

'The people?' Edensun says.

'Yes, the fucking people, will they win? Will they overthrow the exploitative system?'

'Probably,' Edensun says. 'Many will fall in the process, but what do they have to lose now they see the truth?'

Lilith points towards the Houses of Parliament. 'They are focused.'

'So it was worth it?' Star asks.

'Evolution, revolution, change is always worth it,' Lilith answers.

'This gives you a buzz, doesn't it?' Star looks at Lilith then Edensun, daring them to argue.

'Maybe you should look in the mirror, Darling. I've never seen you look more energised.'

'So much death.' Star looks across Parliament Square at the charred and bloody remains.

'Just so one regime can fall and another can rise,' Edensun says.

'Oh God.' Star holds her hand over her chest.

Edensun puts his arm around her shoulders. 'What is it?'

'What the fuck have I done?' Star's body shakes.

'You've changed the world, Mum.' Edensun answers.

Chapter 67

Star watches explosion after explosion. Her head vibrates with the deafening sounds of bombs, helicopters and human screams. She looks to Lilith and Edensun and wishes she had never been born.

Bodies tumble around her. Static electricity tugs her hair towards the sky. The pores of her skin prickle.

Her eyes focus on a helicopter hovering above the people. Weapons flare as missiles rain down on the insurrection. She imagines rotary blades folding inwards. The helicopter jerks and splutters. The blades stop spinning and it falls like a boulder, hitting the lawn in front of Parliament and bursting into flame. Citizens race from the wreckage. When they reach a safe distance, their voices rise in celebration.

Star concentrates on a second helicopter. As that too falls to the earth, the other pilots flee with their cargoes of soldiers. Turning their war-birds around, they head for safety.

Free from the overhead threat, people swarm across the grass. Songs of freedom resound. Men in suits are dragged from buildings. Some are torn to pieces by the crowd, while others are thrown, screaming, into fires.

Star wonders what will happen when the old leaders are all murdered. Will the crowd turn on each other to continue the violence or will the people re-establish order and work together to rebuild the city for themselves?

'At least they have a chance, now,' Star mutters.

She looks at Lilith and Edensun. Neither appears to have heard. Certainly, they provide no answer. She shrugs. *Is this better?* The aroma of blood and burned flesh fills her nostrils. Her question will not be answered for years. The final result, harmony or escalating violence, will not be apparent until decades have passed. *Will people, like my parents, cling to old ways and an oppressive, demanding god, or will they embrace their new freedom? Will they survive?*

Star touches Lilith's arm. 'Will God be angry?'

'I already told you, he doesn't care what humans do with their lives, only that they are born. He will neither rage nor rejoice. He may not even be aware of what has happened.'

'Are you angry?' Star asks.

'No.'

'Disappointed?'

'Do you want me to be? Why do you wish to be judged?'

'I need to know if I did the right thing.' Star stares at the floor.

Lilith hooks a finger under Star's chin and pulls her face upwards until their eyes meet. 'Star darling, that is something only you can decide.'

'This is freedom. All is one and everything is nothing.' Star kisses Lilith then embraces Edensun. 'I love you both.'

They smile at her and she smiles back.

'See you.' Star steps forward. Careful to avoid the dead and injured, scattered across concrete and grass, she walks towards the centre of the square. The broken helicopter is a pyre. Flames warm her. Their fingers beckon her to join them. Lifting her arms, she steps into their midst. Spinning through the flames, she laughs until her throat crisps. She dances while her flesh becomes ash which rises from the fire towards the stars.

Lightning Source UK Ltd.
Milton Keynes UK
UKOW05f1147201113

221474UK00001B/52/P